GARDEN OF SERPENTS

The Demon Queen Trials—Book Three

C.N. CRAWFORD

SUMMARY OF PREVIOUS BOOKS

In September, Rowan was a mortal college student, struggling with student loans. All very ordinary—until a gorgeous demon known as the Lord of Chaos crashed her birthday. Orion had silver hair, blue eyes, and a bizarre certainty that she ruined his life. Apparently, Rowan looked exactly like an an ancient succubus named Mortana, who was an absolute nightmare.

Orion—as always, certain he was right—kidnapped Rowan and threw her in a dungeon in the Demon City. There, she spilled her most embarrassing secrets to him, and she also found a mysterious carving: *Lucifer urbem spinarum libarabit*—the Lightbringer will set the City of Thorns free.

Only when Orion bit her and tasted her blood did he finally accept that she was mortal, and they teamed up to kill the demon king, Cambriel.

Cambriel had murdered Rowan's mother by lighting her on fire, giving Rowan a lifelong terror of fire. He'd stolen the throne from the rightful heir, Orion. Incubi and succubi were a particular type of demon known as Lilu, hunted out of existence by mortals and the previous demon king.

Orion, however, was secretly an incubus, a creature who fed off lust. After the rest of the Lilu were murdered, he had lived for centuries in a dungeon, completely forgotten. He watched his whole family die before his eyes, and he blamed Mortana for their death. She was the last living succubus—or so he thought.

When Rowan's demon mark showed up—a glowing sign on her forehead showing that she was a demon all along—things go sour for the pair. Her parents had used magic to hide her true nature, because succubi like her were hunted and outlawed. Now that it was clear she had the same demon mark as Mortana, Orion became convinced this was all another trick played by his worst enemy. Just like Orion—and Mortana—Rowan had the rare skill of fire magic.

Making things more complicated—Rowan's demon mark proved she was also an heir to the throne. Rowan was now Orion's rival.

And yet he could not bring himself to kill her; he had started to fall in love with her.

The pair travelled to the underworld to break a blood oath Orion had made to murder Mortana's entire family, which would have compelled him to kill Rowan. While there, Rowan learned that Orion had also made an oath to another incubus in the dungeon—a man named Ashur. Orion had promised Ashur that he would get revenge on mortals for their role in the slaughter of the Lilu.

This made Rowan determined to stop Orion, to prevent the slaughter.

When Orion left the underworld, Rowan stayed behind to train with a chaos god named Tammuz— secretly, Orion's father. Tammuz was the one who marked them both with the sign of the Lightbringer, because he thrived on chaos.

Time passed differently with Tammuz, and Rowan learned to fight and hunt like a demon, until she was ready to take the throne.

But when she returned to the City of Thorns, Orion managed to take control of the city, and he banished her to the mortal world.

Devastated, Rowan retreated to Osborne. In her home town, she was forced to hide from the demon hunters.

While in hiding, an elderly family friend name Mr. Esposito dropped off a book for her. The book was about the *Demon Trials*, and detailed exactly how she could win the throne for herself.

❧ I ❧
ROWAN

Sunlight streamed through autumn leaves, lighting them like tongues of flames against the sky. I stared out a third-story window, watching a little boy stuff his mouth with cotton candy on the brick sidewalk across the street. Just next to him, his mom chatted with a friend, her hair the same bright red as the autumn leaves above her.

The little boy reached out to grab his mom's pinkie finger—one hand on mom, the other on his treat. Crystalized pink sugar smeared across his cheek, striking against his pale skin. From the oak tree above him, a bright orange leaf drifted onto his tufted auburn hair, then slid off to the bricks. His green eyes followed the leaf's motion.

My chest felt tight.

Any day now, Orion could be ripping through this town to murder everyone. This sugar-covered toddler with Band-Aids on both knees wasn't responsible for anything that happened four hundred years ago. He just wanted his mom and dessert.

I watched the peaceful scene, my breath fogging the glass.

This could be the last moment of peace in a while.

By midnight tonight, my head would either be resting on a silken pillow or hanging from the gates before the Tower of Baal. After the first night of the trial, those two paths lay before me. Nothing else.

But if Tammuz—the dying god—thought I had a chance at winning the crown, who was I to argue?

When I took a step back from the window, a ray of light caught on the word *love*, etched in the glass with a diamond long ago. I could almost see a version of this world where an unbroken Orion would welcome me into the city. A world where we could rule together. But that wasn't this reality, was it? Because he'd thrown me out on my ass to fend for myself against demon hunters as my magic faded.

In reality, Orion's soul had never left the dungeon. Even if his body made it out, he was trapped there still.

With a tight throat, I turned, taking in the eighteenth-century mansion. Shai's aunt's house was one of the most beautiful places I'd ever seen, the floors delightfully crooked and creaking with age, the walls carved mahogany. One half of the living room opened into a kitchen with marble countertops. On the other side of the room, diamond-pane windows looked out over the churning, sun-kissed Atlantic.

Amber sunlight streamed through the old glass, falling on the portrait of one of Shai's relatives, a New England merchant sea captain with brown skin, a white cravat, and a brass-button navy coat. Impossible to tell if he was part demon, like Shai.

I absolutely adored this place, and it had become my hiding spot while Shai's aunt was away in Paris. I had the whole house to myself.

Breathing in deeply, I closed my eyes for a moment, relishing the calm before the storm. I'd been awake all night, my mind whirling. The mortal police were still after me for killing a congressman, and I knew what horrors Orion had planned.

I crossed to the antique sofa, and I pulled out my phone to check the time. Nearly noon. Shai should be here any minute with something I desperately needed.

When I looked up again, a chill rippled over my skin. Shadows had spread through the room, and an electric crackle of magic skimmed up my spine.

I jumped up again and crossed to the window. Unnatural iron-gray storm clouds had claimed the sky.

The little boy still held his mom's hand, but now worry creased his brow. He stared up at the darkening clouds, wiping his sticky hand on his shirt, leaving behind smears of pink.

A gust of wind swept through the trees, tearing leaves off the oak's boughs. All at once, clouds opened above, unleashing a wild rain storm that hammered against the window.

My heart started to race as I craned my neck to peer down the hill through the old glass.

It's starting. I couldn't breathe. Already, they were coming—the demon horde, their silver claws extended, eyes black as pitch. The earth seemed to rumble with their approach. This was it—the vengeance that obsessed Orion, his lust for mortal blood.

I banged on the glass, screaming to get the mom's attention. Why wasn't she running? She needed to get that little boy the fuck out of here. My voice seemed trapped in the room, and I bitterly regretted that I'd let my magic run out.

At last, the boy's mother turned to see the horde, and her face went white. She grabbed him by the wrist at first, then under his armpits, and started to run. But she was slow and human, no match for the demons. I couldn't watch this.

I pivoted and raced for the stairs. They creaked as I thundered down, my body shaking with adrenaline. By the time I flung open the front door at the bottom of the stairs, the mom's screams had gone quiet, and the little boy's, too—

My heart stopped as I turned to look in the direction of the City of Thorns.

Dressed in a cloak, Orion stalked closer, his face half shrouded. He was death incarnate. Blood dripped from his claws, and my heart twisted in my chest.

The question was, what made me so fucked up that I was drawn to him?

2

ROWAN

I woke, gasping, my face pressed against embroidered chartreuse silk. My heart lurched. Slowly, I sat up on the sofa and clutched my chest.

Holy hell, that had seemed so real.

There's still time.

I was still in Shai's aunt's house. The sun still shone outside.

As my gaze slid around the room, I took in the calm swirls of mahogany, the portrait on the wall, still washed in gold light. Slowly, the nightmare began to fade.

A book lay on the coffee table before me. Gilded stars and letters were engraved in the deep blue surface: *Trial by Combat in the Demon World*.

I opened the cover to the first page, staring again at the strange text inscribed within.

> *I will always help you when I can.*
> *-Sabazios*

This was my gift from the elderly Mr. Esposito—and also the only way to stop the nightmare I'd just seen. In the past few weeks, I'd learned everything I could about how to dethrone Orion.

With a heavy sense of dread, I padded barefoot to the window. The sun shone through leaves the color of pumpkins and honey. A woman with pink hair walked with a ginger cat in her arms, a flat-faced and sleepy creature, its eyes blinking slowly.

No demons, no blood, no cotton candy–covered little boy. No oncoming demon horde rumbling over the street. Just a beautiful October day in New England.

Outside, the pink-haired woman pivoted, and her gaze slid to my window as she stroked her orange cat. Unease flickered through me. I'd seen her before, hadn't I? I had the disturbing sense that she was spying on me, and I wondered if the demon hunters were finally catching up.

I slipped back out of her eyesight and dropped onto the sofa again. After another minute, I heard the sound of someone climbing the old, creaking stairs. Relief flooded me as the living room door swung open, and Shai stood in the doorway.

Her hair was a halo of brown curls, and a little leather bag rested against the houndstooth fabric of her skirt. "Hey girl. Are you just waking up?"

"Is it that obvious?" When I looked down at myself, I saw my tangled red hair hanging over wrinkled pajamas. I rubbed my eyes. "I couldn't sleep last night. I passed out here sometime after the sun came up, I think. I just had the worst fucking nightmare about Orion."

She crossed the living room to the kitchen. "I'm making us cappuccino."

"I love you," I called out.

"You'll love me even more when you see what I brought back for you."

Excitement lit me up. "Is it the iron gauntlet, by any chance?"

"Sure is," she called out from the kitchen over the sound of frothing milk. "And I already started spreading the word that you're not Mortana. The whole city is abuzz with the gossip."

A few minutes later, she crossed back into the living room, holding two white coffee cups on saucers, and slid them onto the table.

I picked up my cup, delighted to see that she'd powdered the frothy milk with a dusting of cocoa. Gods, it was really nice to be taken care of. "How did you get your hands on the gauntlet?"

She sat in the armchair across from me but made no move to open her bag. "Are you sure you want to do this *tonight*?" she asked, ignoring my question. "It seems so soon to take on the son of a demon god."

Any moment, that glorious buzz of caffeine would hit my veins, jolting me awake. "It's never going to feel like a good time to challenge a demon king, and I don't have a ton of time. There's a woman with a cat who keeps walking past the apartment like she's spying on me."

"Okay..." Her voice trailed off, and then she said, "I know you're the Lightbringer." She didn't sound convinced, though.

"Shai. Tonight's the night." I stared at the velvet book.

"It's the moonlight festival. It's perfect. Everyone will see the trial by combat. If I win, there will be thousands of witnesses."

She tapped the side of her cup. "Well, if you're going to go ahead with it, let's not say *if* you win. Let's say *when* you win. Anything else is unacceptable and simply cannot come to pass. Do you understand?"

I had the sense that Shai was annoyed at me for putting my life at risk, but I didn't have much choice.

"It'll be fine." I still had that little boy's pink-sugared face in my mind. "I'm a Lightbringer, remember?"

She took a deep breath, her expression relaxing. "If you say you can do it, then I believe you."

At last, she reached into her bag and pulled out an ancient-looking iron glove, a piece of carefully crafted armor. She gently placed it on the table next to the book. I stared at the hinges and delicate metal plates that had once allowed a warrior's fingers to move, to grip the hilt of a sword. In a ray of honeyed sunlight, Lucifer's star gleamed from the back of the gauntlet—a bright spark of gold on the iron. I reached out and traced my fingertips over it, surprised by the jolt of ancient magic that shot into my fingertips when I touched it. A smile curled my lips. That felt like a sign from the demon god himself.

"Shai, how, exactly, did you get the gauntlet? I thought it was hidden in a secret temple."

"Legion helped me."

His image flickered in my mind—the black-haired demon with golden skin and tattoos that twisted over his muscular forearms. "So the leader of the Sathanas Ward knows I'm coming in for the trials."

"*Everyone* knows. The rumors already spread. They know Mortana is dead and that you're her sister. Or whatever. They know you're a Lightbringer." She sipped her coffee, then licked the froth off her upper lip. "Everyone saw your mark when you were about to kill Cambriel. You have a claim to the throne. Any demon would try it." She leaned back in her chair, peering at me over her coffee cup. Steam curled before her face. "Even if they don't know you're coming tonight, they think you're either going to challenge Orion or marry him. Either way, if you live, you'll be queen."

"Marry him." I snorted. "Did they miss the part where he kicked me out of the city?"

"No, but you're a succubus. Hard to resist. And everyone knows he's an incubus." She slid her coffee onto the table. "And since he didn't kill you, people still think there's a chance it all ends in marriage."

"Yeah, that's not happening. Orion is fundamentally broken. I don't think he actually has the capacity to love anyone. All he cares about is murdering people. Revenge. That's it."

She peered at me over her coffee cup. "Yeah, I think people are pretty terrified of him. You know, some of them were around during the Lilu massacre, and they didn't stop it. No one knows if he's going to rip their heads off like he did with King Nergal." She smiled faintly. "That's why Legion helped me find the gauntlet."

"I'm surprised Orion hasn't started the bloodbath already."

She took a sip of her coffee. "No one really knows what he's been up to. Tonight will be one of his first public events." She gave me a measuring look. "And you're going to show up and...what, exactly?"

I took a deep breath. "It's very simple. We fight, and the first person thrown to the ground loses. All I have to do is throw Orion to the earth, and then I become shadow scion. His official challenger."

She sank back into her chair, considering this. "Alternately, the first person to be killed loses."

A bit of fear danced up my spine. "Well, that *is* one way of falling to the ground."

"That's the point I'm stuck on," she said. "I mean, you literally just said he's broken and bloodthirsty, so it doesn't fill me with a great deal of confidence about his level of restraint. He's going to try to murder you, right?"

"Shai! I'm trying not to think about the worst-case scenario. I'm trying to envision success. If I win tonight, I'm in charge of the second trial. I'll have an advantage." Nodding at the book, I said, "There are a whole bunch to choose from in there." I dropped my coffee onto a coaster and cracked open the soft blue volume, flipping through the ancient pages. "It could be a quest. An endurance test. A battle of magic. Jousting. I've read through every option. But they all require magical spells in Demonic, so I'll need your help with that part."

She smirked. "Please tell me you're going to joust."

"Yeah, I'm gonna pass on that one. But I'm not committing to anything yet. I want to see what it's like to fight Orion first."

"I *do* want to be besties with a queen." Shai took the old book from me and began paging through it. "I can totally lend a hand with the spells. But I also have two friends who can help. Legion and his friend Kas have been teaching me magic. They're, like, the best professors in the history of the demon world."

I narrowed my eyes. "I've only been gone two weeks, and you have a whole new friend group. Do I need to be jealous?"

"Absolutely not, because you're going to love them, too. They're very easy on the eyes. And they helped me discover my hidden demon powers."

I arched an eyebrow. "Okay. Can I get a demonstration?"

She stood and crossed the creaking floor to one of the windows overlooking the sea, then turned to face me, her brown eyes glinting. "Watch and be amazed." She faced the window again and lifted her hands toward the glass, then started to mutter under her breath.

At first, nothing happened, and I just drank my coffee, waiting. But after a few minutes, an electrical rush rippled through the room, raising the hair on the back of my arms. Magic hummed along my arms and legs. Around her body, the air glowed silver, and her curls rose higher off her shoulders.

A chill ran up my spine. Outside, shadows began to creep across the clouds. The air thinned and grew darker.

Outside, the ocean waves churned against the rocky shore. Just like in my nightmare, storm clouds unleashed fat drops of rain. Within moments, they were hammering against the window, sliding down in rivulets.

Stunned, I held my breath.

Slowly, Shai lowered her hands. When she turned to look at me, her eyes shone with a certain wildness.

"Holy shit, Shai."

"I've been trying to summon lightning, but it's not happening for me yet." She dropped into the velvet armchair once more. "Cool, though, right? I'm not just an ordinary mortal student anymore."

"You were never ordinary."

She leaned over to pick up her coffee. "I wish I could help you in the trials. I could just hit Orion with lightning." Rays of sunlight peeked through the clouds, gilding Shai's brown skin and rose-gold cheekbones. "Exactly how broken and bloodthirsty is he?"

My breath quickened. "I mean, he spent centuries in prison thinking of nothing but avenging the Lilu. He feels like he died in that dungeon. Where his soul used to be, there's now only lust for revenge."

"Shit."

"And that's where you have to keep me on track, Shai. Because if I win this trial, he's going to use every trick in the incubus playbook to throw me off. An incubus is seductive and charming, and he's going to use all that to try to get me to quit. Not because he cares, or because he likes me. An incubus uses his beauty and magic as a weapon to control other people, and that's exactly what he'll do with me. An unrelenting, seductive charm offensive of sensual magic and pretty words."

Shai arched an eyebrow. "Unsettling. But also weirdly hot at the same time?"

"The Lord of Chaos is all about mind games, but I absolutely cannot fall for it. If I seem like I'm going soft on him, please remind me that he shoved me out of the City as soon as he no longer needed me. He killed the man

I'd been hunting, even though he knew it was my life's goal. Remind me that he said I'm boring and that he doesn't respect me."

She narrowed her eyes. "Okay, he might be broken, but he doesn't think *you're* boring. Like, it's obvious—he's kind of obsessed with you, I think. Otherwise a king wouldn't let his rival live. But yes, he's all messed up, or he wouldn't have said something so insane in the first place."

He'd sort of taken it back in a moment of passion, but that wasn't exactly trustworthy, was it? "That's because we're both Lilu. We feed off lust, and we're the only two left. Our feelings aren't real, just the deceit of magic."

"Absolutely. Forget about Orion, because I really think you'll like Kas. He's got these huge muscles and these tattoos—"

"I'm all done with men, Shai," I said, interrupting. "You know Queen Elizabeth I, the redheaded queen who never married? That's going to be me. She was the best monarch England ever had because she didn't have a man around getting in her head and trying to take over. She was married to her kingdom. That's gonna be me."

"Cool, but get back to me after you hear Kas's voice. It's deep and rough. You can't have Legion, though. Legion is mine."

"*Really?* You have something with the duke?"

Her lips curved. "I will. And if you go out with Kas, he might help you melt away this whole 'bitter, sad woman' vibe."

"I'm not bitter," I protested. "I just think most romance is bullshit. It's cotton candy. It looks nice, and it tastes kind of good at first, but ultimately, it just makes you want to puke."

"That's a lot of rage you have for cotton candy."

Our feelings for each other were an illusion, the product of Lilu lust magic. They were spun sugar that dissolved at the first sign of a storm.

She nodded. "No more Orion. I'm just saying there are better, less genocidal options who are also hot as fuck. You know, once you win the trials. Get yourself in a positive headspace before you come into the City of Thorns. Find a new man, one less murdery."

Every inch of my body was tightening with resolve. "I'm perfectly happy. But what matters now is stopping a tyrant before he slaughters all the humans." I lifted my coffee in salute. "And that all starts tonight."

She heaved a deep breath. "Okay. But you should probably know that the demon hunters are completely staked out by the entrance, waiting for you to walk up to that gate."

Anticipation crackled over me. "Good thing Orion showed me the tunnel system, then."

❧ 3 ❧
ROWAN

Beneath the City of Thorns, the world was quiet as death. I stalked through the shadows in borrowed clothes, all black. A bag bounced against my hip as I walked, heavy with the weight of the gauntlet.

From under the city, I could hear vibrations through the stones—the sounds of dancing and singing.

In the initial trial by combat, no weapons were allowed. Fortunately, Tammuz had trained me to fight like a demon: unarmed, but using my claws as a weapon.

Just beneath the demon city, the promise of magic beckoned me closer. Once I was in their world—*my* world —power and grace would flow through my body. Images flared in my thoughts: Orion's eyes darkening to black, his lip pulled back from his fangs as he lunged for me...

Hard not to hear his words replaying in my mind. *You don't have it in you, love.*

My fingertips curled, and ice-cold anger rushed through my body, chilling me to the marrow. My fury was a hurricane wind that drowned out all the thoughts in my mind.

As I reached the place where a few cracks of light pierced the darkness, I no longer had words with which to think.

Fingers and toes gripping the spaces between the rocks, I climbed up the tunnel wall. With one hand, I pushed the metal covering aside. The star-dappled night arched over me, and I breathed in the fragrant, humid air of the City of Thorns.

When I pulled myself out onto the dark riverside, my magic slammed into me, spreading outward from my lungs. Power skimmed down my thighs, my calves—hot and delicious, a buzzing warmth. Faintly, I was glowing, overcome by the urge to run and fly and tear through the air, singing to the stars. The return of my power was like taking the first breath of air after being held underwater —*glorious*.

Forcing myself to focus, I crouched down and slid the cover back over the opening, then straightened to take in my surroundings. The Acheron River rushed past me to the left, and the dark Elysian Wilderness spread out behind it, its shadows strangely inviting. My mouth started watering. I hungered to sprint through that primal darkness—to hunt like I had in the underworld.

I'd fought there once, but I was no longer the Rowan who needed makeshift flame throwers to survive a battle. I'd journeyed to the underworld. I'd died at the hands of a raving mob. I'd come back to life. I'd learned lessons at the hands of a god.

I wasn't stupid enough to think this would be easy, but I had a *chance*.

I turned, eyeing the apartment I'd stayed in—the one with a view of the pool. A little blade pierced my chest when I recalled the alliance Orion and I once had when he was teaching me to *act* like a succubus. Didn't really need those lessons, as it turned out.

I started to hurry toward the festival, my nerves sparking. I moved quickly past the Asmodean Ward and into the ward of Abaddon. As I turned away from the river, golden stone buildings towered over me. When I drew closer to the Tower of Baal on the eastern edge of the city, the sound of the festival floated on the wind, rhythmic and intoxicating.

My skin tingled with anticipation as I stalked through an alleyway, and I felt my hips swaying with the confidence of a succubus. Through an archway, I crossed into the broad square before the Tower of Baal. A glittering, bejeweled crowd spread out before me.

I had to hand it to Orion. Seemed like he knew how to put on a party, even after all those years in isolation. In the air, glowing lights hung suspended by magic, some shaped like crescents and some like full moons. On the other side of the square, rays of silver light projected the moon's cycles onto the walls outside the tower.

Demons whirled and danced to a mesmerizing beat, with the sound of vocal harmonies layered over it. Most of the guests wore white and silver, and their flutes of champagne seemed to shimmer, opalescent. A tree stood in the center of the square—one that hadn't been there weeks ago. It towered above the revelers, and pearly lanterns hung from its gnarled boughs like plump jewels.

Tonight, the stars seemed brighter than ever, and the vibrance of the full moon almost made it seem like it had shown up to party along with its worshippers.

No one had noticed me yet, lurking in the shadows. Unseen, I reached into the bag at my hip and pulled out the gauntlet.

From the corner of the square, I scanned the crowd, searching for the king. Most new monarchs would relish the limelight and take center stage. But apparently, that wasn't Orion's style. A festival honoring night was perfect for him, when he kept as much as possible cloaked in darkness—including the truth about himself.

I dropped the empty bag at my feet.

Gripping the iron gauntlet, I took a few steps into the square. Slowly, the eyes started to turn to me, and one or two people yelped, smacking the arms of their dancing partners. A hush spread over the festival as whispers began to spread. The music faded to silence, and the crowd parted around me. Tension thickened the air.

At last, the only noise remaining was a quiet murmuring in the crowd, and the slamming of my heart against my ribs. How would Orion handle this?

"Rowan." The king's voice from behind me was a stroke of velvet up my spine, and a hot shiver ran through every inch of me.

I turned to see him standing behind me, a lock of hair falling in his eyes. He didn't wear a crown, and he looked perfectly relaxed, his hands in his pockets. He wore a simple dark blue button-down shirt that stretched across his muscled arms and shoulders, and dark gray trousers.

Shadows wrapped around him, but his eyes glowed with icy light. If it weren't for his shockingly beautiful face and silver hair, he'd have blended with the darkness behind him.

I tossed the gauntlet down, and it clanged at his feet. Nevertheless, he kept his eyes locked on me.

With a practiced tongue, I invoked the archaic Demonic challenge to the king. "*Parzilu Sarrum Tahuzu.*"

"You've come for the crown," he said, a faint smile curling his lips.

"You don't seem surprised."

He shrugged slowly. "Maybe I was starting to miss you."

Ah. There it was—the incubus charm. The façade. It was a trick that Tammuz had taught me: confuse your opponent until they can't figure out how to respond, get them to let down their guard.

Orion had no choice now, though. The trial was starting either way.

He cocked his head. "You don't seem scared, considering what you're about to undertake."

My fingers twitched. "Of course I am," I said quietly, so only he and I could hear. "But I'm gonna kick your ass anyway."

His response was what looked like a truly dazzling and genuine smile. Disarming. Throwing me off guard.

He arched an eyebrow, taking a few graceful steps forward. "You don't think we should join forces, love?

Everyone else seems to think so, including Lucifer himself. After all, he did mark both of us."

Was that a hint of mockery in his tone? Hard to tell with him.

According to the ancient courtly customs of demonic fighting, I was supposed to wait until he was ready to begin the fight—when he picked up the gauntlet, formally accepting the trial. But that part wasn't a *law*, per se, just a convention. And the longer I waited, the greater the opportunity I'd give him to flirt with me until I no longer knew what was happening.

I lunged forward. Lightning-fast, I slammed my fist into the side of his head.

❧ 4 ❧
ROWAN

The force of the blow echoed off the stones, and he nearly lost his balance. He regained his composure well enough to retaliate with a punch, but I blocked it with my right forearm. I brought down my left fist hard, into his shoulder.

My feet landed on the ground, and my claws shot out from my fingertips. In a fraction of a heartbeat, I made a move for Orion's throat, but he arched his back, his head dodging out of the way. As he did, he grabbed my wrist, *hard*. For just a moment, the world seemed to slow as we stared at each other, and a briny wind toyed with my hair. Why did he look so fucking exhilarated by this? Like he was enjoying himself?

"I wanted revenge," I whispered. "You took it from me."

His pale eyes had a sorrowful expression that *nearly* made me feel bad for him...that is, until he twisted my arm behind my back, spinning me away from him.

Pain shot up my arm, and he leaned down to whisper in my ear, "I'm sorry."

My jaw clenched. *Fucking incubus mind games.*

I brought my left arm back into his ribs with enough ferocity that he dropped his grip on my arm. I spun, then slashed my claws through his gut. But something stopped me from going deeper, pushing harder—even though he'd live. It was an instinct I couldn't overcome.

Orion still hadn't brought out his claws, and he punched me again—but I blocked it. The force of his wrist against my forearm was like a sledgehammer falling from a thousand feet, and I was pretty sure my bones fractured for a moment. But as a demon in the City of Thorns, I healed quickly.

As my wings burst from my back, I lifted off the ground. Orion was up in the air faster than I'd expected, his wings pounding the night.

If I'd expected him to look fearful or enraged, I'd have been disappointed.

In the air, he was giving me a look of pure mischief, pale eyes glistening. We might as well have been dancing. "Did you miss me as much as I missed you?"

"Only if you didn't miss me at all." My claws glinted in the moonlight—but before I could strike, he soared past me, blending into the darkness itself. Had he just...disappeared?

I'd never seen him do that before. How many hidden powers did this cocky fucker have? And how was I supposed to win if I couldn't even see him?

I inhaled, trusting my demonic instincts to help find

him. Soon enough, his exotic magic thrummed faintly along my skin, and I detected his scent. *Cedar.* He'd moved closer to the tower walls. Soaring through the air, I followed his seductive, fragrant trail, but I still couldn't see him.

I turned, scanning the night air, the crowd below. That was when he appeared again—a powerful warrior's body materialized out of moonlight. He rushed forward, and I started to fly to meet him, to strike first.

But his velocity was so intense that he slammed me hard into the tower wall. I flinched, anticipating the shock of pain that would splinter my back. But the pain didn't register. Orion had deftly managed to cushion the blow— one hand around my waist, holding me closer to his rock-hard chest, and the other pressed against the stone wall itself to stop me from making contact.

His warm magic swept around me, singing over my skin. The night wind whipped over us. I'd never felt so alive.

"I shouldn't have kicked you out," he said softly. Up here, the silver light washed over his perfect cheekbones and sparked in his eyes. For the first time, I noticed that the pale blue in his eyes was shot through with silver flecks like moonlight. "I'm sorry I took the revenge that should have been yours."

"Here it is," I hissed, pressed against him. "The incubus's most confounding weapon. Charm."

His fingers were tight around my waist. "Do you know what I like about you, Rowan? This city is full of powerful demons, and not a single one of them has the balls to admit that they're scared of anything." His eyes seemed to be searching mine. "And that's a lie we're living. Because we're all terrified of something."

"What scares you?" I breathed.

His mouth was an inch from mine now, and he was staring at my lips as if he were going to kiss me. "You." His eyes flicked up to meet mine again. "Among other things."

"What other things?"

His breath warmed the crook of my neck. "Someday, I'll tell you."

Throwing me off guard. I slid my palms up his chest, then pushed him away from me with all the force I could muster. He flew back into the air, but he managed to stay suspended, looking startled.

I rushed forward, angling my wings for speed. I brought out my claws, ready to strike again. But Orion rushed forward, caught me around the waist, and pulled me in against him again. Our wings pounding behind us, and we hung suspended in the air like the moon itself.

I wrapped my arms over his shoulders.

Staring deep into my eyes, he murmured, "Why not join me, love?" His breath warmed the crook of my neck.

"Because, *love*," I said, "you want to fucking murder everyone."

No denial from him. Instead, he cupped the side of my face, and he stroked his thumb gently over my cheek. "Don't you want to be free?" he purred. "Demons were never meant to be caged. Cambriel might have been the one to murder your parents, but the mortals are the reason they were in hiding in the first place, vulnerable without the power that belonged to them."

The little boy from my nightmare flashed in my mind,

and a surge of protectiveness lit me up. A long-buried animal instinct sent aggression snapping through my nerves.

I wasn't mortal anymore.

Demons hunt.

I wanted to devour the beautiful thing before me, to feed off his essence.

My fangs lengthened, and I sank them deep into Orion's throat. His blood surged into my mouth—deliciously sweet and with a metallic tinge, a dark sort of ambrosia. This was life. This was power. I dominated him.

No *wonder* demons liked drinking blood.

With a snarl, he pushed me away.

He held his hand against the puncture marks, his brow furrowed. "No one's ever bitten me before."

Remember when you said I didn't have it in me? That you didn't respect me enough to hate me?

I wiped the back of my hand across my mouth. "Fair's fair. You drank my blood the first night we met."

I'd learned something from this fight—Orion was still stronger than me, still faster. But he was vulnerable to the element of surprise.

The corner of his mouth quirked. "You've changed, Rowan."

Force your enemy to let down his guard.

I flew a little closer, eyebrows rising. "Of course I've changed. I trained with the Dying God. The *Chaos* God. Bit of a dysfunctional family you've got, isn't it? He's your father, and he taught me how to kill you."

His faint smile faltered with uncertainty.

Now.

The night wind swept over me, and I swiped for his throat with my claws. Blood arced through the air, and I used my wings to give me the speed of a hurricane. I slammed into Orion, and we hurtled toward the ground together. We hit the stone with a force that cracked the rock beneath him. It sent shockwaves across the square as the ground fractured. Orion's wings were still out, spread beneath him in dark arches of feathers. I was straddling him, legs wrapped around his waist. He stared up at me, catching his breath.

I'd won.

Around us, the crowd of onlookers gasped.

It must have hurt like a bitch when his wings met the rock, but the pain didn't even register on his perfect features. "Tammuz," he said, his voice rasping.

It was glowing now—the star of Lucifer on his forehead. I reached down to touch it.

"Your real father," I said. "He's the one who gave us these marks. To cause chaos."

He grazed his fingertip over my forearm, and I realized it was the spot where the tattoo of the skeleton key marked my skin. "Is it true?"

Orion's blood had spilled down his front and started to dry on his neck, but the gash in his throat was healing already.

I shrugged. "It's what he said. But I don't trust either of you to tell the truth, so who knows?"

"He told me you were after my crown."

I leaned down, so mesmerized by the thrill of victory that I nearly forgot the silent crowd around us. "He was right."

He cupped my jaw and whispered, "This was a painful way to get your legs wrapped around me again. But maybe it was worth it."

I slid off him and rose to my full height, surveying the hushed crowd around us. Orion got to his feet by my side.

The crowd of onlookers stared at us silently, as if they were still waiting for more bloodshed. I almost had the sense that this trial had been a disappointment for them, that they'd craved a fresh, beating demon heart pumping on the stones, and all they'd gotten were some broken wings.

I caught Shai's attention as she stood near the front of the crowd, her eyes wide. She beamed at me, grinning. Legion stood by her side. The leader of the Sathanas Ward wore a crisp white shirt, his sleeves rolled up to show off his tattoos. His long black hair was tied up. On the other side of her was a blond demon with piercing amber eyes and thorny tattoos coiling over his forearms, spiky swirls that wound all the way up to his neck. With a faint smile, he nodded to me—almost a bow. Shai's new friend, I assumed.

By my side, Orion's body faintly glowed with silver like the moon we were celebrating.

I raised a hand. "City of Thorns! You have two leaders now, a king and a shadow scion. And when the trials are completed, I hope to be your queen."

"Do not try to win my favor by hurting her." Orion's voice boomed. "The ancient laws of the demon trials protect her, and I will personally tear out the heart of anyone who lays a finger on her." He held my gaze for a moment before turning back to his subjects. "The woman you see before you is not the monster who murdered the Lilu. Don't make the same mistake I did. This is Rowan Morgenstern, not Mortana, and the two of them could not be more different." He cast a sidelong glance at me. "Rowan is welcome here, and as king, I will be giving her the best I have to offer until the trial has ended." His smile was truly dazzling.

The incubus charm offensive.

And with his gracious speech concluded, darkness swept around him. He slipped into the crowd again, enveloped in the shadows.

Lucifer was the original Lightbringer. His twin, Tammuz, reigned in darkness. And here was Tammuz's son, a creature of chaos and night.

Was there anything else I didn't know about him? Another godlike power I hadn't yet seen?

As ever, Orion was always keeping the truth about himself hidden in the darkness.

❧ 5 ❧
ROWAN

Orion had disappeared without explaining what I was supposed to do, so I figured I might as well enjoy myself. This was, after all, a festival. Long ago, a Lilu like me would have been to plenty of these. The music swelled in the air again, and mortal servers rushed around with trays of pastries and champagne.

Even if I was only a shadow scion, I was being treated like a queen already. A small crowd had formed around me, and someone handed me a champagne flute. Another person handed me a small crescent-shaped cake with silvery frosting. I bit into it, delighted to find that someone had decided the moon should taste like chocolate and raspberry.

Shai stood by my side, and given the way she was swaying, I guessed she was on at least her third glass of bubbly. "I swear to the gods, Rowan. My heart was in my throat the whole time. I really can't handle this shit."

Next to me, a woman with platinum hair and a silver

dress leaned in closer. "What was he saying to you when you were fighting? Was he proposing a truce?"

Orion was predictable, even to them. He'd been fine with exiling me weeks ago, but now that I'd returned to challenge his power, he'd decided that teamwork was the way to go, and maybe I could drop the whole idea about taking his crown from him.

I shrugged. "Oh, you know. He was just being his usual charming self. Trying to distract me from winning."

Around me, the other demons craned their necks, listening to every word I said.

"You look radiant!" said another woman from the back.

A male demon with bronze horns lifted his champagne flute. "Truly regal, Shadow Scion."

I cast a quick look at Shai, who just shrugged. I wasn't used to being showered in compliments, and I had no idea how to respond. Of course, they were only hedging their bets, hoping to be on good terms with the next ruler. As soon as I walked away, they'd be doing the same to Orion.

"Do you need anything, Lady Morgenstern?" someone asked from behind.

What I really needed right now after that exhausting fight was not to be the center of attention.

I lifted my empty glass, and before I could say another word, someone snatched it away to refill it. But I'd been in a dark underworld for what felt like a year, and then in a quiet apartment by myself. I wasn't quite used to all these people yet. Even the moon seemed too bright, somehow. Why did I feel like I could hear everyone's breathing?

I held up my hand. "Thank you, I've had enough champagne. I'm going to get some rest and think about the next trial."

I forced my way out of the crowd, desperate for space. Once I reached the edges of the festival, my gaze flicked toward the river. Following the Acheron was always the easiest way around the City of Thorns, and walking west along the bank would take me back to my apartment that overlooked the pool. Towering stone buildings loomed over me on one side. On the other, the forest seemed to beckon. When I'd first arrived here, the wilderness had struck me as sinister. Now, it looked like heaven. The sight of it made my fangs lengthen and my heart beat faster. I ran my tongue over my teeth, dizzy for a moment with hunger.

What was I hungry for? Something I couldn't name, a power I'd once possessed.

I glanced down at the tattoo on my arm and traced my fingertips over the dark contours of the skeleton key. In the underworld with Tammuz, I'd lived like a real demon. With just the two of us there, I'd trained in a primal world, becoming a predator. A memory flashed in my mind: I'd taken down a stag with my bare hands, sinking my teeth into its neck to feast on it.

I swallowed hard, shocked to remember I'd eaten it raw.

I started toward the stone river walk, breathing in the humid air. For now, the ball was in my court. As the shadow scion, I would choose the next trial. The time, the location, the task...

What I'd learned from tonight was that anything

involving physical strength was a risk. Maybe I'd win, maybe not.

As I crossed onto the river walk, I heard Shai calling my name, and the sound echoed off the stones. I turned to see her walking between Legion and the blond demon. They really did make a gorgeous trio.

"I wanted to introduce you to my friends," said Shai breathlessly as she drew closer.

The blond held out his hand, and I shook it, my gaze trailing over the tattoos that snaked around his arms. His eyes were the color of whiskey. "I'm Kasyade. But almost everyone calls me Kas. And I am absolutely delighted to meet a real succubus." With his messed-up hair, he had an almost boyish look—which made his deep, gravelly voice unexpected. "I was already intrigued by Mortana, but I didn't want to get anywhere near her, given her reputation."

This close, I got a better look at him. He was styled much more casually than most of the demons I'd seen, in dark jeans and a T-shirt that gave him a kind of tattooed, muscular, James Dean look.

I glanced at Legion, who was clean shaven and dressed more formally. "We've met before," I said, "but I suppose I was Mortana then."

Moonlight glinted in his angular brown eyes. "It took a long time for Shai to convince me that you were someone different. But then I suppose if you were the real Mortana, a Lilu king would have ripped out your heart by now. And he still might, of course, since you're trying to take the crown from him."

Kas sighed. "Please excuse my blunt friend." He

glanced over his shoulder. "But he's right. You're not safe here, no matter what the king said."

I shook my head. "I'm sure Orion knows the rules are very strict. He's not allowed to hurt me outside the trials."

Shai hooked her arm into mine. "We'll escort you home anyway."

Kas quirked a lopsided smile, his cheek dimpling on one side. "I didn't want to miss the chance to meet our city's first queen."

"I like your confidence in me, Kas," I said.

As we started walking, the music from the festival faded into the distance.

Legion's black eyebrows knitted together as he looked at me. "The Asmodean quarter...don't you find it a bit..."

"Haunted?" asked Kas.

I glanced between them. "Do you two always finish each other's sentences?"

"We've known each since we were little boys," said Kas. "Since before the city was founded."

"So you're older than Orion?"

"Old and wise," said Shai. "Exactly why they'd be perfect to help you prepare for the next trial."

My gaze flicked between the two male demons. "What if I lose? And what if Orion takes out his rage on you two?"

"We survived the mad king Azriel," said Legion. "We can survive the mad king Orion."

"All things being equal," said Kas, "we'd prefer someone sane. That's why we'll help you."

The wind rushed off the river, giving me goosebumps.

On our right, we passed a stone building with turrets and windows lit up with warm light.

"What do you think of Orion, then?" I asked.

"They know he wants to murder all the mortals," said Shai. "Because I told them."

Legion's dark eyes slid to me. "I remember what it was like back then, when the mortals invaded our City after the war. First, they weakened our magic. Then they cut off the heads of the Lilu who resisted and stuck them on pikes. Anyone who survived was marched past the remains of their families. We thought the Lilu were being led to their deaths. None of us ever imagined some of them survived. We never spoke of them. We all felt guilty. We had no clue Orion was still down there. The idea that someone was locked up by himself in a dungeon after all that—there's no way he could be sane."

Kas ran a hand through his messy hair. "Honestly, the thought of someone enduring that is unbearable."

"Stop," I said. "You're going to make me feel bad for him, and then I'll lose."

"Just remember," said Shai, "he said you were boring. It's really the worst thing a person could say, even if he didn't mean it."

Kas's brow furrowed. "King Nergal told us that the mortals' revenge on the Lilu was the price we had to pay for losing the war. It was a sacrifice. But the truth was, he wanted the Lilu gone, too. They were a threat to him. They were too powerful, and he had no conscience whatsoever. And that is why, sometimes, I wonder if the mortals have it right. Maybe we should, I don't know, *vote* for a leader instead of letting people decide it by ripping someone's heart out of their chest." He smiled at me. "But if I have to support someone's brute strength, let it be yours. You've at least lived among the mortals. You know how they think. They modernize. We don't. You have that advantage, don't you?"

I narrowed my eyes. "And why should I trust you two ancient demons?"

"Because I said so," said Shai.

"Well, that's your first lesson." Kas's expression had turned serious. "You shouldn't trust us. In the City of Thorns, you shouldn't trust anyone or anything except your own senses."

"And sometimes," added Legion, "don't even trust those."

"True," said Kas. "You can hide things from yourself. Like, you didn't know you were a demon, right?"

"When did you first feel your magic?" asked Legion.

I bit my lip. "I guess the night my mom died was the first time. I saw the reflection of my demon mark in a puddle. But I lost that memory for years, so yeah, you can't always trust your senses or your memories."

"Ah," said Kas quietly. "*Gaze no more in the bitter glass.*

The demons, with their subtle guile

Lift up before us when they pass,

Or only gaze a little while;

For there a fatal image grows

That the stormy night receives."

His words made my skin tingle, and a hush fell over us for a moment.

"No quoting Yeats," said Legion, breaking the silence. "I've had enough of random poetry from you."

Kas leaned in close, his voice low. "The thing about demons is that we keep most of our powers hidden until we really need them. It's part of our culture. We all do it." Kas crossed in front of me, walking backward to keep his twinkling amber eyes on me. "Everyone keeps secrets here. I'm sure you have some of your own." The wind caught his hair as he walked, his movements graceful as a dancer. "So don't trust anyone. Not even me."

My gaze slid over his tattoos, the wild swirls and patterns covering his muscular forearms.

A mournful thought nagged at the back of my mind. I never did find out what Orion's serpent tattoo was about, and at this point, I doubted I ever would.

In front of me, Kas stopped walking abruptly, and I nearly bumped into him. His gaze was on something over my head, and shadows slid through his golden eyes. I looked up, and in the next heartbeat, I knew exactly why.

Orion's tantalizing magic sang over my skin, and I spun around.

Here was the king, draped in shadows, the wind toying with his silver hair. "Thank you for escorting our shadow scion home, but I will take it from here." Underneath his smooth, velvety voice, I heard a distinctly sharp edge. He prowled closer and rested his hand on my waist.

To my surprise, I heard the sound of Kas and Legion growling behind me, and tension crackled the air.

❦ 6 ❦

ROWAN

I stared up at Orion, who was looking over my head at the two other demons. The entire time I'd been fighting him, his eyes had remained pale blue. Only now, when we were standing by the side of a river without a single hint of a threat, did they darken to black.

Orion's gaze slid from Kas to Legion like he was about to murder them both. "As king," he said quietly, "it is my job to keep the shadow scion safe."

"From *whom*, exactly?" asked Kas.

Orion's hand tightened on my waist. Maybe it was time for me to stop this macho display of possessiveness before my new friends ended up as piles of ash on the stones.

"Okay, everyone—" I began.

A flash of hot magic interrupted me, searing the air. Heat slid through my blood, and I stumbled back from the force of Orion's magic.

For one horrible moment, I was certain that Orion had just incinerated everyone around us until I realized I'd been thrust back into Kas's powerful chest.

When I turned to look at the others, I found them staring, dazed and open-mouthed. Shai swayed, a little smile playing on her lips.

I touched her arm. "Shai?"

Ignoring me, she stepped closer to Orion, fluttering her eyelashes. She reached out, touching his chest. "Your Majesty! Do you work out?"

With a low growl, Legion's hand snapped out, and he grabbed Shai's bicep, then spun her around to face him. "Why don't you forget him and show me your room?"

She bit her lip, staring dreamily into Legion's face.

My jaw dropped in disbelief as I realized what he'd done. Orion had slammed them with his incubus magic, and now they were all lust drunk. Somewhere deep down, I had this power, too. I'd just never learned to use it—nor would I ever use it on my friends, because *what the hell?*

When I caught Kas's gaze, the look he was giving me was searing, carnal, his eyes dark as jet. His gaze shamelessly swept down to take in every inch of me. "Rowan." His voice came out as a deep, husky rumble.

In a rush of shadows, Orion swept in front of me and gently wrapped his fingers around Kas's throat. "I *suggest* you find someone else for your attention."

Kas swayed on his feet for a moment, staring into Orion's eyes in a stupor. He sighed deeply, then repeated, "Find someone else."

"Orion. Stop fucking with them," I snapped. "This is why everyone hates the Lilu."

I could feel the effects of his lust magic, too—a warmth that coiled tight in my core, the sensitivity of my skin—but as a succubus, I had more control over myself.

Kas turned away from him, stalking back to the festival. I felt a twinge of disappointment. It would actually be nice to have a group of friends for once.

I cut Orion a sharp look. "This is a little stalkerish, don't you think? Following me and chasing off my new friends?"

He cocked his head. "Everyone hates our kind. We are the last two left, and I'm not letting anything happen to you. Besides, I need to show you to your new room."

"You're not letting anything happen to me?" I started walking quickly, even though I had no idea where my new room was. "Not long ago, you kicked me out of the city and left me to fend for myself, with no magic, surrounded by demon hunters who want me dead. And I'm supposed to suddenly believe you care about my safety?"

"I didn't leave you," he said smoothly. "I had guards watching over you. First in the hotel, then in Shai's aunt's house."

I swallowed hard. "Guards?"

"Anna, with the pink hair. And her cat, Taffy. I thought you would have noticed them."

"Hmm." *Don't trust him, Rowan.* I'd come prepared for his charm, and my iron defenses would withstand it. "So nice of you to look out for me. And yet, you killed my half brother Cambriel, knowing that all I wanted was to avenge my mom."

When he met my gaze, his large blue eyes gleamed. "I made a promise, too, Rowan. A vow to *all* the Lilu dead that I would avenge them. It's why I must be king. And I knew you'd try to stop me, but I made an oath of vengeance to Ashur before I watched him dragged to his death. I promised it to the memory of my mother. To each of them."

I inhaled deeply. "But that's not what's best for the demons who live. Starting a war with the mortals."

Silence stretched out between us, and I listened to the sound of the Acheron rushing past. "I went to find you, Rowan," he said at last. "When you were still in the underworld, and I finally realized you weren't Mortana. I woke one night with this terrible realization that you'd died. Not Mortana, but Rowan. And I felt like my heart had been ripped out." He touched my elbow, leading me away from the river and under a dark archway.

A shiver of pleasure rippled through me from the point of contact, where his fingers were brushing against the back of my arm. Clearly, his incubus magic was still affecting me, because desire swept down into my belly and settled there, making it hard to concentrate. "Okay," was all I could muster.

"Why would I feel your death, Rowan, unless we were connected? We are the twin stars. Our fates are entwined."

My heels clacked over the stones and echoed off the narrow alley. *Iron defenses.* "I'm not giving up the trials, Orion, if that's where you're going with this. Where are you taking me, by the way?"

"To your new palace."

"Palace?" I repeated.

"In the Luciferian Ward, near me." He turned to look at me, his eyes piercing the dark. "Listen, when I thought you were dead, I traveled to the underworld. I was desperate to find you again if I could. And I really didn't know I could feel like that anymore."

"Like what?"

With a sharp intake of breath, he looked away. "Anything," he said vaguely. "I didn't know I could feel anything for the living. And after I passed through Purgatory and found Tammuz, he knew exactly how to get inside my head. He knew exactly what to say, because it had been my mantra for centuries. He knew all along exactly what I'd experienced with Mortana. Tammuz didn't lift a finger to stop it because the chaos delighted him. He played us both, don't you think? He just wanted to be entertained."

"What did he say to you?" I asked.

Orion stopped walking and turned to me. "He said, 'Orion, don't you know that you should never let yourself hope?' He knew that was the lesson I'd learned from Mortana. Letting myself hope was what killed me slowly in the dungeon. Mortana used to promise me I would be released, only to laugh in my face every time I believed her. But maybe it's time I stopped taking my lessons from her."

"Does that mean you no longer want revenge?" As soon as the question was out of my mouth, I was already wondering if I was simply falling into Orion's seductive trap again.

Instead of answering, he led me into an alleyway that opened into a rounded courtyard where myrtle trees bloomed. Their crimson petals scattered over the stones like drops of blood. Here, the air smelled of salt and lemons. It smelled like home to me.

On one side of the courtyard was what I could only assume was the palace—three stories, with turrets and narrow, glowing windows. A few chimneys rose from the roofs, and the star of Lucifer was engraved above enormous oak doors. Buildings ringed the courtyard—stone with steep peaked roofs, some with balconies. Cute place.

Orion turned to me. "I made a promise to Ashur that I would get revenge. I didn't specify what it would be. But I believe the demons must be free, or it could happen again."

"Setting the demons free would start a war."

He studied me. "You mean the mortals would start a war. But we would win. And it's my responsibility to protect demons, not mortals. If mortals want to engage in a suicide mission just because we're no longer trapped in here, then that sounds like their problem."

I shook my head. "I feel like you're repackaging your revenge as 'freedom.'"

He arched an eyebrow. "The demons in the City of Thorns must be set free. It's what a Lightbringer is supposed to do. *Lucifer urbem spinarum libarabit*—the Lightbringer will set free the City of Thorns. It is our destiny, whether you realize it or not."

"Free so they can feed on mortals again?" I asked. "Like you once did."

"Yes, I like the idea of restoring the world to the way it once was. You know something is missing, don't you? We're creatures of the forest, of the wild. We're not meant for cities of stone." He reached for my cheek, then pulled his hand away, his fingers tightening. "We are supposed to hunt—and yes, sometimes that means hunting mortals. That is our nature, love. And we are meant to terrify."

My eyes narrowed, and I took a step closer. "Demons seem happy here. This place is fucking amazing."

A lock of his silver hair grazed his cheekbones. "But it's not enough, is it? This place is a prison of *civilization*." Disdain laced his tone. He leaned down, and his breath warmed the side of my face as he whispered, "Why not give in to what you desire? I know that you feel it, too." The warmth rolling off his muscled body made my breath catch.

Maybe it was the leftover lust magic, but my pulse was out of control.

"I don't want people to die." I was reminding myself, wasn't I?

"And yet, I could hear your heart racing at the thought of freedom."

I pulled myself away from him, heading for the wooden doors.

Of course I couldn't expect Orion to change—he'd been like this for centuries.

Don't you know that you should never let yourself hope?

From the stairs, I turned to face him. "I'm going to sleep, Orion. I'll let you know when I've decided on the next trial."

"Don't trust those demons you were with," he called out.

"I don't trust anyone." I gave him a wry smile. "Least of all you."

✤ 7 ✤

ORION

By my library window, I sipped a scotch. Books and candles littered my desk. From here, I had a view of the Abraxas courtyard, dappled with red petals, and Rowan's palace just on the other side. Inside, the windows of her new home glowed with warm light.

I'd watched as she'd stepped inside the heavy oak doors and they'd closed behind her.

I rose and ran a hand through my hair as I crossed through the library. Three weeks ago, when I'd become king, I'd moved into this house.

I always hated the ostentatiousness of the Tower of Baal, and I had no intention of living there. Ever. I didn't want to be the center of attention—that was for people like Cambriel and Nergal. And now that I was no longer pretending to be a duke, I didn't need the swanky seaside apartment. I just wanted a little cottage in the shadows.

But I wasn't exactly deprived here. I had a library, a balcony, bedroom walls lined with books. Everything was tidy, in exactly the right place.

In the evenings, I ate dinner with my cook at the dining room table with a roaring fire. Amon had been my family's cook before the Lilu massacre. He'd returned to me as soon as he'd learned who I really was. He was the only person here who seemed willing to talk to me about the Lilu, and the only one who talked to me like I was a normal person.

Every night, his two black Labs would curl up under our feet as we ate, hoping for scraps. Castor and Pollux, they were called.

I stepped into my bedroom. This was an old home, built around the time when I was born. The walls were dark wood, with two carved mahogany columns in the center. A little fire burned in the fireplace. In my room, the balcony doors were open, making the flames dance. A single painting hung on the walls: the succubus Lilith, with a snake climbing up her bare leg. Her hair was bright red.

Whisky in hand, I stepped out onto the balcony and glanced up at the stars. I settled into a wooden chair that overlooked the Abraxas courtyard.

With my free hand, I traced my finger over my throat. Even though I'd healed, I could still feel where she'd ripped it open with her claws. When she'd done that, I'd had the distinct impression she'd enjoyed it. The viciousness suited her.

The problem was, she wasn't going to let herself give in to her true nature.

I heard the little clicks of Labrador claws on the tile floor, and I turned to see Castor ambling over to me, a silvery sheen on his black fur. Moonlight glinted in his dark eyes, and he looked up at me with a distinctly guilty expression. When I noticed the smears of butter on his face, I understood why.

"Castor," I said. "You absolute glutton."

He lowered his head and crossed to my feet, where he made himself at home, curling up with a sigh. A salty wind swept over us, rustling his dark fur.

Behind me, the sound of footfalls echoed off the wooden walls.

I turned to see Amon crossing toward me, a glass of whisky in his own hand. His dark brown hair hung over broad shoulders.

Drinks on the balcony—our nightly ritual in these past few weeks.

As he sat down in the chair next to me, my gaze snagged on the jagged scar that ran down his face, from his scalp, across his nose, to his bristled jawline. When the mortals had come for us, he'd tried to protect my mom. I remembered when they'd split his head in half, and I'd assumed he'd died.

He took a sip of his whisky. "You could have won that fight tonight."

I glanced at him out of the corner of my eye. "I'll convince her to come around to my side."

His eyebrows rose. "You still think you can charm her after everything you said and did?"

As soon as I'd kicked her out of the city, I'd started to regret it. Rival or not, I'd *missed* her.

I sucked in a deep breath. "The problem is, she objects to the idea of freeing the demons."

Amon flashed me a sly smile. "Is that maybe because you told her you were after a bloodthirsty revenge crusade against the mortals, and that you wanted to slaughter all of them, even though they had nothing to do with events four hundred years ago? Can't imagine why she'd take issue with that plan. Seems perfectly reasonable."

I grunted, irritated that Amon agreed with her. "It might have something to do with it." I sipped my whiskey. "Fine. Maybe she has a point. But we still need to break the spell trapping us here. The mortals are after her, and they won't relent until I hand her over. As long as we're stuck, they could keep escalating."

"Is it actually possible to break the spell, Your Majesty?"

"Stop calling me that, Amon."

"Fine. Orion, if that's what you want to be called. But why that name? It's not your real one."

I stared at the night sky, so bright here in the City of Thorns. "I was comforted by thinking of the stars in the dungeon. It was the one spark of brightness—thinking of constellations like Orion. I tried to carve them so I could look at them."

My gaze slid over to the constellation of Gemini, the twin stars that beamed near Orion, seeming to reach across the darkness for each other.

I didn't remember my old name, nor did I want to. Whoever I was before had died in the dungeon. When I made the memorial for the Lilu dead, I'd include a nameless silver-haired boy.

Amon breathed in deeply, staring at the sky. "The twin stars. The two Lightbringers. Rowan and Orion."

"I used to dream of them at night when I wasn't

dreaming of food. The twin stars. I never knew what it meant."

"Ah," he said quietly. "And is that why you are sitting out on a balcony staring at your ex-lover's house like a heartbroken lunatic? You are quite literally written in the stars."

I cleared my throat. "It's better if she stays close to me. There are many people here who fear the return of the Lilu."

When I'd thought she was dead in the underworld, it had nearly broken me. I couldn't handle the thought of her dying when she was under my protection here.

Rowan terrified me every bit as much as Mortana did. Mortana had been a sadist with my life in her hands. Rowan, on the other hand, has my heart in her hands.

When I'd first met her, she'd been fragile, easily scared. Innocent. Now, she looked like she wanted to rip my head from my body. But it wasn't death that terrified me. It was the look in her eyes, her anger with me that made me so scared, I could hardly breathe.

In the dungeon, revenge was the promise that had kept me sane. Without a purpose to it all, I would have gone completely mad. That blood oath had been the only way to make meaning out of the horror—a single pinprick of light in the darkness.

Vengeance was the righting of a wrong.

"Orion," said Amon, his voice gravelly, "when are you going to tell me what happened to you?"

Unlike me, Rowan wasn't afraid to tell the truth about herself. My secret would die with me, but Rowan wasn't like the rest of us demons. She was better.

"What happened to me?" I said. "Nothing. Just a lot of boredom and starvation. I ate more than a few rats." Another sip of scotch. "What do you know about Legion and his friend Kas?"

When I'd seen her walking with the two demon males, I'd felt an overwhelming urge to vaporize both of them.

Amon stared at me. "You really don't remember them, either?"

A hazy, distant memory danced in my mind—a dark-haired boy with brown eyes, leading me into the Elysian Wilderness. Older kids I'd once looked up to.

"Oh. A little." But I didn't want to remember that time.

"So many secrets," Amon muttered. "Even keeping secrets from yourself."

I had one other secret: I would love Rowan until I died.

And that was why I deeply regretted what I had to do next.

✣ 8 ✣

ROWAN

I didn't need to follow Orion's orders here. As a shadow scion, I could make my own decision about where to stay. But as much as possible, I wanted Orion to think of me as the clumsy mortal he'd first encountered. I wanted him to let down his guard and completely fail to prepare for the next trial. Which he probably would, because his ego would get in the way.

The palace's lower floor had looked positively medieval. In the entryway, I'd found soldiers lined up on either side of a stone, each one wearing the blue uniform of a soldier, and the royal insignia of the king on their lapels—a crown with a star above it.

All the king's men...

As I'd entered, the king's men stared at me silently, still as statues on a floor of black and white tiles. Without a word, one of them had marched me up to my room.

When he'd shut the door behind me, I'd felt relieved.

My room faced the sea. In here, oak bookshelves lined two of the pale stone walls, and a few candle flames cast warm, dancing light over the room. A bed stood by the open balcony doors, covered in a cream duvet and enormous pillows. A wood table stood next to it, and a brass lamp for reading.

When I surveyed the whole room, my heart squeezed *hard* in my chest. On one of the walls hung two portraits of my parents, taken from their mansion in the Asmodean quarter.

In a daze, I walked closer to them, staring. Before me was the father I'd never known, Duke Moloch—the same red hair as mine, fading to blond around his chin, plus high cheekbones and dark brown eyes like mine. Next to him, my mother looked out over my head, her dark hair piled high—elegant in a way I'd never known her.

The gilded frames looked brand new.

Why, exactly, would Orion reframe these and bring them here? He hadn't known I was coming tonight, I thought. He must have left the festival after the trial and rushed around to get this room set up.

I stared up at Mom. Of course Orion was trying to make me comfortable. He would do whatever he could to get me to let down my guard.

When I glanced at the bedside table, I saw a pen resting beside a small pad of paper, which seemed like an odd touch. But when I moved closer to it, I realized it wasn't just *any* pen. In a daze, I traced my fingertips over the little glittery rainbow symbol on the side, slightly worn with time. Here it was—my lucky pen. I'd been carrying it the night I'd met Orion. Which meant, of course, that it hadn't been very lucky at all.

Still stunned, I turned it around in my fingertips. He'd

kept it all this time? I'd even asked him for it in the prison cell, and he hadn't given it back.

All these charming attempts to win me over...

I dropped it on the table and turned to eye the rest of the setup.

On the wall overlooking the sea, light streamed through a glass door. When I looked outside, I had a view of a balcony made of sand-colored stone. Beyond a low stone wall, the dark silver-flecked sea stretched out forever, blending into the night. Gorgeous.

I opened the door and stepped out into the salt-tinged air. As a demon, my vision was so much better, and I could even see stony islands far out to sea, silvered in the moonlight. The waves pounded against the rocks below me. Tucked in one corner of the balcony, a small, heated pool released curls of steam into the dark sky.

When I peered over the balcony, I found soldiers lining the shoreline. Who did they expect to be coming out of the water? If I had to guess, Orion had probably told them to report to him if I flew off this balcony.

With a sigh, I crossed back into my new room and shut the balcony door, then ripped a piece of paper off the pad. I scribbled a note to Orion:

I don't need this anymore.

WITH THE NOTE FINISHED, I PULLED THE DOOR OPEN. In the dark palace hall, two guards stood across from me. I walked up to one of them and thrust the note and pen into his hands. "Please give my regards to the king when you return this pen to him."

❧

THE MORNING SUN WASHED OVER ME AS I WALKED through the meandering streets of the Luciferian Quarter, looking for somewhere to get breakfast. A servant had knocked on my door this morning, offering to bring me food, but I wanted to get out and stroll around in the daylight.

On one side of me, a canal ran between stone walls, sparkling with gold morning light. On the other side, vine-covered stone homes lined the cobbled road, their roofs sharply peaked. I paused to look in the window of a shop selling curiosities and magical items for witches—a human skull, vials of blood, and large books of magic, their spines etched with silver writing.

Mortal witches learned magic from demons at Belial University and at universities in other demon cities. If a mortal became very, very good at magic, he or she could become a witch.

And for the next trial I had in mind, we would be summoning a powerful dead witch from the underworld. Thus, I had nine days to master necromancy.

I pulled the door open, listening to the tinkling of bells as I stepped inside. The walls in here were painted black, and bell jars lined crooked shelves—stuffed birds, a brass hand with contorted fingers, and jars of herbs and potions.

A mortal man with a long beard sat behind the counter, staring at me. "Shadow scion..." he muttered.

When the bells chimed behind me, I turned to see Kas in the doorway, leaning against the frame. His sleeves were rolled up, revealing tattoos of stars on his forearms. His chin was tilted down, and a smile ghosted over his lips. A lock of his messy blond hair fell before his eyes. "Shadow scion," his deep, rough voice rumbled over the room. "We've been looking for you."

My eyebrows rose. "*We?*"

He turned to step outside and held the door open for me. "Shai and Legion. Breakfast awaits you."

I followed behind him, squinting in the bright sunlight. "Do we have plans?"

He turned back to me with a little smile. "We do. I'm making us pancakes and coffee, and then we're going to figure out how to make you queen."

Intrigued, I walked beside him. "You told me not to trust you."

"Absolutely do not." His eyebrow quirked. "But I'm going to help you anyway."

❧ 9 ❧
ORION

I t felt haunted in here, in the old brick mansion where my family had once lived. My footfalls echoed off the dusty tile floors. I could have this place cleaned, but something stopped me from bringing it back to life. It was a mausoleum now, the air musty and stale. This home was a grave.

So why the fuck was I in here?

I supposed this was the only place where I could douse the fire of my lust for Rowan. Because when she was around, I couldn't think. I couldn't breathe when her image came into my mind. Every time I thought of her, my heart stopped. Her deep brown eyes, with the faint ring of gold at the edges. Her full lips painted red, the tiny smattering of freckles on her nose, the curve of her hips. The way she'd moaned when I'd fucked her—

Anyway, what sort of king would I be if I couldn't get my mind off her?

This was the only place I could find respite from

thinking of her. Sadness twined through this place like a heavy mist.

From the tile floor, I eyed the old busts in the hallway alcoves, their faces smashed, some shattered on the floor.

I felt the world tilting beneath me as my gaze roamed over the deep red stain on the floor. That was where my brother, Molor, had been murdered while I watched.

My breath sped up, and I couldn't quite get enough air in here.

He'd tried to stand in front of our mother because he was so strong—

At least, my older brother had *seemed* so large and powerful to me then. I was shocked that the soldiers had knocked him down. Back then, I'd thought of him as a god. A titan. Someone who would always protect me. And maybe that was why I hadn't unleashed the fire I had in me, because if only I'd been thinking clearly, I could have burned the mortals to ash. They'd weakened our power before invading, but I'd still had some.

But surely Molor would stop them.

Molor had been the one to teach me curses, and he'd tried to teach me to land a punch. Every time he'd left the house, I'd screamed that I wanted to go with him.

In a daze, I walked through the hallway to his old room. He'd always been tidy, and it was neat even now, despite the dust and cobwebs. His was a simple, elegant room with white walls and dark wooden beams across the ceiling, an old flagstone floor and a threadbare rug. Stags' antlers jutted from the wall above the mantel. His bed was a four-poster, the mahogany posts etched with thorns. Pale light streamed in through mullioned windows onto a desk stacked with old books.

I opened his wardrobe, stunned to see how small his clothes were. Had he really been that *small?*

And the children's toys in here—a doll in a white dress with black beads for eyes, and a wooden top with black numbers on it. I picked the top up, turning it over between my fingers. If the mortals hadn't come, Molor would have taught me how to play this game. As it was, I had no idea what it was for.

When my gaze flicked up at the clothes, I felt my breath leave my lungs. How could he have been so tiny? So delicate?

I pulled out one of his old suits, one with black velvety fabric trimmed with gold. I remembered this one...Molor had been so proud of it. He'd planned to wear it at his fourteenth birthday. Fourteen was a big deal for demons, and my parents had been planning the party a year in advance.

I laid it on the bed, staring at it. He hadn't quite grown into it by the time he was killed, and he never would.

With a lump in my throat, I crossed to the window and stared out at the Asmodean clocktower. At some point, it had stopped working, the hands frozen at six p.m. I couldn't help but wonder if time had frozen there when the mortals had arrived at dusk, because that was when the world had stopped. Or maybe it stopped with Molor's death—

When the Puritans cut out Molor's heart on the living room floor, it had really felt like they were taking mine with it. The pain had been blinding.

Clouds crept across the sun, casting the abandoned town square in shadow.

I stared through the old glass at the clock tower, a beautiful work of art for its time—a stone structure with gold-painted discs that had once moved. It had not only told the time, but also the position of the sun and moon and the astrological signs. A stunning feat of technology, learned from the mortals. A faint memory flickered at the recesses of my mind—mechanical statues that had once appeared from doors on either side of those gleaming discs: a figure of the king, and one of the god Lucifer, appearing to hand him a crown.

Long ago, everyone in the town had set their pocket watches by those gold hands. I remembered staring at it, waiting for the king to slide out from the door. Captivated by the magic.

I couldn't breathe in here anymore.

When the mortals came, my world had stopped, the sky had gone dark, and the air had turned to ash.

I could never let myself feel loss like that again. And what if I caused *her* to feel that pain because I let her love me? Because there really was nothing worse.

I turned, desperate to be out of this tomb.

I'd tried to create prison walls around me to keep myself safe, but Rowan was breaking them down. This was a problem.

I pulled her pen from my pocket, staring at the absurd chipped rainbow symbol on the side. A ridiculous thing. It shocked me how much it had hurt when she'd returned this to me. What the *hell*, Orion?

Furious at myself, I threw the front door open and stepped into the stone square.

One of my soldiers stood by the door, always protecting me—as if *I* needed protecting. With his pale skin and long, black hair, he looked like a spirit from the underworld. "Jasper," I said, "I have a very important task I need you to undertake."

Because I would do whatever I could to avoid feeling that agony of loss again.

ROWAN

K as lived in a home on a crowded street, a house with a white Tudor-style front and crisscrossing wooden beams that overlooked the busy lane. Unlike Orion's pristine apartment, this place was littered with trinkets and oddities: a desk strewn with books before a mullioned window, a telescope, an old globe.

Kas stood at an iron stove before the kitchen window, making us pancakes, and the scent of butter filled the air. It all seemed almost...human. Normal.

Shai and Legion sat across from me, sipping coffee at a table littered with handwritten notes, plates, and a little pile of cutlery. A window to my right overlooked a narrow city street and shops covered with climbing ivy.

Shai picked up one of the papers, frowning at it. "What's this?"

"Oh, gods." Standing above the frying pan, Kas glanced over his shoulder. "That's my art. Don't look."

Of course we looked. I saw beautiful pencil drawings of the natural world—birds, trees, butterflies. A self-portrait lay among them, perfectly rendered. His skill was truly remarkable, almost photorealistic.

Legion sipped his coffee and picked up a sketch of two toadstools. "Are you ever going to do anything with your art?"

"More tattoos, maybe," Kas grumbled. He carried a heaping platter of pancakes in one hand, and he forked two onto my plate. "But we're not here to discuss my hobbies, are we?"

The corner of Shai's mouth quirked. "Legion's hobbies, then? Because he looks like a giant, tattooed badass, but he's been painting little pewter figurines of soldiers."

Legion pinned her with his gaze. "I wouldn't expect someone from the mortal realm to understand the fine art of miniature battle recreation."

"Just admit you're a dork." Kas dropped pancakes onto his plate.

My mouth watered, and I poured out a thin stream of maple syrup onto my pancakes. "What's on today's agenda?"

"We're planning for your trial," said Shai. "Have we decided what we're doing yet?"

"*We?*" I bit into the pancakes—thin and buttery, just the way I liked them. "Well, I've decided. I'll be announcing it later today. The trial requires summoning a witch from the underworld and stealing his magical talisman. In this case, a crown of blackthorn that enhances his magical powers."

"Spellcraft," said Shai. "Invocations in Demonic. You've never been to school for that."

"Neither has Orion. I heard him use a Demonic spell

once, in the underworld, but he never had any formal education." I picked up my coffee cup, warming my hands. "In any case, *all* the trials involve demonic invocations. They're supposed to test not only physical strength and strategy, but the ancient art of Demonic spellcraft, too. And tonight is my deadline to announce it."

"How do you win?" asked Shai. "You just steal the crown?"

"The person who is successful at the summoning will have an advantage. I'd be linked to the witch, and that would make it easier to find him. But it doesn't guarantee a win."

"Summoning the dead requires extremely powerful magic," said Legion. "Can you compete with Orion in how much power you have?"

Shai caught my eye. "She's a Lightbringer, just like him. She has as much power as he does, and she has the advantage of not being insane."

"True," said Legion. "But none of us really know what Lightbringer power does. We've never seen it or experienced it."

"Magic is new to me," I admitted. "But there's no way around it. All the trials involve some sort of invocations, magic summoning. And since this one doesn't involve direct combat between Orion and me, it's one of the least dangerous options."

"Okay." Kas watched me over his steaming coffee. "Summoning requires precision. How good is your pronunciation of Demonic spells?"

I winced. "Maybe the three of you could help me practice."

"Who is this witch you'll being bringing back from the dead?" asked Shai. "Is he dangerous?"

"He was a king sixteen hundred years ago, Alaric of the Visigoths. Powerful enough to sack Rome. So here's how it works. First, Orion and I mark our foreheads with the blood of a dead witch. That will help break down the barrier to the dead people. Then we do the creepy demonic chanting. Whoever summons the dead witch first will have a bond with him, and the bond will help us locate him. So hopefully, I summon him, use the bond to find him, bind him up with magic, and snag the crown. And rule over a golden age, as your unmarried ginger queen."

Legion stared at me over his coffee. "We maybe have to go over some of the magical terms."

"Sure," I said.

"Taking a crown from a mortal isn't hard," he added. "It's the necromancy you'll struggle with."

"Not hard?" Kas's eyebrows rose. "He's a witch, not an ordinary mortal. Do you have any idea how dangerous the most powerful witches are? Those from the greatest generations long ago?"

Outside, the sky was growing darker, shadows sliding across the sun.

Legion frowned. "Are you scared of mortals?"

"I am." Shai's eyes flashed. "And if you're not, you're underestimating them. Have you heard of *la sorcière de Brocéliande*?"

"Who was she?" I asked.

A cold tingle of magic shivered over my skin as I sipped my coffee. Outside, a light rain started pattering the windows and sliding down the glass in rivulets.

Shai leaned forward, her mahogany eyes gleaming. "She was the most terrifying witch who ever lived. In the fifteenth century, she singlehandedly killed an entire army of demons in Rennes-le-Château. She blamed them for murdering her family, and she had them ripped to pieces by ravens, and their flesh crushed under stones." Lightning split the darkness outside, and rain started to hammer the windowpanes. "She absolutely loathed demons."

Thunder boomed, and Kas startled. "Is that you, Shai?"

She shrugged and picked up her coffee. "I wanted to add a bit of atmosphere."

Legion shrugged. "Well, she's dead now. That's what mortals do. They die."

Kas met my gaze. "Until they're raised again by a Lightbringer."

"I'm not raising *la sorcière* de whatever," I said. "Alaric is wily and powerful, but not insane and murderous. The demons who compiled the trials didn't want the whole city slaughtered. We're supposed to find the best leader, not end the demonic species."

The rain still pattered against the windows, a gentle sound.

"And you think you can win this?" asked Legion.

"It's possible," I said. "I've heard Orion use invocation spells before, but I don't think he's spent much time actually practicing magic. Magic didn't work in the dungeon, and he had no one to learn from once he'd freed himself. And I have you all to help me. Orion doesn't understand the concept of asking others for help, or even preparing for anything."

"Raising the dead always works best in the wilderness,

where magic is most powerful," said Shai. "Learned that freshman year."

I nodded. "So I'll go there to practice."

Kas rubbed a hand over the back of his neck, looking worried. "Before you practice raising the dead, let's just go over some of the basics, shall we?"

⟡

FOG WOUND BETWEEN THE LARGE, SINUOUS OAK TREES IN the Elysian Wilderness.

To start, I'd been practicing the name *Alaric* with the correct pronunciation. "Alaric," I said for the twentieth time.

"More emphasis on the *Ala*," said Legion. "Pronounce it like German."

It was adorable that he thought I knew German.

In a black buttoned coat, Shai stood with her arms folded, leaning against the trunk of a gnarled oak. "She's almost there." She flashed me a wicked smile and walked closer, crunching over the leaves. "Can't we try out some real spell magic? I want to see what she can do."

"What do you have in mind?" I asked.

The breeze washed over us, lifting curls of Kas's blond hair. "There are three types of magic that we practice," he said.

Shai cleared her throat. "Excuse me, Kas. I was about to show off." She lifted a finger. "So, we've got medicine—when we use natural materials in magic, like the blood you'll be putting on your forehead. Then there's thaumaturgy. Only demons can use that, not mortals. That's the innate, elemental power that you have, like when you explode with fire. And then finally, invocations. Using language to draw on the magic of the gods and channel it to your will."

I wasn't entirely sure I'd taken all that in. "So can I try raising something from the dead?"

Shai stood directly in front of me. "Magic is connected to emotions," she went on. "If you're dead inside or apathetic, you won't be able to use your elemental fire magic. When I want to control the weather, I think of something that pisses me off, like how my mom forgot to mention that I might be a demon because she's deeply committed to conformity among the mortals." She smiled brightly.

I nodded. "Okay. I've got plenty of intense emotions to choose from."

With his hands in his pockets, Kas took another step closer, crunching over the leaves. "Everyone's magic has a different feel to it. Mine is smooth and silky," he said, "like ribbons gliding over my skin."

Legion held up his hand, and I watched as dark silvery magic played about his fingertips. "Mine feels ice cold."

"And mine vibrates." Shai held up her hands to the side of her mouth to stage whisper. "Now you know why I've been practicing so much."

I cracked a smile. I already knew how my elemental magic felt—hot and bright, just like Orion's.

Legion gripped a thick book of spells, the spine etched with gold letters. "As a demon, your spellcraft is all about trying that innate power you have and using language to create something new. The pronunciation and syntax are key, but you have to have a clear intention, too. You're taking a raw force—your innate power—and shaping it to your will."

"Go ahead." Shai waved a hand at me. "Put it in psychology terms. I know you want to."

I exhaled. "It's like how creativity works," I said. "There are the dreamlike states in your occipital cortex. That's like the gods' power, the raw, unshaped creativity. And your prefrontal cortex at the front of your brain needs to organize them into something meaningful."

Legion stared at me, then blew a strand of black hair out of his eyes. "Sure. Whatever. Maybe just try the spell."

He handed me the book, opened to a page with a short spell, and I took it from him.

I scanned the text, inhaling deeply. The Demonic alphabet was different than ours, and I had no magical ability to read it, sadly. Luckily, there was a phonetic translation on the right side of the pages.

"What does this do?" I asked.

"It's a simple spell," said Legion. "Just bringing clouds into the sky. Anyone should be able to do it."

Shai glared at him. "It's not that simple."

Legion smiled at her. "In the future, I'll remember that you have all the sensitivity of a mortal, and I will phrase my thoughts more carefully."

"It's okay." She smirked at him. "Someday, I'll learn to be condescending and emotionless like the rest of you."

"But emotions and passion are our source of strength," he murmured. "We just save them for the most important occasions. Like magic, and...other things."

They stared at each other, holding eye contact for so long, it was starting to get uncomfortable.

"Right." Kas sighed and pointed at the book. "Ignore them, and channel your emotions. As you read the spell, keep your intention in mind. Envision the clouds. You're directing the magic of the gods. There are two fundamental pillars of magic, power and control. Understood?"

First, the power. That came from emotions, so I held the book open in my hands and envisioned Orion's face. Always good for stirring up some feelings. Anger mixed with regret when I conjured the perfect contours of his face. My blood started to warm up, and I felt the air grow more humid around me. A faint glow beamed from my fingertips.

With my magic summoned, I started to chant the spell as it was written out, careful with my pronunciation.

But when I glanced up at the sky, I was frustrated to find that sunlight still streamed through the leaves.

"That was good," said Shai. "Maybe just a bit more emotion."

I stared at the book, summoning more magic. This time, I thought of Orion swooping down to murder Cambriel. Kicking me out of the city. My mind was aflame with a sense of loss.

Fire sparked in my chest, and it began coursing through my blood as I read the spell. Around me, the wind began to pick up, rushing past. My gaze flicked up again, still seeing blue.

I chanted the spell again and again, and in the hollows of my mind, I heard Orion speaking, his voice cold and emotionless: *Escort this woman out of my realm.*

As I read the spell, light started beaming from my body, illuminating the book's pages. They began to flutter and flip in the wind. Magic crackled around me, and my chest beamed with power. The wind whipped at my hair, and iron-gray storm clouds spilled like ink across the sky. Lightning cracked the clouds, searing the air. As it touched down at the top of a nearby oak tree, an electrical charge sparked from the soil up into my feet.

"Rowan," shouted Shai above the wind. "Too much! Too much!"

Above, the sky opened up, unleashing torrents of ice-cold rain and pelting us with hail. As the wind lashed the trees, leaves caught in the currents and tumbled through the air. The lightning strike had lit the oak on fire, and it blazed like an enormous torch under the dark sky.

"Fuck." Kas pushed his dripping hair off his forehead. "We're going to need to work on that control part."

❧ 11 ❧
ROWAN

S oaking wet, gripping hot cups of tea, the four of us sat around the roaring fireplace in Kas's home. He'd given each of us soft blankets with which to warm up. None of us had managed to stop the rain and hail, and it still hammered the windows, threatening to crack the glass. On the plus side, the ice storm had managed to extinguish the blazing oak tree very nicely.

The two men sat shirtless, showing off their muscles in the dancing firelight. Shai and I weren't complaining.

"Why don't we start next time with something less dangerous?" asked Shai.

"The floating paper," said Legion. "It's one of the first things students learn in magic school. A simple spell, and no trees will catch on fire."

Kas slid me a devious look. "I wouldn't rule it out."

"We have time," I said. "There are still nine more days."

"You'll be fine." He nodded. "Only those blessed by the gods can get this far. At least, that's how the story goes."

"The story?" asked Shai. "You're not a true believer?"

Kas shrugged. "The gods seem a little insane to me. Any being as old as time must be demented. I sometimes wonder what it would be like if we just *voted* for a leader instead of leaving it up to trinkets and the whims of the gods."

"Don't be ridiculous," said Legion.

"You're right," said Kas. "It makes much more sense to see who can hunt down the magic crown from a dead witch first."

"Hey." I shrugged. "I didn't make the rules."

Just as I finished my sentence, something caught my eye in the rain.

I let out a long breath, annoyed to see a demon in a navy blue uniform lurking outside. With his milky white skin and long black hair—wet in the rain—he looked like *he'd* been raised by the dead. "One of Orion's soldiers is spying on us."

"Not a very good spy," said Legion, "if he's hovering right there in the window like a Peeping Tom."

The creepy man disappeared, and a moment later, a knock sounded at the door.

Bare-chested, Kas pulled open the door and lifted his chin. "Can I help you?"

The man's dark eyes slid to me, and he nodded curtly. "The king requests the shadow scion's presence this evening at a memorial service for the Lilu dead. It begins in the Asmodean Ward by the clock tower."

Of course Orion had sent someone to follow me here, no doubt trying to learn what I was doing, in order to gain an advantage.

Kas leaned against his door frame, and his blanket slid off him. "Sorry, who are you?"

"Jasper. Loyal servant to the king." He cut me a sharp look. "May the true king reign until the sun consumes the earth with its flames."

"Okay," said Kas. "Thanks for...that." He shifted from the doorframe and slammed the door. "Weirdo," he muttered.

I met Shai's gaze. Did Orion really want me there to remember the dead, or did he have something up his sleeve?

༒

AT MY SEASIDE PALACE, I'D SELECTED A LONG BLACK dress with capped sleeves.

As I'd arrived in the square just before six, some of Orion's servants had handed out little silver model ships with a candle in the hull. Each one had a handle so we could carry them along. I didn't know what the ships were for, but I held mine now in the hushed silence as a crowd gathered around the old clock tower. Overhead, the setting sun stained the sky with crimson.

This must be the first time the Asmodean square had been filled in hundreds of years.

As I looked around me, I felt like Orion was as remote as a star. An adoring crowd gathered around him. Jasper was right by Orion's side, looking tense, his jaw clenched. He reminded me of a guard dog. Orion, on the other hand, looked perfectly at ease, his beautiful face gilded by the dying sun. Taller than most of the other demons, he leaned down to speak to anyone who approached. All around him, a sea of candles flickered and bobbed in the silver ships.

I was quickly starting to get the impression that apart from my little crew, everyone favored Orion.

I held up my model ship, studying it. For something that looked metallic, it was surprisingly light, and its surface was etched with Demonic words. "These things are beautiful."

Kas leaned closer to me, whispering, "Once, this was how the Lilu mourned. They were creatures of the night and sea. The memorials were called *challariu*. It meant..." His eyebrows drew together. "To be called home. The gods called them home when they died." Kas held my gaze for longer than seemed normal, his amber eyes studying me. He reached up and brushed a flyaway strand of my red hair from my face. "The candles are supposed to light their way to the underworld. It's a path from this world to the next."

I pulled my gaze away from him to find that King Orion was no longer paying attention to the other people in his orbit. Now, his eyes were drilling into Kas, his jaw tensing. The look he was giving Kas sent a chill through my blood.

Orion stalked closer, his eyes locked on my new friend. "I will be escorting the shadow scion. You may find someone else to amuse you."

Rude. I thought I caught a hint of an eye roll from Kas before he stalked away.

"Let's walk to the river," Orion said gruffly. "I know a shortcut. We need to talk. Away from everyone."

He led me toward a narrow street carved between two stone buildings. I should feel nervous that my bloodthirsty rival was leading me into an isolated alley, but I just never felt scared around Orion. This close to him, I breathed in the scent of burnt cedar, heady and masculine. Fuck. I'd forgotten how good he smelled, and I was very much trying not to stare at the broadness of his shoulders or think of the dark shirt stretching over his ridiculously large muscles.

As we walked, I glanced behind us. "Are we going to talk about the spies you have following me?"

"Spies? Think of them as protectors."

I arched an eyebrow. "Right. War is freedom, and spies are my protectors. You have an amazing skill for making words mean different things."

A line formed between his eyebrows. "As long as I am king, Rowan, it's my responsibility to make sure you are safe. And speaking of which, do you really trust two ancient demons you've only just met? You know they were around when the rest of our kind were slaughtered."

Of course he knew they were training me. "Except for Shai, I don't trust anyone. And that includes you, so forgive me if I don't take everything you say at face value."

"Will you at least come to me if you're in danger? When I thought you were dead, Rowan—" A muscle flickered in his jaw, and his eyes darkened. "As I said, it's my job to keep you safe here. That's why I've sealed up the tunnel so no one can get in—the demon hunters have become obsessed with you, and someone has told them that you're in here."

I let out a long breath. "But there's an agreement, right? If a mortal enters without permission, he can be killed."

"And yet, they're willing to risk death just so they can drag you out and kill you. But in the meantime, they're lobbying politicians to put in emergency measures to attack us."

A shudder ran through me. "Attack the whole city? Just because of me?"

"Not just because of you." Orion stopped walking and turned to look at me. Across the river, the shadows from the forest's trees crept over the grass. Clear, crystalline water rushed past us. I tilted up my head to meet his cool gaze. "My spies followed you and the demon hunters in Osborne. I didn't let them get anywhere near you. But unfortunately, that has created new problems. Some of their agents learned of your location. We had to deal with them before they could relay the message."

I sucked in a sharp breath. "You killed more demon hunters."

"It's usually how I deal with things, yes, but it also happened to be the only way to stop them from murdering you in Shai's aunt's apartment. It was only two days ago. I was about to bring you back here when you decided to show up on your own." His expression darkened. "If you win the trial against me, if you become queen, you need to know what you're up against. If they're successful in convincing mortal politicians that we're a threat, they could wipe out this entire city. And all I can do for now is try to head off an attack using our magical wards to keep us safe."

I closed my eyes. "This all started with me killing the congressman."

"You had to, Rowan. He was going to slaughter you like

an animal. And the fact is, it was always going to come to this—us against them. This was always going to happen."

And there he went, sowing doubt in my mind.

I turned away from him, staring at the river as it rushed past. "But they haven't waged war against us yet. You don't need to start one."

"For now, I'll be asking my strongest spell casters to protect us from the mortal missiles that could rain on us at any moment. But as long as demon power fades without these city walls, we will always be at risk. It wasn't the case centuries ago, but now they have weapons that could take down all the walls at once. So, Rowan." He touched my arm, and I turned to face him. "If I die in the trial, you need to carry on that work of protecting the city."

His words took my breath away, and I stared at him. "Don't be ridiculous. You're not going to *die*."

"Why not?"

Good question. I mean, that was usually a primary component of these trials. And yet...I grabbed his arm. "We don't need to kill each other to win the trials. The trial I'm choosing involves summoning a dead sorcerer and stealing his crown. I'm not going to kill you, I just plan to win. Nine days from now. This is your official notice. We're raising Alaric." I did the math in my head. "October thirty-first."

The fact that the trial would fall on Halloween was either a fantastic omen that I was destined for success or a terrible idea. I couldn't yet decide which.

He cocked his head, his pale eyes glinting in the darkness. "You would let your rival live? You don't worry that this would cause problems?"

"I'll deal with those problems later," I said, and let out a long breath. "I don't want you to get hurt."

His expression was serious, transfixed on me. "I don't want to hurt you, either."

"But that doesn't mean we're on the same side. We both know that freeing the demons is an act of war. The streets will run with blood, and innocent people will die. And I know that's what you want."

He turned away from me, shrugging. "If mortals decide our freedom is a pretext for their aggression, that moral failure is on them, not us. And Rowan, the tensions have already begun. You and I were the tinderboxes that lit the spark. The revelation of your presence scared the shit out of them. A demon embedded in the mortal world, one who spent years around a demon hunter, no less—they're feeling extremely vulnerable right now. They no longer know who's mortal and who's a demon, and panic is running through their world like wildfire. They're terrified that there are more of us out there. They're not going to let us live."

I swallowed hard. "Do you have any evidence, or am I supposed to take everything the Lord of Chaos says as truth?"

"You'll have to trust me."

Nope. "Sure. But how about we let the gods decide who should rule? Through the trials, like we agreed. And as for whatever happens next—we'll just cross that bridge when we come to it."

"Fine." The corner of his mouth twitched in something like a smile. "The gods will decide. Since they're always so fucking rational."

❧ 12 ❧

ROWAN

Distantly, I heard the sounds of mournful singing echoing off the city's stones, beautiful and eerie at the same time. My heart felt heavy.

"It's starting," said Orion quietly.

He reached into his pocket and pulled out two objects, a pale white clay pipe and a pearl necklace. "On the night of *challariu*, this is one way to honor the dead. The Lilu used to believe that rivers and the sea connected us to the underworld. Before we began singing, we would give the river something that belonged to the departed so that the ones we mourned would have some of their favorite things in the afterlife. Then we'd walk along the water and sing the songs of the dead. We believed it would help them have an easy journey to the underworld."

"Did those belong to your parents?" I asked, staring at the pipe and the necklace.

He shook his head. "No. These belong to yours. I found them in your parents' house. You can keep them, of course, if you want, or you can give them to the river. It's your choice."

I found my eyes stinging as I took the necklace and pipe from him. My mom never had anything this beautiful in Osborne. "Thanks," I said quietly.

This seemed...oddly thoughtful of him?

Tears brimmed in my eyes as I took a few steps to the river's edge, and I thumbed the smooth pearls on the necklace, imagining how it would have looked on Mom. Maybe she'd look beautiful wearing this in the underworld...

I dropped it in the river, watching as the dark waters claimed it. Then I turned the pipe over in my fingertips—a man I'd never known, but one who'd been looking out for me when he died. I let that go, too, watching it tumble in the waters. Now that the sky had grown dark, moonlight shimmered over the river's surface.

On the river bank, Orion knelt beside me. Warmth radiated from him. "The silver ship goes in, too," he murmured. "It's supposed to light the way."

I dropped the model ship into the river and watched it float along the surface, swirling a little in the eddies.

"One for each soul," said Orion. He let his go in the water, too, and our twin sparks of light moved toward the ocean.

I glanced at him through blurred eyes. Had he known I wouldn't want to do this in front of the crowd?

I couldn't read his expression as he held out a hand to help me up.

When I felt a tear slide down my cheek, I wiped a

hand across my face. "What did you bring for your family?"

His mouth opened and closed, and he took a moment to respond. "I already let them go in the river earlier today. For my mother, I brought her favorite book. My stepfather, I gave him back his pocket watch. My big brother, Molor, had a suit I returned—" His voice broke, and he looked away into the alley from which we'd come. He cleared his throat. "The others should be here soon."

Without entirely realizing what I was doing, I found myself putting my hand on his chest. He turned to look at me, his lips parted in surprise. I started to lift my hand, but he covered it with his. He breathed in deeply as the crowd grew nearer.

An ocean of candles floated toward us, like stars in the night, the sound of singing floating on the wind.

"We will lead them now to the yew grove in the Elysian Wilderness," said Orion. "I've made the memorial there."

When I'd first heard the news that we'd be spending the night at a memorial, it felt like a distraction from my preparations, or maybe a trick of some sort. But now that we were walking under the starlight, with the sorrowful music filling the air, it seemed necessary...and right. As we passed, some of the demons dropped their model ships into the river, and the waters carried them away.

"Are you all right?" Orion asked.

"Yeah. You?"

He held my gaze for a long time, his expression unreadable. "Same as always."

I had no idea what that meant. "Full of quiet rage and loud confidence?"

"Not quite."

We crossed the bridge. Illuminated silver ships were streaming down the river now, bobbing over the water. Just across the river, lanterns hung from tree boughs, swinging a little in the breeze. Orion led me into a yew grove, where the dots of warm light illuminated tree trunks. Around the grove, large, rough stones had been carved with Demonic letters, the shapes serpentine and elegant. A fitting resting place for a culture that belonged in the wild.

I stepped through the mossy forest, wishing I could read the names. The stones seemed to go on endlessly, which in itself was heartbreaking.

"It's a beautiful memorial," I said.

"Spell casters worked on the lanterns. The candles will never go out." He touched my lower back lightly. "Here." He nodded at a couple of large stones by one of the river's tributaries.

I crossed to look at the stones, and my eyes stung when I saw the names. These were the only ones here carved in both Demonic and English. I crouched down and ran my fingertips over Mom's name: *Aria Morgenstern, Duchess of Asmodeus*.

How strange that I'd never known her full name, nor my father's name at all. *Baal de Moloch, Duke of Asmodeus*, next to her. Gold and shadows danced over the stones from the lanterns, making the carvings come to life.

My throat felt tight. "Why are these in English?"

"They're for you. They're your family."

But there was a third stone here, too, tucked off to the side, hidden in shadows.

Lady Mortana de Moloch.

"You made a memorial for Mortana," I whispered. "Unexpected."

"I made one for every dead Lilu."

I turned to look up at him. "Why her?"

Again, a line formed between his eyebrows. "Once I learned that she'd died in the underworld after losing her mind...I don't know. The threat is gone. Maybe she helped Nergal because it was the only way to survive. Or maybe she was truly evil." Shadows danced back and forth over his features. "I don't really know what she was thinking, and I no longer care. She's dead, and I'm not. Every dead Lilu gets a marker."

I rose, staring out at the forest of glittering lights and the stones beneath them. "How did you dig up all their names?"

"I remembered them. There wasn't much else to do in the dungeon except think of their names, engrave them on my heart, and promise to avenge them."

I swallowed hard. "You were only five."

He slid his hands into his pockets, his expression serious. "I had Ashur to help me remember every name."

My heart felt like it was cracking. Orion would never break his promise to Ashur. And I wasn't even sure I could blame him, but I'd try to stop him anyway.

Closer to the river, demons were filling the forest. He turned away from me, and his face fell into shadow. "We should join the others for the memorial songs."

Mom must have known all the words to these songs once, but she'd never taught me.

"I don't know the Lilu songs," I whispered.

"You'll learn them," he said quietly.

Those didn't sound like the words of a man who intended to get rid of me. Then again, how could anyone ever really know what someone as unpredictable as Orion was really thinking?

13
ROWAN

I stood on the balcony outside my room, staring at the sea. After the *challariu*, I felt emotionally drained. I think I was exhausted from the mental puzzle of trying to figure out what was real and what was a lie. So I'd eaten by myself on the balcony, under the stars. Orion's servants had brought me a bottle of Malbec and grilled salmon with delicately spiced rice.

Now, my head was swimming, my mind racing with worries about the upcoming trial. On the one hand, I'd demonstrated a bit of control today. Just before the memorial, I'd managed to make a piece of paper float across the room to Shai without lighting anything on fire.

On the other hand, Orion was such a wild card, I couldn't predict him as well as I'd thought.

As the sea wind skimmed over me, I poured myself another glass of wine. Sipping, I glanced up to the sky. Clouds were creeping over the moon now, and the wind started to pick up. A sudden gust of wind knocked over the wine bottle, spilling a little stream right onto my dress.

Yikes. Had I already finished most of that bottle? On my own? Let's hope demons didn't get hangovers like mortals did.

As I hurried to clean it up, lightning speared the sky. Clouds had blotted out the stars, and a heavy rain started to fall. I grabbed my glass of Malbec.

I needed to get my shit together and clear my mind. I *could* win this and become queen.

Except at this point, I was certain of only one thing: despite all my warnings to myself, Orion was deeply, firmly messing with my head.

When I thought you were dead—

Something was making my cheeks heat, and that was bad news, indeed.

DAMP FROM THE RAIN, I LAY IN BED WITH THE SHEETS pulled tightly around me. A storm was raging outside, and the sea sounded violent and angry. Thunder boomed across the ocean, making the walls rattle. Every time I started to drift off, a flash of lightning ignited the sky, waking me again.

I rolled over, imagining the gentle bobbing of the silver boats down the river. I closed my eyes, listening to the rain hammering against the windows and the stone walls.

At last, I started to drift off, and I almost thought I could hear the funeral song of the Lilu washing in from the sea...

My heart skipped a beat as an unnamed panic stole my breath. The room felt unnaturally cold.

My eyes snapped upon, but shadows had consumed all the light. I started to sit up in bed, but when I was only halfway up, my airway constricted sharply. What the *fuck?* Someone or something was crushing my neck, and I started to thrash wildly, unable to see my attacker. Fear snapped through my nerve endings. Already, my lungs were burning from the lack of air.

Panic summoned my magic, and golden light flared from my body—enough of it that I could see the person choking me. Pale skin, long black hair, and eyes to match. *Jasper.* The king's right-hand man. How was he so fucking *strong?*

With one hand around my throat, he raised the other above me. Long ivory claws shot out, aiming for my heart. Frantic, I blocked the strike, and his claws carved into my forearm, slicing against the bone.

Pain electrified my arm, igniting my survival instincts. I kicked at Jasper as hard as I could, knocking him off the bed. When I summoned my fire, it raced down my arm to my fingertips. But as I did, the room went cold, dark...and the flames snuffed out on my fingertips. Shadows enveloped me.

Shit. I could no longer see Jasper. Glacial air stung my lungs as I inhaled.

When lightning flashed again outside, I caught a glimpse of him.

Flames burst into life in my palm, and I hurled a fireball at the corner of the room where I'd just seen him. But before the fire met its target, the flames sputtered and died in the icy darkness. Arctic air stung my lungs and skin, making my limbs shake.

My heart was a wild beast. "Why are you trying to kill me, Jasper?" Somehow, the cold air seemed to swallow up the sound of my voice.

"Because I follow King Orion's orders," he hissed.

"The king?" Heat started to erupt inside me. Cracks of light were splintering my skin. Once I let go, I could burn the world to ash. Flames rose and guttered to life on my fingertips—

The door burst open, and a muscular frame stood silhouetted against the hallway light.

"What the fuck do you think you're doing?" Orion's voice came low and controlled from the doorway, and his eyes were on Jasper.

Jasper's eyes glowed from the shadows. "I will not relent until your orders are complete. As you said, Your Majesty."

Orion's muscled body looked coiled with tension—a snake about to strike. "I commanded you to keep her *safe*." He turned to look at me, glowing with golden light. "Did he hurt you?"

Furious magic still crackled through my body. Whatever was going on here, it only reaffirmed one thing: in the City of Thorns, things were never quite as they seemed. "Nothing that will last."

Jasper's dark eyes were intent on me. "Even if you tried to stop me, Your Majesty, you said I must—"

The air went icy, and Jasper lunged for me, his ivory claws drawn. But in one swift move, Orion swung for him, using his claws to slash Jasper's heart out of his chest.

With a snarl, he threw the heart onto the floor, and Jasper's pale body crumpled to the tiles.

Blood covered Orion's arm and chest, and he turned to look at me, his body beaming with light. "What happened to all the soldiers I stationed around the palace? Why did none of them intervene?"

I stared at him. "You're asking *me*? They're under your command. I was asleep."

"Come with me," he said abruptly. "You can't stay here, obviously. It's not safe."

"He just said that you ordered this." I followed after him anyway, eager to get away from Jasper's corpse.

In the hallway outside, a single soldier stood in the marble hall. Orion stalked over to him and gripped him by the neck, lifting him high into the air. "Why did you let someone in here? You were tasked with keeping the shadow scion safe."

The demon's green eyes were open wide, his mouth moving wordlessly. Orion was crushing his throat.

"I don't think he can answer you like that," I said.

Orion dropped the soldier, and the force of his body hitting the floor cracked the tile. The demon's face turned white as milk as he stared up at Orion. "Your Majesty? You asked us to let him in. You ordered all the other soldiers to leave, and you asked me not to intervene, no matter what."

Orion stared down at him, and he took a step back like he'd been hit. "When did this supposedly happen?"

"Thirty minutes ago..." the soldier stammered, looking baffled.

Orion stared at the solder, then at me, as if he was expecting me to answer this conundrum for him.

I folded my arms. "Did you stage all this, all by any chance, so you could swoop in and save me?"

A flurry of emotions crossed his features. "And what purpose would that serve, exactly?"

"To get me to trust you."

His withering look drilled into me. "If I wanted to create an opportunity to save you, do you really think I would have done such a terrible job? If I'd set this up, do you think I'd leave all these loose ends of people telling you about it?"

He had a point... I shrugged. "I don't know. Maybe you're preoccupied with panicking about how I'm going to steal your crown."

He narrowed his eyes. "Clearly, someone enchanted my soldiers. This is obvious mind control spellcraft. Someone is trying to put us at odds with one another. Someone is trying to make you think I'm a threat."

My nose wrinkled. "That would be a waste of time, considering we already are at odds with one another."

Orion's eyes dipped down for just a fraction of a moment, his jaw clenching. Only then did I realize I was braless, in a tank top and underwear that were still wet from the rain. Ah, but that was power. I stepped closer to him. "Tell me, how did you know I was in trouble at that exact moment?"

He pinned me with his intense gaze. "The same way I knew you were in trouble in the underworld. I felt my heart racing, and for a long time, I didn't remember what that sensation was. But then you reminded me. It was fear. And I feel it when you're in danger. We are connected. We are the twin Lightbringers, and I know when you're not safe."

"Hmm. I've never felt *you* in danger."

"I'm never in any danger," he said impatiently, like it was a ridiculous concept. "Not since I got out of the dungeon." He stalked down the stairwell. "You'll be staying with me now. I can't trust anyone but myself."

"But can you even trust yourself, Orion?" My voice echoed. "Because maybe you're losing your mind."

He pivoted and marched up the stairs again toward me. With a stony expression, he scooped me up in his powerful arms, like a groom carrying a bride, and carried me down the stairs.

Warmth from his skin slid over me, and I felt acutely aware of all the points of our bodies that made contact. Orion wore a thin black sweater, underneath which I could feel his muscles moving as he carried me. Outside, the air was a cool salt mist—and Orion's body was all steel and heat wrapping around me.

"I'm perfectly capable of walking," I said. "And I was also about to kill Jasper on my own."

Orion's pale eyes stared straight ahead as he carried me out of the palace. "You were moving too slowly."

Maybe he was just trying to keep his enemy close. But that worked both ways, didn't it?

Living in his house, I'd get a firsthand look at what my rival was up to. I wrapped my arms around his broad shoulders.

"I hope you realize," I said, "that I'll need my own room. You can't be around me when I'm planning for the next trial. And I don't want your spies watching me, either."

"Rowan." He looked at me evenly and pulled me in close to whisper in my ear. "I promise to play fair," he said in a velvety tone that I didn't trust at all.

✿ 14 ✿

ROWAN

Orion's house was surprisingly small—and surprisingly close by. A two-story stone cottage, it looked more like a gatehouse than a palace. He had no soldiers protecting the exterior, but as we crossed through a wrought iron gate, the sizzle of magic over my skin told me that it had been protected with charms.

Inside, two black dogs followed us up dark wooden stairs.

As he carried me up to the second story, my gaze flicked up to meet Orion's eyes. I felt a strange flutter in my belly. I shouldn't be here, of course, and yet, I felt safe with him. My insane animal instincts trusted him and told me he'd protect me, even if the rational side of me knew better.

"I didn't order that to happen." His silver hair was rustled and sticking up, and he seemed unusually rattled.

"I don't really know what I believe anymore," I admitted.

"Rowan." His voice sounded rougher than usual. "I was here with Amon. He can tell you that. I'll find out who was behind that attack."

Upstairs, he carried me into a tidy bedroom, then into a second bedroom that connected to it, one in the corner of the cottage. Dark beams scored the ceiling. Like Orion's apartment, this place was neat and tidy, and sparsely decorated—just white walls and elegant mahogany furniture. A cream-colored cashmere blanket covered the bed. The only color in the place came from the spines of books on a large bookshelf, and a few stacked on a desk by the window. Another door was open to a small bathroom with a shower.

Orion set me down on the hardwood floors and pointed back to the first bedroom—just slightly larger than this one, with a four-poster bed and darker walls. "If you need anything, I'll be in there."

"Cozy." I crossed to a large mullioned window and peered out at the moonlit garden below. "So if I'm going in and out of the house, I'll be walking past you?"

"More importantly, if anyone tries to come *in* the house, they'll be going past me."

For a moment, I indulged in a fantasy—one where Orion and I were two normal people in a cottage like this, with two black dogs. We had no marks of Lucifer, no murdered moms, no horrific memories, or centuries of imprisonment. In this phantom world, we were two normal people who could wake up tangled in each other's limbs and wander out to have morning coffee in the garden. We could live surrounded by books and quiet...

But it was stupid to let myself indulge in that fantasy.

I turned to find Orion watching me. Studying me closely, he crossed to me. "He left a bruise on your throat." He cocked his head. "That makes me wish I'd killed him more slowly."

"I don't even feel it anymore."

His eyes had darkened to black. "Rowan, I returned to the dungeon today. Do you remember that cell I kept you in the first night we met?"

"Being imprisoned by the Lord of Chaos isn't the type of thing a person forgets, Orion."

"That cell was the exact cell where my mother and I were first kept. Right before she was killed, the guards moved me to a different cell by myself. But when I looked in the first cell, I saw that she'd carved something in the wall."

"*Lucifer urbem spinarum libarabit,*" I said, finishing his thought. "The Lightbringer will set free the City of Thorns."

His dark eyebrows drew together. "That's what I'd thought, too, when I first saw it. But some of the lines were worn, and ivy was covering part of it. When I was mulling everything over, trying to understand my destiny, I went back to read her carving. I pulled the vines away. It says *Luciferi urbem spinarum liberabunt.*"

I swallowed. "It's plural. The *Lightbringers* will set us free."

"We're meant to do this together. It just took me a long time to see it."

I ran through my promise to myself, all the reasons that I wouldn't let him sway me. "You told me you didn't even respect me enough to hate me. You called me neurotic, dull, and unskilled at everything. 'Apart from our one little tryst,'" I said, mimicking his British accent, "'I find you tedious and pathetic.' And then I died, and I learned I'm a lot stronger than I ever realized. I should be ruling here, not you, Orion."

His jaw flexed. "None of those things I said were true. I was trying to keep you away from me. I didn't think I had the strength to resist you, so I was trying to keep you at arm's length, because I'm terrified of what could happen..."

My fingers tightened. "*What*, exactly?"

"That it could happen again!"

I stared at him, not understanding. "That *what* could happen again? What are you talking about? There are no more Lilu left to murder."

"There's us." He seemed uncharacteristically at a loss for words, and he raked a hand through his hair. "Rowan —of course I respect you. Of course I—" His mouth closed, and his gaze slid down my goosebump-covered arms. The next thing I knew, he was wrapping me in the soft cream blanket from the bed. "We can turn the heat up in here."

The cashmere felt amazing against my skin, but my thrill also came from his warm, smoky scent curling around me. This blanket was my armor. I could resist his charms. Unwilling to let him off so easily, I glared at him. "Okay, so let's talk about avenging the Lilu. I want you to understand something about mortals and your theory about how they're the root of all evil."

He sighed and leaned against one of the bookcases, folding his arms. Annoyingly, that only served to show off his biceps, which seemed to strain the fabric of his white shirt. "I'm listening."

My eyebrows rose in surprise. He was actually willing to hear me out? "Demons and mortals are alike. It's not that complicated. Some of us are evil, some are good, and some are fanatics who want to destroy anyone different."

"Are you calling me a fanatic?" he asked dryly.

"Yeah, I am. You're the demon equivalent of Jack Corwin."

His muscles tensed. "I'm *what*? That is, I think, the worst thing you could have said to me."

I shook my head. "I meant only in fanaticism. Not your charm or intelligence or whatever else. His demon hunters want to kill all of us, and you want to kill all of them. You're both extremists."

He seemed to relax a little. "Go on."

"And yes, I know you've catalogued every instance in history of mortals committing atrocities, and there are plenty to choose from. The same goes for demons. But what about the good things mortals have done?"

He cocked his head. "Do you have a single example?"

I bit my lip, wishing I'd prepared a little better for this conversation—maybe I could have used a PowerPoint and academic references. "Keanu Reeves," I blurted. "He's amazing. He donates money to cancer research, to children's hospitals. He gives up his subway seat on trains! What kind of maniac wants to kill Keanu Reeves?"

"I have no idea who you're talking about."

My eyes widened. "Right. Of course you don't! The world *stopped* for you four hundred years ago. For you, time froze, and you came out wanting to murder the people who hurt you. And you know what? The mortals you encountered back then fucking *sucked*. No one likes Puritans. No one. But they're gone, and the world kept moving on for everyone else. You missed several centuries of human existence. So maybe you should learn more about the people you want to murder, you know? I have more examples." I lifted a finger. "Steve Buscemi."

"These are friends of yours?"

"Ha! I wish. No, but he was a firefighter, and then he became an actor. And when some fanatic mortals flew airplanes into skyscrapers in New York City, he got on his old firefighting gear, and he put his life at risk to help save people. Not just him, but lots of firefighters made a huge sacrifice trying to get people out of a burning and collapsing building. Tons of them gave their lives to help people they didn't even know." I was on a roll now. "And in Fukushima, a nuclear reactor was melting down after an earthquake, and people actually volunteered to help clean it up, even though they would die of cancer. These were mortals saving other people. Saving strangers."

His eyes shone brightly as he listened to me. "I haven't read about these things."

"It's all pretty new. It wouldn't have been in your ancient dungeon books, and it's not like you use the internet." Now that I'd started thinking about heroic mortals, I couldn't stop. "John Robert Fox! A lieutenant in World War Two, he intentionally gave his own coordinates to the Nazis to give the rest of his unit a chance to escape. He died in enemy fire to save his crew. These were all mortals, Orion. As a whole, they're not any better or worse than us. Some of them are fucking terrible, and some are heroic.

The only difference I can see between mortals and demons is that mortals kill with weapons, and demons use magic. And the mortals out there now are not the ones who killed your family. Killing them isn't vengeance. It's insanity."

His gaze slid to the window, and I had no idea if I was actually getting through to him. "You and Amon both," he said quietly.

"What do you mean?"

"He's on your side." He let out a long sigh. "But the fact is, Rowan, the mortals have too much control over us in the modern world. One bomb could take out our walls, and then we're done. That's what the curse means. And what sort of king would I be if I didn't prioritize the safety of my own subjects over outsiders?"

He was almost sounding reasonable, which was making it hard for me to keep my resolve. So reasonable that I *nearly* forgot that several people were claiming he'd sent someone in to try to kill me tonight.

And here was the real question: what did I have to lose by taking the crown from him?

The simple fact was, if I were in control, I wouldn't have to worry about who to trust.

I straightened and lifted my chin. "Listen, Orion. There are only two options for this trial. If I win, I decide what happens. Or you win, and that's when you can prove to me that you do really want me to rule with you. Because right now, you have all the power. Of course you want me to give up. Let's see you offer me an alliance when it actually counts."

His eyes sparkled, and he took a step closer. He gave me a slow, dazzling smile that made my heart skip a beat.

"I'll be happy to prove it to you when I win the trial. And do you know what?" His voice was low and silky. "I like being challenged by you."

The vulnerable side of Orion was gone, and he'd turned on the charm again. So I can't say I was shocked when he left the door open between our rooms. He crossed into his own room, pretending to ignore me as he unbuttoned his shirt. When he pulled it off, I told myself not to stare at the absolute masculine perfection that was his body—the thickly corded muscles, the visible V in his abs just over the top of his pants.

But telling myself not to stare was just about as useful as telling the moon to stop shining.

When he turned to me, his lips curled in a beautiful half-smile, I was momentarily mortified to realize my mouth had been hanging open.

He crossed to the door frame and leaned against it. My gaze roamed over his snake tattoo, then down to his chiseled abs again. "Something the matter, Rowan?" And here was Orion's cocky attitude, replacing that brief glimpse of his vulnerable side.

I took a deep breath, trying hard to ignore the heat sliding through my belly. "Are you trying to seduce me? Because I don't care how pretty you are—I'm still going through with the trial." I'd somehow lost control of my voice, and it had come out louder than necessary. One of the dogs poked his head in the door, looking between us to make sure everything was all right.

Orion's eyebrows rose. "I simply took my shirt off because I'm getting ready for bed." The look he was giving me was positively smoldering. "Love, surely you know by now that if an incubus were seducing you, you'd be writhing beneath me and begging for more right now."

I felt my cheeks flush, and my mind clouded with a haze of lust. I wasn't exactly sure what was happening, only that Orion was getting the upper hand. Throwing me off my game, getting me flustered.

But I was a succubus, and two could play at this game.

I let the blanket drop from my body, knowing that my wet tank top was falling off one of my shoulders and that my underwear hardly covered a thing. As soon as I did, I felt the atmosphere in the room change—a flash of heat and light that seemed to pulse from the demon king himself.

❧ 15 ❧

ORION

As soon as she dropped the blanket, I knew I was in trouble. All the blood seemed to rush from my head, making my cock harden until I could no longer think straight.

I stared down at her—big brown eyes, her full, peaked lips, nipples straining at the wet fabric...

In the salt breeze off the coast, I knew that if I kissed her, she would taste of the sea. I loved kissing her, and the way she looked at me. I loved...

Stop it.

Only a thin sheath of fabric covered her naked body, and I could see her perfect contours beneath it.

As a succubus, she could feel me drinking in her beauty, and her chest was faintly flushed.

"Not trying to seduce," I managed, forgetting the basics of language.

I was repeating myself, though, wasn't I?

And yet, it was the truth. I couldn't seduce her—not when I risked everything.

I'd simply wanted her to realize that little blond pretty boy Kas had nothing on me. Quite simply, jealousy was making me act like a fucking idiot.

She sat on the bed and leaned back. The damp tank top stretched over her breasts. She was quite obviously not wearing a bra, and her nipples were hard against the fabric. What I wanted to do, more than anything, was to throw her down and rip that cotton off her body. I wanted to kiss and lick her between her thighs until she screamed my name loudly enough for him to hear...

"Of course you weren't trying to seduce me. My mistake." She looked up at me from under her long eyelashes and rolled over, giving me a view of her ass. I was desperate to run my fingers over that fabric, to feel her heat.

Her cheeks were lightly flushed. "Something the matter, Orion? You look...dazed."

She was using my exact phrase against me. *Smart-ass.*

I didn't feel entirely in control of myself as I found myself moving closer, back into her room. A moth to a flame. I sat next to her on the bed, but my eye was drawn back to that fucking bruise on her neck.

I reached out to brush my fingertips over it. At the contact of my fingertips against her skin, she gasped slightly.

My heart was ready to explode.

"Just making sure you're healing properly." My voice sounded husky, and I pulled my hand away from her.

Her lips appeared full, slightly pouted. There was something about how she looked right now—seductive and adorable all at once—that was robbing me of rational thought. I wanted to taste her so much, it hurt.

She bit her lip and brushed her fingertips over my wrist. "I'm fine. I'm a demon now, Orion. You don't have to worry about me breaking."

She was right, of course, and yet, I'd never felt more compelled to keep someone safe. All I could do was thank the gods she trusted me enough to come with me here, into my home. I stood, trying to force myself to move away from her, to douse the fire in my thoughts.

"I want to kiss you, just once." The truth tumbled out of my mouth before I could stop myself. "But that's all, Rowan. Just one kiss tonight."

One kiss was fucking dangerous enough.

"Just one?" She cocked her head. "What are you so afraid of?"

One more heartbreak, and it will be the end of me. My sanity already hung by a thread. "You," I said softly. "I already told you that."

With her big brown eyes locked on me, she rose from the bed and wrapped her arms around my neck. Under the thin cotton, her breasts brushed against my bare chest, making me stiffen even more.

I cupped the side of her face. Fire swept through me as I leaned down to press my mouth against hers.

When our lips made contact, I immediately knew this was a mistake. If she rejected the real me, I'd lose my mind. If I fell in love completely and lost her, I'd also lose my mind. But around Rowan, I made fucking terrible decisions, and my tongue swept in to taste her. My whole body had come alive for her. I savored the way her tongue welcomed mine, and her muscles became soft and pliable in my arms. Oh, *gods*.

For the first time, I felt her succubus magic entwined around me, an inviting caress that stroked my back. I slid my hand up her spine, gripping her hair to tilt her head. I was overwhelmed by the urge to strip her naked and make her scream.

She would ruin me.

Arching into me, she moaned lightly, and that sound nearly made me lose the little control I had. I needed to fuck her hard against the wall. I wanted her to remember how perfectly we fit together—

I hardly knew what I was doing as I lifted her higher off the ground and she slipped her legs around me. One of her hands gripped my hair. With her back against the bedpost, I pressed my hard length against her. Had I ever been this desperate for anything before? Not even after centuries in prison.

The sound of one of the dogs barking interrupted us. Rowan broke from the spell first, pulling away from the kiss. Her lips were swollen, her cheeks pink. She'd never looked more beautiful.

"Don't really know what I'm doing here." She caught her breath. "You're my rival."

I pressed my forehead against hers, trying again to remember how to form a sentence. What had she said?

Ah…the rival thing. She thought I was dangerous.

As it happened, I thought the same about her.

Rowan had shown up in my life and thrown everything wildly off course, and when I was around her, I felt as if the world were tilting beneath my feet.

My plans for vengeance had always been the light that shone a path through madness, like the little illuminated ships floating along the river. Without vengeance guiding my way, I was in the dark again. Chaos. She brought that into my life.

"You're the Lady of Chaos," I breathed.

She touched the side of my face. "What?"

"Lady of Chaos. Ever since I first ran into you in that bar, you've lit every one of my plans on fire. You've destroyed everything I thought I understood."

"Sounds dangerous. Maybe you should put me down, then."

By the racing of her heart and the hot pulse of the magic around the room, I knew she wanted me as much as I wanted her. But how much of her desire for me was real? She was a succubus, responding to my lust magic. Lilu power thickened the air. That didn't mean she *cared* for me one bit—it just meant she was high on desire.

Meanwhile, I cared about her far more than I should. And that was why I was burning my centuries-old plans to the ground.

It wasn't her descriptions of John Robert Fox or the other mortals that had planted seeds of doubt in my mind —it was the fact that the mortal world had created Rowan. Could mortals be that terrible if they'd produced the perfect mix of terrifying and adorable, sweet and fero-cious, that was Rowan Morgenstern?

"Right. I'm putting you down." My whisper sounded choked, and it took a shocking amount of effort to release my grip on her.

She narrowed her eyes at me as she slid down my body,

and my stomach turned in knots. "If you were trying to get into my head, it's not working. The trial is still on," she said coldly.

She moved away from me, climbing over the bed, and I felt a sharp sting at the loss of contact.

"I just wanted you to think of me and not Kas when you're going to sleep." Sweet Lucifer, why had I admitted that out loud? *Idiot.*

She shifted back under her covers, staring at me in disbelief. But I caught a hint of a smile, and then it deepened into something truly dazzling. "Hang on. Is the incubus king *jealous?*"

"Don't be ridiculous. Why would *I* get jealous?" Gods below, exactly how often did I lie to everyone?

"Sure, you don't."

She saw right through me, of course. Which was strangely refreshing.

I leaned against her bedpost, unwilling to let the night end just yet. "Rowan. You saved my life in the under-world..." The rest of my thought died on my tongue before I could bring myself to say it out loud: *Do you really think I was worth saving? And more importantly, would you still think that if you knew the truth about me?*

She stared at me for a long moment, and a little line formed between her dark eyebrows. "Yeah, of course I did. And I'd do it again. I don't trust you to run a kingdom without murdering everyone, but I want you alive."

I could still taste her on my lips, sweet and salty. "What if you were wrong about me?"

"Oh." Her expression shifted, eyes glistening. She

looked sad enough that I wanted to climb over the bed and gather her in my arms again.

I was holding my breath as I waited for her reply, until her expression shifted again. Becoming more guarded.

"I can tell you want to say something, and you're holding back," I said.

"How can you tell that?"

"Your nostrils flare when you're frustrated."

"I can't tell if you're saying all the right things to try to get me to let down my guard, or if you're genuine. But assuming you're being real here...Orion, did you try to make me hate you on purpose? Because you wanted to beat me to the punch before I realized what you were like?"

The accuracy of her words was like a fist to my throat, and all I could do was swallow hard.

She bit her lip. "Because you *do* love to tell strangers that you're terrible as soon as you meet them. It's like you're constantly trying to warn people."

My chest tightened. She really could see right through every one of my defenses, and it left me feeling confused, completely without my armor. "I don't have a lot of experience with people."

She gave me a sad smile. "I think you're crushed by the guilt of what happened to you. I still have hope for you. But I'm still going to kick your ass in the trial and become your queen." She arched an imperious eyebrow. "*Then* we'll figure out how to fix you."

"We'll see about that, love," I said, almost to myself.

And maybe—now—it was here before me. The light in the darkness, the new plan.

At some point, I would take the greatest risk of my life: finding out if she still cared for me when she really knew me.

But I was getting ahead of myself. I wouldn't play too much with the dangerous fire of hope, or I risked letting my last shreds of sanity go up in flames. Letting myself hope that Rowan could love me when she knew what I'd done—that was just about the scariest thing I could imagine. If she truly cared about me, then maybe I was meant for something other than avenging the dead. Maybe I had actual fucking worth.

My heart was about to beat right out of my chest with fear.

"I'll see you in the morning, Rowan." I brushed my fingertips over my lips as I crossed back to my room, still replaying the memory of that mind-blowing kiss. I knew I'd be thinking of it until the sun rose over the sea at dawn.

Maybe that last little thread of sanity had already gone up in smoke.

❧ 16 ❧

ROWAN

Eight days until the trial.

Last night's conversation had left me so deeply confused that instead of sleeping, I'd simply replayed his words over and over in my mind.

And not just the conversation, of course. That *kiss*. The way he'd kissed me had been as intense and hot as fucking, and I couldn't stop thinking about it. Something had changed in the way he kissed me—a sort of reverence that wasn't there before.

In the morning, I'd woken early, sneaking out past a sleeping Orion. On my way out, I'd stolen a glance at his muscular back, and I'd briefly met his sweet friend. Amon had sent me off with coffee and scones. I peered out the door cautiously before leaving, surveying the square for any errant assassins. I found nothing amiss, but I kept scanning the streets as I walked.

As long as I was around Orion, I risked getting so distracted that I'd fail the trial. And the depressing truth was, I was still struggling to push him to the back of my mind.

What are you so afraid of?

You.

I sipped my coffee and replayed it for the millionth time. Was he trying to tell me that he was scared I would reject him? That I'd break his heart?

Someone—Mortana, I supposed—had well and truly convinced him that hope was the most dangerous thing of all.

Unless...

Unless, of course, that was all an act.

I blew out a long breath, trying to center myself by focusing on the world around me. My gaze skimmed over the flowers gently blowing in the salty breeze—pink peonies, violet foxglove, lavender...

As I walked through the garden, a fountain burbled gently. I breathed in the humid scent of wildflowers, and my mind cleared at last. Sunlight warmed my cheeks. Another sip of coffee sent a jolt of caffeinated life into my veins.

I pulled my phone from my pocket, relieved to see a text from Kas. Our magical lessons were beginning soon. I really had lucked out with teachers who were so willing to help me.

I crossed the bridge toward the forest, glancing at the sun sparkling off the river. As I approached the wilderness, the humid scent of moss and soil filled my nostrils.

I found Kas and Legion in the oak grove.

Legion stood with a large spell book in his hands, while Kas sat on the mossy forest floor, leaning against a tree trunk. He wore a crown of ivy and blue primroses that rested—crooked—over his delightfully messy blond hair.

I smiled at him. "Looking regal."

His cheeks dimpled when he smiled. "Not all of us are born royal. Some of us have to make the crowns ourselves from Mother Nature."

"Where is Shai?" I asked.

"Uh..." Legion's gaze moved from me to the spell book. His hair was pulled back, but a few strands of black caught in the breeze. "She's on her way."

I raised an eyebrow. "Everything okay, Legion?"

Kas rose, and he dusted off the back of his jeans. "Everything is fine. But we have a long day ahead of us because Legion decided to give you the most tedious possible task, and we're all going to be sitting through it for hours."

I took a deep breath. "As long as it helps me win the trial, I'm fine with tedium."

"Good." Legion flashed me a faint smile. "First, you will practice control of your magic. Then you can practice summoning more power. But first comes mastery. Understood?"

"Otherwise, we could all die in a fiery hell-world of your exploding magic," said Kas.

"Of course." I held out my hand for the spell book. "What spell?"

"Sifting soil," said Legion.

I frowned. "What is that, exactly?"

"Really, just what it sounds like."

Kas crossed his arms, his caramel eyes gleaming with amusement. "Legion has decided that you will spend the entire day making small piles of twigs using magical spells, and maybe trying to build tiny structures with them."

Good thing I'd brought the coffee.

BY THE TIME SHAI SHOWED UP, I'D MADE TWO TINY twig houses, and I was ready for an afternoon nap. On my twentieth recitation of the spell, I was yawning uncontrollably.

Shai was rubbing her eyes as she crossed into the grove in wrinkled clothes.

"Late night?" I asked.

She exchanged a quick look with Legion, then shook her head. "The storm kept me up."

It was so brief that I nearly missed it, but the look she'd given Legion made me think they'd been together.

"What's your excuse?" she asked.

I let out a long breath. "Now that you're all here, there's something I should maybe mention...don't freak out, though." I touched my throat, right where Jasper had tried to crush it last night. "Orion moved me into his home."

Shai glared at me. "*What?* You can't stay with your rival."

"Did he give you a choice?" asked Kas, anger lacing his voice.

I shrugged. "Well, I didn't say *no*. He saved me from an assassin." Why was I feeling so defensive on Orion's behalf?

Shai raised a hand. "Hang on—"

"An *assassin*?" Legion finished her thought.

"Do you know who it was?" asked Kas.

I felt that unwelcome sense of protectiveness again for the demon king. "It was Jasper. The king's right-hand man. But Orion killed him." I let out a long sigh. "The weird thing was, Jasper thought Orion had ordered him to do it. And some of his other guards said the same thing. Orion thought that maybe they'd been enchanted. Mind control magic."

Shai's nose wrinkled. "Only Lilu have mind control power, and even then, it's rare."

"A spell, maybe?" I offered.

"Rowan," she said sharply. "You said that if he started to seduce you, I was supposed to remind you about Queen Elizabeth and the cotton candy."

Kas pulled off his flower crown and dropped it on the ground. "Seems like a brilliant ploy to get you to trust him. Maybe he even hoped you'd call off the trials."

Of course that was the most likely explanation. And yet...if Orion were going to stage some kind of ruse, he wouldn't be dumb enough to leave all these people telling on him. "At this point, I know one thing and one thing only for certain: I need to win the trial, and nothing else matters."

Kas stared at me. "Nothing else matters except that you're now living with a psychotic king who probably wants you dead."

"I'll be fine," I said sharply. "I really don't think he wants me dead." What would they think if they knew I'd kissed him last night? If *kiss* was really sufficient to describe what that had been.

Legion pinched the bridge of his nose. "You don't think your rival for the throne wants you dead? What, do you think the mad demon king is...*too nice?*"

He managed to make the entire concept sound insane.

"Look, I have eight days left," I said. "So am I going back to the twigs, or what? We're wasting time."

Legion glanced at the mounds of soil. "I think you've mastered those. I have something new for you."

I smiled. "Exciting. Are we going to raise the dead?"

"You're going to summon ants."

I took a deep breath. "You remember that I only have eight days left until I need to summon a dead witch, right?"

Legion nodded. "We're getting there. No shortcuts in magic."

"I mean, they exist," added Kas, "but if you take them, sometimes, a whole lot of people die."

I held out my hand for the book. "Ants it is, then."

❦

I WAS ALMOST DELIRIOUS WITH FATIGUE BY THE TIME Kas offered to walk me home. After the initial twig successes, my magic had grown unfocused, flames bursting out in trees around me. I'd accidentally summoned red ants instead of black, and Shai has shrieked at me every time she was bitten.

And yet, tired as I was, I still didn't want to go back to my new room. The problem with Orion's cottage was that Orion lived in it, and I desperately needed to avoid him.

So as we walked, I slowed the pace, rambling to Kas

about my favorite morbid facts. "Mary Tudor burned several hundred people at the stake. Did you know how long it took them to burn on average?"

"I think I'd rather not."

"Forty-five minutes," I answered anyway.

Kas smirked at me. "Aren't you just a ray of sunshine?"

I grinned. "Well, I *am* a Lightbringer, so I've got to have some sunlight deep down. Somewhere. Buried under lots of horrific trivia and obsessive fears."

"They say you get the leaders you deserve. Our two Lightbringers are a genocidal maniac and an absolute neurotic downer who tends to light things on fire when practicing magic—"

"*Excuse* me, I'm not always a downer." I racked my brain to think of something fun, though I'm not sure I fully understood the concept. "Tomorrow, when we practice, I'm going to bring cupcakes. With sprinkles. Like, rainbow...flower cupcakes. Very fucking *fun*."

His cheek dimpled. "As we eat them, will you tell us how many small children choked to death on cake last year?"

"If you don't think that's useful knowledge, I don't know what to tell you."

His eyes twinkled. "I'd gladly take you over a genocidal maniac. A ruler's job is to keep everyone safe, and I have no doubt that you will keep us all from harm with your wealth of knowledge about ways to die."

"I'm glad someone understands my true value."

He slid his hands into his pockets and scowled at Orion's cottage as we approached. "Did the king *order* you to stay in his house? Is he allowed to make demands of the shadow scion?"

"There's no protocol for that in the books." I sighed. "But there *is* a protocol for attacking each other. If one of us murders the other between trials, we get executed by the Council."

A pulse of warm electrical magic washed over me, and goosebumps rose on my skin.

I turned to see Orion stalking from the shadows, his pale blue eyes sparkling in the moonlight. "Ah, Rowan. Are you and your pretty friend weighing the consequences of murdering me?"

I narrowed my eyes at the king. "No. But *Your Majesty*, out of curiosity, are you ordering me to stay with you, or do I have the option of leaving?"

He pinned me with a heated stare. "I'll keep you safe, Rowan, whatever it takes."

"That's not really an answer, is it?" said Kas.

The air thinned, and Orion cut him a sharp look. "I don't owe you an answer, Kasyade." Darkness slid through his eyes, and he took a step closer. "Lest you forget, I am still your king. Rowan is a Lightbringer. You are not."

Kas held his gaze, and thorns grew in the silence.

Menace rippled off Orion. I was starting to get worried that he was going to rip Kas's heart out—his usual method of dealing with inconveniences—and I sucked in a sharp breath. "Kas wasn't questioning your authority. He just pointed out that it wasn't a real answer."

Orion's violent gaze was still locked on Kas, and the air around him heated. "You were around then, during the purge of the Lilu."

Oh, here we go.

The low, quiet tenor of his voice sent a shiver up my spine. An unspoken threat laced the air.

Kas lifted his chin. "I was a child then, same as you."

"Not *exactly* the same as me." Venom under that velvety voice. "I remember you, Kasyade. You were older than me. So lucky not to be a Lilu, weren't you?"

Gently, I touched Orion's arm. "Many of your subjects were around then. You can't threaten them all."

Orion had to realize he couldn't fight a war on two fronts. If he was truly expecting a confrontation with the mortals, he'd need every demon on his side, whether or not they'd stood by during the purge of the Lilu.

Orion tilted his head. "Then don't consider it a threat, but I do have a warning. You, Kasyade, are not qualified to help a Lightbringer learn to practice her magic. You have no idea the kind of danger you're playing with."

And with that, he stalked off into his house.

I stared after him. "Any idea what he's talking about, Kas?"

"If I had to guess," Kas replied dryly, "he's going to try to tell you that your magic is too dangerous to use, and that you should probably just let him win the trials so no one gets hurt. And that it's all too complicated for you to understand."

I snorted. "Right." So why did I feel this sharp tendril of unease at Orion's warning? "Don't worry, Kas. I'm ignoring everything he says." *Liar, liar.*

That *should* be the truth, but it wasn't.

"See you at dawn," Kas said, and then he leaned in and

lowered his voice. "Keep ignoring him. You've got this, Sunshine."

I ignored the nickname, and my chest unclenched a little at his reassurance.

When I crossed inside, I found Amon sitting with his dogs by the fireplace, a book in his lap. Over a steaming cup of tea, he raised an eyebrow at me. "The king is in...a *mood*."

Delightful.

❧ 17 ❧

ROWAN

I climbed the stairs and crossed into my cozy little room, surprised to find he wasn't in his. So I shut the connecting door and flicked on the lights.

Exhausted, I closed the wooden shutters, in case any rogue assassins were watching me. My clothes smelled faintly of woodsmoke from the accidental fires I'd lit in the forest today.

A buried worry snagged at my thoughts as I slipped into a pair of shorts and a tank top for sleep. Orion had never had the chance to learn magic, either, but like everything else, it came naturally to him, easy as breathing.

My ears perked at the sound of the door opening in his room. I crossed to the door, pressing my ear against the wood to listen.

And I nearly fell into his room when he pulled the door open. He arched one of his dramatic black eyebrows. "Yes? I heard you breathing against the door."

You'd think I'd be used to it by now, but the sight of him shirtless took the breath from my lungs. His skin looked bronzed in the warm light, his silver hair lit up from behind like a halo. I forced my gaze from his muscled chest to his devastatingly perfect face. His skin was so *golden*.

I leaned against the doorframe, trying to look casual.

He opened the door wider, motioning for me to enter. Of course, it was extremely stupid to step into his room when he was shirtless, but here I was, walking in anyway.

"Cotton candy," I whispered to myself. "Queen Elizabeth."

He turned, his glacial eyes striking in the warm light. "Did you just whisper *cotton candy* and *Queen Elizabeth* to yourself? I remember recently you suggested that I was losing my mind, but I now wonder if you were *projecting*. That's the word, isn't it?"

"Have you been reading psychology books?"

He shrugged. "I read everything I can."

"How did you hear me breathing on the other side of the door?"

"Demons have incredibly good hearing."

He sat on the edge of his bed, leaning back. His posture, unfortunately, highlighted his perfect body, gilded in the candlelight. I thought of that kiss—deep and sensual, like he was fucking me with his tongue.

"Rowan?"

"Yeah. Here." I dragged my eyes up again and tried to put my thoughts together. "My hearing isn't that amazing."

"You've lived your whole life as a mortal. It would probably be overwhelming for you. Maybe you just need time to get used to it...like you need time to learn how to manage your Lightbringer power."

I sat as far away from him as the room would allow and found myself perched awkwardly on the edge of a chair. Why did I find it so hard to relax around him, as if we hadn't already had sex and traveled to the underworld together? As if I didn't—at this point—know him better than probably any other living person? As if we hadn't *just* kissed passionately last night?

"What did you mean about the Lightbringer power being dangerous?" I asked. "And how have you learned to manage it? You've hardly had much more time than I have with your magic."

"No. But I'm naturally good at things, and you're...not."

"Oh, my *God*," I muttered.

"Really, Rowan, you needn't address me that way, although I suppose I am technically divine. Thanks for telling me about that, by the way. But *Your Majesty* is perfectly fine for me."

I stared at him, uncertain if he was joking. But what difference did it make? I was here for one reason alone: information. "Tell me how you know the Lightbringer power is so dangerous if you don't actually have firsthand experience of this danger, since—according to your theory—you just naturally do everything perfectly."

"Oh, I didn't say I do everything *perfectly*. I make plenty of bad decisions. I'm just good at things. Like you said, I'm basically a god—"

"I didn't say that."

"But to answer your question, I've felt it happening. The power of starlight streaming from my body. And the things it touched...it was like all the matter around me was falling apart. Turning into dust that could be swept away with the breeze. It was like the world crumbled around me."

I sucked in a sharp breath at this horrifying image. "So how did you control it?"

He rose. "Stand up, love. I'll show you."

At what point did I stop hating that he called me "love"? As I stood, I caught a glimpse of his eyes brushing down my body.

Heat rippled off him. "I think magic is different for us than it is for other demons." He spoke quietly, and his deep voice was making my pulse quicken. "Most demons are simply trying to call on their magic and make it as powerful as possible. For us, I think we have to temper it. Some emotions are hot and full of energy. Anger, passion, love. Even fear. Others are dark and cold, like sorrow and loss. And it's the cold emotions that temper it."

Just hearing Orion speak the words *passion* and *love* made my blood pump harder.

"When you want to summon magic," he said, "you draw on the hot emotions. That's why you were able to call up enough magic to kill the congressman. Try it now. Think of something that fills you with an intense emotion." He reached out, gently touching me just above my belly button. "This is where you feel it first, right? Between your ribs?"

Heat radiated from the point where his finger contacted my white cotton tank top, and my gaze flicked down to the V just above his trousers.

"Yes."

"Try it. I want you to summon your magic but try to focus on an intense emotion as you do so."

My pulse raced as I stared up at him, meeting his gaze. He must *know* the effect he had on me because his incubus powers would tune in to that. But could I hear *his* heart racing, too?

Better to think of something else. I closed my eyes and replayed the worst things he'd ever said to me.

I don't respect you enough to hate you... I find you tedious and pathetic... You don't have it in you...

Anger simmered in my blood, boiling away the desire. And the coup de grâce for any positive feelings, the memory of him saying *Escort this woman out of my realm.*

Power swirled between my ribs, just at the point where Orion was touching me. After all that, how dare he try to seduce me again? Molten wrath swept through me.

"Rowan," he barked.

My eyes snapped open, and I found Orion gilded in light that was emanating from my own body.

When I looked down at myself, I *glowed*, the light nearly blinding. I gasped at the sight. I'd seen this happen to Orion before, but never to myself. He was still touching me, and the heat from his fingertips helped to center the magic in my body. Tracing his fingers up a little bit, I felt the electrical buzz of magic move with them. Now, it spilled into my chest.

"Rowan," he whispered. "You are *shockingly* powerful. You need to draw on one of the colder emotions before you destroy my house. Think of something sad."

Ah, but there was so much to choose from there. And the first thing that popped into my mind was an argument

I'd had with Mom the week before she died, when I'd told her that she was always annoying me with her paranoia. I'd told her if she kept it up, she'd make me as crazy as she was.

I still vividly remembered the look of hurt on her face...

God, I was an asshole. Guilt and sorrow slid through me, and I watched the golden light fade from Orion's features. Tears stung my eyes, and I tried to blink them away.

Reaching out, Orion brushed a strand of my hair out of my face—a gesture so natural I nearly forgot I was supposed to be keeping my guard up.

"For Lightbringers," he said softly, "our power is different. Overwhelming. If it feels too intense, you could shut it down. Or it could explode out of you and incinerate everything around you, which is what would have happened just now if I hadn't been helping you center it."

He seemed sincere, but I could already hear Kas's response in my mind. Kas would tell me he was trying to convince me to lose.

I sighed, still trying to shake off the devastating image of Mom. "Okay. Well, if it seems like I'm losing control, I know what to think about."

His pale eyes searched mine. "What is it?"

"Guilt."

"Ah," he said softly. "I know that one well. It's with me always. And maybe that's why I will never lose control of my magic completely."

"Thanks for the help." I swallowed. "I guess." I blinked. I was having a hard time putting coherent thoughts together, which wasn't wildly unusual around Orion.

But right now, I was particularly confused.

The world seemed to be dimming. Each word, each phrase, was floating by like a puff of dandelion seeds blowing on the wind. I almost wanted to fall right into his powerful chest and let him wrap his arms around me. "Something doesn't feel right."

He put his hands on my shoulders. One of his thumbs moved back and forth slowly, giving me clarity again. "It's not just the risk of the damage you can do to the world around you. Powerful magic like that has a cost. When you release your light magic, you leave a vacuum. And chaos magic slips in to fill the void."

With his touch, my mind started clearing again. I reached up and pulled his hands off my shoulders. "Why would you help me steal your crown?"

"Because we're on the same side."

Exhaustion washed over me, and I wanted desperately to curl up into his bed. But my own was just a few feet away. "I should go to sleep." I turned, my muscles like lead. "Good night."

"Rowan?"

When I turned to look at him, I thought I saw a flicker of sadness pass across his perfect features—but it was so fast.

"Yeah?"

"*Sunshine*." Disdain laced his voice. "What is that?"

I rolled my eyes. "It's sarcastic. Because...you know..." Suddenly, I found myself desperate to know what he thought of me. "Because I'm a downer."

He studied me closely, and I expected him to say something mildly insulting. Instead, he said, "A downer?"

Given Orion's history, I probably *was* a veritable ray of sunshine. "You know, I have a lot of stored facts about death and general fears."

A line formed between his brows. "But of course you'd need that. Mortals die so easily. And you seemed particularly accident-prone."

"Thanks for the vote of confidence."

"You're not a downer. You are one of the most entertaining people I've ever known."

"You only know, like, four people, and one of them had his head split open with an axe."

A smile played about his lips. "See?"

I swallowed, then turned to walk back into my room, distinctly disturbed by the warm glow his words had given me.

I was, after all, ignoring him completely.

❧ 18 ❧
ROWAN

Five days until the trial.

After Orion helped me learn about my magic, I'd been rigidly controlled about avoiding him. Leaving the house at dawn before he woke, returning home when he was out. For the past three days, I'd managed to stay perfectly focused, envisioning a crown on my head and a peaceful demon city spread out before me.

With my teachers, I'd worked my way through one magical task after another.

At last, Legion allowed me to raise a monarch butterfly from the dead. Now it fluttered around my head, ignited with apricot light in the setting sun.

"Pretty zombie butterfly," cooed Shai.

"Brilliant." Kas beamed at me. "What do you think? Head home for the night, or do you want to go for gold and try summoning a witch?"

"I'm ready for the witch."

"Let's get the blood," said Shai, looking perfectly witchy in a long black gown with lacy sleeves.

"I think she's ready," said Legion. "We have four days left. If there are problems with the witch summoning, we'll need all that time to fine-tune it."

"Oh, thank the gods." Kas grinned. "I was getting incredibly bored."

I inhaled deeply. "I'm going to need to recite the spell quickly, too. Belial University's head witch will signal us to start, and then we'll be racing to get to the end of the spell first."

"Hmm." Legion pulled a small crimson-filled vial from his pocket. He turned it over between his fingertips, then met my gaze. "So, you're ready for this?"

I shrugged. "Might as well try it. But can you do me a favor and back up? Behind the trees, at least. In case I lose control of my magic."

Legion arched a dark eyebrow. "You haven't set anything on fire in days."

"Right," I said. "But none of us have much experience with Lightbringer power. Who knows what will happen?"

He shrugged. "Okay. Well, when you get to the summoning spell, let's try with a witch we know. Someone gentle and forgiving. Someone who won't mind being summoned from the dead."

I took the blood from him and opened the vial. "Do you have anyone in mind?"

"Goody Pendleton," said Legion. "Also known as Chemosh. I knew her long ago. She studied here in the eighteenth century."

"Ah, good choice." Kas's deep voice seemed to hum off the tree trunks. He wore a dandelion behind his ears. The combination of a flower with his tattoos was very fetching on him. "Chemosh is lovely. She used to make me hot cross buns every Sunday. I think she had a thing for me."

Legion sighed. "You say that about every woman."

"Her Demonic name is Chemosh," said Kas, ignoring him. "You'll need to call her at the end of the spell."

"Chemosh," I repeated, with a sound like a hard H.

"You've got the pronunciation down." Shai was flipping through one of the spell books. "Hang on, I'm finding the summoning spell."

I pulled open the cork on the vial of blood. "Just so you know, once you begin the summoning spell, you could see a few visions of the dead."

A little dread flickered in my chest. I'd seen enough visions of my dead mom to last a lifetime.

Legion took a deep breath and glanced at Shai. "I suppose we should hide."

She handed the book to Kas, and he held it open to the right page.

I raised my eyebrows when he didn't leave the grove. "You're not staying, are you? What if I explode with fireball magic?"

"You don't need to be worried about me. It's the benefit of being a demon, isn't it? Even if I burn to ash, I'll recover—it'll just take a few days. I only ask that you refrain from cutting out my heart, Sunshine, and I'll be fine."

I dipped my pinkie into the blood and carefully drew a five-pointed star on my forehead. The coppery scent of mortal blood filled my nostrils. As soon as the liquid was on my skin, I could feel my body reacting to it, my magic heating in my veins. I closed up the little vial and tucked it in my pocket, then wiped my fingers on my jeans and took the book from him.

Kas's amber eyes glowed.

With the blood on my skin, the world seemed to grow brighter, even though twilight was upon us. Light beamed through the oak leaves, and little motes of dust floated in the rays. All around me, sunlight heated the air. I felt *high*.

Kas himself seemed to glow with light, beautiful as an angel. "How does it feel?" he asked.

I sighed, my breath shaking. "Euphoric."

He let out a low chuckle. "Good. Connect to the earth, and see if you can intensify it."

I blinked in the golden rays of sunlight. "What?"

He stepped around me, and now his lovely gravelly voice was coming from just behind my back. "Take off your shoes."

Shai was right about his voice. It really *was* nice.

"Take them off," he said, "and feel the earth beneath your feet. It can help to intensify the power."

I slipped off my little brown flats and stood on the soil. An earthy forest breeze rushed over me, raising goosebumps. From the ground up, I started to call my magic, heat spreading through my body. "Okay. Here I go."

I started reciting the spell as I'd learned it in Demonic, and power thrummed up my nape.

I closed my eyes, thinking of a *hot* emotion. And as much as I tried to focus on bringing to mind the masculine sound of Kas's voice, Orion's sensual whisper kept intruding...

I wanted you to think of me and not Kas when you're going to sleep...

Warmth simmered between my ribs. I repeated the spell again, thinking of how it felt when Orion had kissed me, pressing me against the bedpost. The way his eyes had looked when I'd dropped the blanket...

A surge of magic kindled in my belly, and I could feel the light heating up my skin—

"Shit," I whispered. "Wait, it's too much." I let the sorrow of loss curl around me, dampening the force of my Lightbringer magic.

When I opened my eyes, I glanced at Kas, catching his worried expression.

He shook his head. "No, you have to use powerful magic for this," he said. "Try summoning everything you have, because I know Orion will."

I frowned, taking a step back from him. "Have you heard anything about a Lightbringer's power being dangerous? Like, if I use all my power, I could make everything around me dissolve, and also lose my mind?"

His forehead wrinkled. "Dissolve?"

"Hang on." Shai stepped out from behind an oak. "Who told you that? Orion?"

I realized how it sounded. "He didn't just tell me. He showed me. When I used a burst of my Lightbringer magic, it left me feeling confused. He said that for a Lightbringer, we can create a vacuum, and chaos replaces the light."

Shai grimaced. "*Rowan*. You can't really believe he's trying to help you, right? You're *rivals*. He tried to assassinate you. He wants to keep his throne."

The sun had slid down below the tree line now, and shadows spilled throughout the forest.

"He *is* the Lord of Chaos," said Kas. "I'm sure he could use chaos magic to make you feel...chaotic."

"Rowan," said Legion, "what do your instincts say?"

My instincts said Orion was right—but who the fuck knew if that was actual instinct or the influence of his mind-blowing kiss?

Shai walked closer to me and cupped both sides of my face. She lowered her chin, our foreheads practically touching. "You wanted me to remind you not to fall for his charm and manipulation, yeah? I'm doing that now."

"Right." I pulled her hands from my face. "Okay, well, just humor me and get further back than you were before."

"Really?"

"There's a small chance that Orion is correct, isn't there? And if I lose control of my magic, not only could I lose my mind, but I could dissolve everything around me."

"Dissolve," said Shai.

"I'm serious," I said. "I don't care if you don't believe it. I felt the Lightbringer power about to explode, and I don't want you near it. I'm talking, like, get on the other side of the Acheron River. I don't care if you'll all recover because you're demons—I don't need more horror burned into my memories." I pinned Kas with a serious stare. "I mean *all* of you. I'll come find you if the spell works."

Shai took a deep breath. "Fine, but we should Face-Time it."

Legion frowned. "Is that a spell?"

She pulled her cell phone out of her pocket and waggled it. "We can watch her through video, and if anyone tries to assassinate her, or on the off chance she loses her mind, we can save her."

"Fine." I pulled my cell phone from my jeans and propped it up against an oak. "Call me when you're on the other side of the river. And if my phone suddenly goes dead, it's either poor reception, or I exploded."

Shai's forehead wrinkled. "Right. Okay."

Night had fallen in the City of Thorns, and my friends quickly disappeared into the darkness, leaving me alone like I'd asked. As the sounds of their footfalls faded, the air seemed to grow colder.

On my forehead, the witch blood tingled.

It seemed like ages before my phone rang, the little screen lighting up with Shai's picture. I crossed to the oak tree and flicked it on to answer.

Shai's face popped up on the screen. "We're here. Hanging out by the river."

I waved at Shai. "I'm ready."

"Go for it, Sunshine!" Kas said from behind her.

Rolling my eyes, I stepped back into the grove. Barefoot, I took a deep, shuddering breath.

As I did, I called up a memory certain to instill fury in me—Orion standing over King Cambriel and slaughtering the man I'd vowed to kill. Taking my revenge from me...

In my mind's eye, I saw the hot splatter of blood on the stone. Anger started to rise, tightening my muscles. Just the right amount of power...

I opened my eyes to see the wind whipping through the trees. A faint golden glow emanated from my body, and I started to recite the spell, reading from the book. As I read, goosebumps rose on the back of my skin. From the corner of my eye, ghostly images flickered past. Between the trunks, shadows seemed to twine with wisps of light.

I glanced down at the page once more, but it took me a moment to find my place again on the page. I started again, pronouncing each word carefully. The hair rose on my nape as I felt I was opening the door to an ancient, powerful world. In the corner of my vision, silvery lights twinkled. From the soil upward, power rushed through me.

Glowing, I felt a primal connection to the world around me—to the generations of mortals and demons who'd come before me, who'd grown from the forest soil, then fed it with their bodies. The night spread its shadowy mantle, and I breathed in the humid, ancient air of the woods. This was where the Lilu belonged—in the wild.

Magic slid around me as I neared the end of the spell. But unwelcome memory started to intrude along with it: Orion's fingers tightening around me as he hoisted me up against the bedpost to kiss me hard. That deep, sensual kiss was too powerful for me to think of—

I tried to push the lust to the back of my skull.

"*Chemosh*," I said, completing the spell once again.

Light poured from me, and I tried to dampen the ardor of my emotions by thinking of the worst day of my life. But I felt like I could smell him now, the scent of burnt cedar wrapping around me. His skin tinged with gold.

Orion's eyes were on me as I leaned back on the bed, darkening because he liked what he saw. He was about to lose control of himself...

What are you so afraid of?

You.

Distantly, I heard Shai calling my name. But I wasn't in her world anymore. My body grew hotter, brighter.

Shaking with the power of the stars, until my mind no longer formed words. I lived in a world of light now.

But I no longer knew where my feet met the earth, or if I had a body at all.

I WOKE IN ORION'S ARMS, TO THE SOUND OF HIM swearing. When I opened my mouth to say something to him, I couldn't remember how to speak, or how I got here. I only knew that I needed to heal, and that I craved his body on mine.

Delirious, I kept my eyes on his square jaw until I could no longer remember his name.

❊ 19 ❊
ORION

I held Rowan in my arms, carrying her into my room. As soon as I'd seen the searing burst of light from the wilderness, panic had begun to claw at my mind. I'd raced through the skies, only to find her in a clearing of dust and ashes. The air still shimmered with gold around her.

Her magic had consumed a large circle of trees, and she lay in the center of it all, her clothing destroyed by the force of chaos. For a moment, I'd been so stunned by the sight of her lying naked on the earth that I could hardly think straight. But once I'd realized how badly she needed me, my thoughts became crystal clear.

I couldn't sense her soul.

She was clearly here—I could see her, feel her weight in my arms, smell her scent of ripe cherries with the mossy scent of the forest still clinging to her skin. Her chest rose and fell with each breath. But I couldn't sense her life. Normally, I could feel her energy, but like the music of the spheres—or an air conditioner that suddenly switched off

—it was hard to notice a constant presence until it went silent.

Rowan's energy had been like that, I think since even before I'd met her. Maybe since she'd been born—my twin star, a vibrating, humming power just at the outer edges of my consciousness.

When the mob had hanged her in the underworld, I'd felt the same dreadful quiet. Fear had stilled my heart.

Now, I laid her gently on my bed, and her arms flopped over her head. Her hair fanned out above her, billowing like a mermaid's. Or like Ophelia in the paintings after she drowned herself with a kingdom at stake. With the mad, murderous prince Hamlet driving her insane...

Regret tightened my throat.

Fuck. I was the mad, murderous prince. And this is what I'd wrought. I should have been there for her always instead of throwing her out of the city walls.

Rowan had been so ferocious when she'd tossed down the gauntlet, and now she looked so delicate—alabaster skin, narrow wrists. Her calves and back were smeared with dirt.

Rowan had used all her Lightbringer power at once, holding nothing back.

Kasyade and Legion weren't proper teachers. They were reckless arseholes so convinced of their own righteousness.

But it wasn't their fault Rowan didn't believe me. The sad truth was *I* was the one who'd convinced her not to trust me. I was the one who'd pushed her away because I was so afraid of losing someone again.

She knew that someone like me would cheat and steal to get the vengeance I'd promised to Ashur.

What she didn't know was that I prized something else above the throne right now. It wasn't revenge, either.

I just wanted her to open her fucking eyes and look at me.

She consumed me, and right now, nothing else meant anything anymore.

Raw fear replaced my anger, and fear was the one thing I couldn't really deal with. This was exactly what I'd hoped to avoid with Rowan, why I'd pushed her away—the dizzying terror of losing someone you cared about. I wanted to avoid that particular horror again, the one that had devoured me so completely, the one that had broken me until I no longer really knew who I was.

I touched her chest, just between her breasts. Whatever light remained inside her was now just a guttering lick of flame. Darkness and chaos swirled around it. That light would be gone for good unless I could heal her soon.

If I fucked this up, she'd be lost to me for eternity to the chaos inside.

A wave of my hand brought the candles in my room blazing to life—I still preferred them to electric lights. And I needed to stoke those flames inside her now, just like that. The Lilu healed by feeding off lust, but it had to be done properly.

Slowly.

Too much lust too quickly would overwhelm her. I'd have to take her to the brink and keep her there for as long as I could. A slow, erotic build-up was the best way to restore a Lilu depleted of power. A simmering heat. And with my hand on her chest, I could already hear her moaning quietly. Even if she couldn't think clearly yet, her body's primitive instincts knew what she needed.

I extended her arms toward the corners of the bed and followed suit with her ankles. I spun my index finger in the air, and tendrils of my magic coiled around Rowan's limbs, holding them fast. If anything went wrong—if I overwhelmed her with power—I needed her under control.

Her heart started to race, her chest flushing. Something in her body liked being bound, which was a detail I'd have to think about later when her life wasn't on the line.

Already, her warm succubus magic stroked over my skin. It invited me in, making my breath quicken. There was still a chance to bring her back.

My gaze raked down her naked body, and I fought for restraint.

I remembered reading about a glutton demon named Shedim who used famine and starvation as torture devices, but with a kicker. He kept mortals on the brink of death, within a heartbeat of the end, for weeks or longer. He'd provide just enough sustenance to keep the mortals breathing. Just strong enough to move and stand, but no more. The twist was that he'd then present the poor fools with a sumptuous feast—a long table filled with all manner of rich meats and cheeses, fruits and desserts, breads and wines. The starving people would inevitably gorge themselves like wild animals, trying to stuff everything into their mouth at once.

Shedim fed off their gluttony.

They'd become violently ill. And some would go so far

as to eat until their stomachs burst, much to Shedim's delight.

And as I stared at Rowan now, tied to my bed, I had some inkling what had driven those starving mortals, because she looked like a feast before me. That same madness threatened to overwhelm me.

But really, this wasn't Rowan at all. Her mind wasn't functioning.

And I'd promised not to kiss her until she trusted me. I *hated* breaking promises, and she had no way to tell me she trusted me in the state she was in.

I threw one of my blankets over her, covering her from her breasts down to her thighs, and she sighed at the contact. Every muscle in my body went taut at the sound, my blood pounding. Already, she was feeding off my raw desire, healing from it. All I had to do was be in the same room with her, and she could drink from my erotic charge. But with the right technique, I could heal her sooner.

I reached down to touch her bare legs, slowly letting my fingertips trace the swell of her calves up to the backs of her knees.

When I reached her thighs, my palms flattened, and her muscles tensed and relaxed involuntarily as I pressed on them more forcefully. She made a tiny, whimpering sound, her mouth opening as she breathed more deeply. There it was—a little more light in her eyes, and her gaze was locked on me. She tugged at the bindings. Already, she was healing—feeding off me. Her body was calling to mine like a siren.

I traced slow, gentle strokes over her thighs. Hungry for me, she breathed faster, and her heart raced.

My nostrils flared as my own arousal stampeded through my body. My incubus magic slid over her as I caressed my way back down her legs to her feet, massaging them one after the other, my thumbs applying pressure up and down her soles and down to the balls of her feet. I took my time returning to her upper thighs, which made her groan as she moved her body against the restraints. The blanket slipped down a little, revealing a nipple that seemed painfully peaked, aching to be touched.

She whispered my name so quietly, I could hardly hear it.

And it took everything inside me not to have her right then and there, to act as one of Shedim's tortured mortals and surrender to my basest desires. I growled, a low, guttural sound, and I moved my hands to the hollows of her hips, pulling the blanket aside just enough that I could stroke her skin. Holy hell, I wanted to rip the blanket aside and see all of her, but this wasn't the time.

Sparks danced where I touched her, as if she were made of steel and my hands were welder's torches. I watched it, entranced. The Lilu were truly amazing creatures.

Light flared in her eyes, and she whispered my name. Relief flooded me as I realized it was working, and I traced my fingertips down her ribcage.

"Rowan?" I whispered back. "Are you returning to me?"

She gasped as I slid them up again, just below her breasts. "Yes," she breathed.

Her hips rose, rocking, as her body sought the sexual release that was the lifeblood of a succubus. When she said my name again, I started stroking her thighs again, stoking her lust.

Every part of me burned for her, and each beat of my heart sent blood pumping to the only place I needed it.

Fuck.

Nothing mattered at that moment except her.

❦ 20 ❧

ROWAN

Hot, velvety, erotic magic charged the room, making my body swell with need.

I *needed* Orion.

I'd never ached for something like this before. Not just one Orion—I wanted two of him. Three? Mouths on my nipples, one between my legs—

I could imagine a whole bunch of them surrounding me, kissing me everywhere, giving me the sex I craved. The silky blanket was a light, torturous friction on my naked skin. Had he done that on purpose?

He'd brought me into this wild state of sexual arousal, but he wasn't finishing the job. Fuck, I'd say whatever he wanted if he just gave me what I needed. If I could remember how to make words...

What I really wanted was to leap on him, straddle him, satiate myself on his body. But I couldn't move—I was held in place, bound at my wrists and ankles with shimmering bands of energy. Gods *damn* it, Orion.

His thumb traced circles over my hipbones just under the blanket, and my body shook, my breath catching. That wasn't where I really needed him.

"Orion," I managed in a hoarse whisper. Light from candles danced on the walls as I tried to put together the wheres and whys and hows of my predicament. I only vaguely remembered how I'd ended up here.

I wanted to ask him to remove the restraints and the fabric off my body, but my thoughts were still a jumble of confusion.

He leaned over me, elbows on either side, his eyes searching mine. He looked golden in this light, and I thought I read relief in his eyes, and a faint smile. "There you are, Rowan."

The way he said my name sounded reverent.

Gods, he smelled amazing. *Kiss me, you hot bastard.*

He stroked his thumb over my cheek. "You drained yourself completely. I guess you had to learn the hard way." A seductive smile curled his lips. "Lucky for you, I'm prepared to bring you back the hard way."

He leaned down, brushing kisses over my jaw, then moved lower to my throat. My body arched into him, my hips moving upward. Every touch of his lips against my skin sent heat sliding through my body, pulsing between my thighs. My breasts ached for him, and the light movement of this silky blanket against my nipples was pure torture. I was on *fire*.

He stopped kissing the tops of my breasts, glancing up at me from under his black eyelashes. His cheeks looked flushed, and the dark look in his eyes said he wanted to devour me. So why wasn't he doing more?

Untying me so I could participate? Holy hell, this was excruciating.

"Orion," I said again, louder this time, like a desperate prayer for salvation. It seemed the only thing I could remember how to say was his name...though another word was rolling around in my mind, the word *fuck*, because that was what I needed.

The ache between my thighs was overwhelming. Slick with desire, thighs spread open with these bindings, I desperately needed him to fill me.

"I said I wouldn't kiss you until you said you trusted me," he murmured into my neck. "But it doesn't count if it's not on your mouth." Another flick of his beautiful, silver-flecked eyes at me. "And this is, after all, an emergency."

"More," I groaned, finally managing a new word.

"Not yet." He kissed my breasts, and I tried to wrap my thighs around him. I *needed* satiation. "Too much is dangerous, love. But you're feeding from me because I'm desperate to fuck you."

That made me shake again, trying to press my thighs together so I could clench them, but they were pulled too far apart.

Gasping, I tugged on my restraints, struggling against my bindings. I could find nothing to provide me with the pleasure I craved. I let my head fall back into the pillows, aroused beyond all reason. I could think only of how much I needed pressure between my thighs that would give me my release.

I felt nearly as empty as I had when my magic left me, just in a very different way.

If he just gave me what I needed, this could all be over. Instead, he pushed himself up so he was sitting on the bed next to me, then slid the blanket up a little higher on my thighs, his eyes burning with dark heat as he stared at my body. I was sure he could see how turned on I was. His jaw was rigid with tension, and he looked as if he was about to snap.

He traced circles between my thighs—too light, not high enough. Teasing me. Making my hips buck as I shamelessly tried to move against him. Higher now, moving over my sex, but too light—

Writhing in my bonds, I hissed, "Please, Orion." Lilu magic charged the room, warm threads of our magic entwining, humming over my skin. And as I moved, the blanket slid off my breasts. His gaze shot to my hardened nipples, and he cursed under his breath. His muscles tensed, and he pulled his gaze away from me.

Then the bastard yanked his hand from me, too. I gasped audibly, certain he was doing this to mess with me. This was torture, wasn't it?

He turned, shoulders tense, fists tightened like he was about to fight. "No more for now, love. Your magic must return slowly, and I'm about to snap."

I gritted my teeth. "You're just doing this to torment me."

His gaze slid back to me, his eyes filled with shadows. "You've already regained enough strength to speak in complete sentences. This was the right way to heal you. Your body can heal itself with our lust magic. But if it goes too far, it will drain you, and then we're back to square one. Trust me," he murmured. "I'm not enjoying this any more than you are."

But did I actually trust him? Now there was a question. And I absolutely could not remember the answer.

I pulled at the restraints as he crossed through a doorway into another room, feeling vulnerable and exposed—and thoroughly unsatisfied.

From where I lay, I heard the sound of a bath filling. Slowly, with Orion out of the room, my heart slowed, and I sucked in deep breaths. I hadn't fully recovered, but my strength was returning.

I hoped my sanity would follow soon after. Begging for sex wasn't my style, especially from a rival I'd been intent on hating.

Orion returned to the bedroom clad only in a pair of black boxers, his tan, muscular physique on display. My gaze swept down to his abs—then lower. From the looks of it, maybe he was as painfully aroused as I was.

"I'm going to release you and carry you to the bath," he said.

"I can walk," I protested weakly.

"Suit yourself."

With a flick of his wrist, the coils holding me captive dissolved into thin air. I curled into a ball before stretching like a cat, twisting my back in every direction it could twist. If he wasn't going to give me what I needed, then what I really wanted was some alone time. But he had warned me that too much sexual pleasure was dangerous. And clearly, it was time for me to start heeding his warnings.

"Promise me you'll be more careful with your magic," he said quietly.

"Oh, I promise." I swung my legs off the bed, then stood to walk to the bathroom adjoining his room. I made it about two steps before I promptly collapsed.

Orion was close enough to catch me before I hit the floor, flinging an arm around my lower back. He scooped me up and carried me to the bubbling, lavender-scented water.

"Not there yet," he said as he gently slipped me into the tub.

The water was divine, and it helped to take my mind off my sexual torment. I surveyed his bathroom, which was as neat and clean as everything else he inhabited. The white tiles and the marble sink gleamed, and sunlight spilled through the diamond-shaped windowpanes. Neat piles of white towels were folded on a mahogany table, and a mirror hung on the wall above it. In the reflection, I watched Orion behind me.

He dipped a white ceramic mug into the bath. "Tilt your head back."

I did as he instructed, and he poured water over my head, careful not to let it splash into my eyes. On the forest floor, I'd been covered in dirt. Now, Orion washed my hair, massaging my scalp to clean me off. In the hot water, my skin started to go pink.

If you've never had your hair washed by somebody while you luxuriate in a hot bath, I highly recommend it, even if you can't find a sexy incubus to do the job.

I relaxed under his expert hands and let the scalp massage become a shoulder massage, then a foot massage, and before I knew it, his face so close to mine that I could feel his breath warming the side of my cheeks. Whenever he touched me, his fingers played my body like a concert-master on a Stradivarius.

But the more I healed—and the more that clarity returned—the more a disturbing thought started to worry at the back of my mind.

I'd fucking exploded, hadn't I?

"Orion, what happened? How much did I destroy?" I asked.

"It's fine, love. You just took out a whole bunch of old oak trees."

"Shit," I muttered under my breath. "But everyone was okay?"

"No one was caught in the blast."

"Thank the gods." My body relaxed, eyes drifting closed as steam curled around my body.

Gods, it was comfortable in here.

My eyes started to drift closed, my muscles turning to jelly. Orion must have noticed, because the next thing I knew, he was wrapping me in the towel and scooping me up. He carried me back into his room and laid me on his bed. He didn't seem to mind that I was making his sheets all damp, and I was too tired to worry about it. I curled up in his covers, delighted to have the smell of burnt cedar—his smell—all over me.

My breath slowed, and I pulled his covers up over my shoulders. The last thing I felt before I drifted off was his arm wrapping protectively around my waist.

But in a surprisingly gentlemanly move, Orion was sleeping on top of the covers, and I was below.

❧

I woke up to the sound of a woman's voice filling the room. I blinked at the sight of the setting sun outside, and I tried to make sense of my surroundings. When I looked down at myself, I saw that someone had dressed me in a white nightgown and underwear.

Bleary-eyed, I blinked at the window—a sunset streaked with periwinkle and rose. I thought I'd slept a full day, and I sat up to drink the water someone had left on the bedside table.

I was in Orion's bedroom, where everything was in its right place. Slowly, the memories started to return to me— the blast of magic, the sexual torture of healing.

But who the fuck was this woman talking?

The fog of sleep cleared more, and I tuned into her words.

"...but Lenore was always an anxious raven..."

I startled, looking back at the bedside table. An old-fashioned cassette played a very familiar book.

How did he remember? We'd talked about this in the underworld. This was what my mother would read to me when I was home sick from school, or she'd play the audiobook for me when I couldn't sleep.

Lenore the anxious raven, who had to learn to slow her breathing before she could sleep.

My mind shot back to a conversation I'd had with him, the things our parents had done to soothe us. It shocked me that he remembered.

My heart swelled when I thought of him finding this for me.

Then it constricted again as I realized I was running out of time to prepare for the trial. And that Orion would be doing whatever he could to throw me off.

If I didn't get my shit together—fast—I'd lose everything.

🎍 21 🎍

ROWAN

vening of the trial.

Rosy sun rays spilled through the trees, and the forest's shadows grew long. As nerves tightened my muscles, I wished I had something to do with my hands.

Twilight was the most powerful time to lower the veil between the worlds.

After I'd recovered my sanity, I'd had three full days to practice. And that was about how long it had taken to summon Goody Pendleton, and to successfully bind her with magic. Just as Kas had promised, she'd been very good-natured about the whole thing, so I'd summoned her and bound her again and again, until my throat was hoarse and Legion yelled at me to get some rest before I lost my mind all over again.

I closed my eyes.

I'm ready.

I'd memorized the spells, and I could rattle them off

fluently. I knew the exact memory to conjure up to summon just the right amount of magic.

I doubted that Orion had practiced at all, which had been my hope. He leaned against a tree, his arms folded, hair falling in his eyes. Insouciant as ever. His gaze slid to me, but his expression was unreadable.

Focus on the trial, Rowan. Not on him.

If I let his pretty face distract me—and the memory of his abs flexing under my fingertips—I'd lose. No question about that.

I scanned the grove of mossy oaks, my heart beating a little faster. When I'd practiced, I hadn't had an audience. But today, half the city was out here in the forest to watch the start of the trial. There was no way to know where this competition would lead us today, but seemingly everyone in town had left their homes and lined up in the woods and city like they were waiting for a parade, hoping to get a glimpse of the moment that might fell a king or crown a queen.

Mist snaked around the ancient boughs and trunks.

I closed my eyes again, mentally reviewing the spells. I didn't *need* to review them at this point, but it kept me from looking at Orion's eyes, and from remembering the feel of his strong hands on me—

Focus.

My jaw clenched. Practicing, I mouthed the words like I was murmuring a prayer for salvation.

The sound of footfalls crunching over twigs pulled my attention from the spell. The dean of Belial crossed into the grove. Mistress Blacknettle, a stunning mortal woman, wore a crown of bluebells and white bloodroot flowers over her long silver curls.

Standing ramrod straight, she lifted her chin. "It has been centuries since a shadow scion has challenged a king. Two Lightbringers, each blessed by Lucifer, vie for the crown tonight, according to the ancient rules of the trials. At dusk, in the boundary between the world of the living and the dead, we will begin. And as night falls over the ancient city, the gods shall decide who will rule the City of Thorns."

A shiver skittered up my spine. Did the gods really have anything to do with this beyond Tammuz's fervent desire to create chaos?

Mistress Blacknettle pulled out two small vials of blood, one for each of us. Inhaling deeply, I pulled the cork open, then dipped my pinkie into the blood and leaned over to draw the star on my forehead.

"Whoever is able to first summon Alaric will have a bond with him, and the other competitor will not," the dean declared. "But the bond does not guarantee a win, only an advantage. The trial will not be concluded until the crown is in someone's hand. Understood?"

As I painted the star onto myself, the shadows thickened around us, and the sultry breeze picked up, catching leaves in the air. Distant thunder rolled across the forest.

The dean took the vials from us and stepped away, her gray eyes flitting between Orion and me.

I inhaled the forest air as I started to summon my magic. Over the past few days, I'd discovered the perfect memory for invoking just the right amount. In my mind's eye, I thought of a happy memory—one filled with love but tinged with just a bit of sadness to keep me from destroying everyone.

I remembered being sick one night with a fever, and Mom lay next to me in bed. The moonlight streamed in the window, and Mom made a shadow puppet in its light. There were two she could make, a dog and a rabbit. She told a little story with them, and it didn't make a lot of sense. But the important thing was that she'd been lying next to me. Thinking of how she looked after me, love bloomed in my chest, and magic glowed faintly from my body.

And as soon as the dean spoke the single Demonic word that heralded the start of the trial, a sense of calm spread over me.

I launched into the spell I'd memorized, desperate to form the bond with Alaric.

As I spoke, the air chilled, mist rising from the frozen underworld. Around us, spirits began moving between the trunks, their forms silvery and transparent. I was pronouncing each word with precision, the words flowing as quickly and fluidly as the Acheron River. It was as if the gods were inhabiting my body...

Shadows pooled in the grove, and a warm fog slid between the gnarled, mossy trees. I no longer worried that Orion would distract me. In fact, I had the power to throw *him* off course. As I recited the spell, I looked up at Orion and gave him a sultry wink.

His eyes widened just a touch. I heard him trip over a single syllable.

With a half-smile, I finished the last word of the spell —*Alaric*.

I'd done it. With that final word, magic crackled over my skin, heralding the arrival of the Visigoth somewhere in the city.

An invisible thread formed, connecting me to him, tugging me north.

My wings burst from my back, and I shot upward, ripping through the oak leaves on my way.

My bond with Alaric compelled me northwest toward the Sathanas Ward, where the gates marked the boundary with Osborne.

Orion raced behind me. Even as I flew, I could feel his hot magic floating on the night air, skimming around me. Beneath us, torches dotted the dark landscape, pricks of orange light that moved toward the bridge. Beneath us, a crowd of onlookers was trying to follow our path.

One way or another, I had to slow Orion down, or he'd just follow me to Alaric. He could steal victory from me at the last moment—again.

So when I reached the outer boundaries of the Sathanas Ward, I angled my wings to touch down a quarter mile from him. I landed fast and hard on a crooked little lane in the old part of the city, my feet slamming onto the cobbles. My wings retracted, and I whirled to see Orion land just behind me. His enormous body was silhouetted against the amber windows of a restaurant.

"You never quite do what I expect, Rowan."

Under my breath, I began chanting the words for the binding spell.

Only Orion's pale, icy eyes pierced the darkness. "You—"

With the final word of the spell, ribbons of darkness

spun around Orion, binding him in place. It wouldn't last forever, but it would give me enough of a head start.

With a smile, I turned to stalk through the darkened streets. The invisible thread felt a little weaker now— moving? I took off on foot, sprinting through the sinuous alleys, past a bakery, past a magic shop crammed with skulls and stuffed birds.

The thread pulled me around the corner to an old, abandoned temple.

And there he was, Alaric himself, a giant of a mortal. He shouted something that sounded like *zookooboos*, which I was guessing was the old Gothic word for "succubus."

Alaric wore a brilliant red cape and gold-plated armor, and he towered high over the cobblestone road. But most importantly, the crown of blackthorns rested on his head.

I summoned my magic again from between my ribs.

As the Gothic king turned to run, I started to rattle off the words of the binding spell. But before I could get to the final word, a flash of vibrating magic burst from the king's enormous body.

From the skies, a horde of ravens swooped down, aiming for me. Some of their beaks dug into the flesh of my forearms, and I gritted my teeth. Their pecking was vicious, down to the bone.

As I shielded myself with my arms, I managed to finish the last words of the spell. I fell to my knees, and the ravens seemed to lose focus. Their wings beat at me, and they started to careen away, veering wildly down the narrow stone lanes. My ravaged arms were healing already.

I glanced at Alaric, finding him frozen in place. Ropes of my golden magic snaked around him. I rushed closer, whispering the only German phrase I knew, "*Tut mir leid,*" hoping the apology bore some similarity to ancient Gothic.

I just needed a little help reaching that crown on top of his towering body.

As my wings burst from my back, I lifted off the stones and reached for it. My fingers grazed the thorns. But as they did, a powerful hand wrapped around my forearm, wrenching my hand away.

22

ROWAN

Orion gripped my arm, his pale eyes gleaming. "You *have* been practicing."

Fast as lightning, I shifted my arm out of his grip and grabbed his wrist. Snarling, I started to twist his arm behind his back—

Behind me, the sound of snapping bindings echoed off the stone as the Gothic king broke free.

Orion twisted out of my grasp, and I grunted with frustration. When I whirled to look for Alaric, the king was already gone.

Without another word or wasted breath, Orion and I lifted into the air, searching for the king. But clever Alaric had cloaked himself in darkness for now.

I turned my attention to the feel of the bond again as I soared over stone spires, over steep-peaked buildings that glowed with warm light. The sea-kissed breeze rushed over me, exhilarating. Gods, I loved flying.

At last, I felt it again—a strong tug between my ribs. The bond was luring me east, toward the sea. I glanced behind me, but I couldn't see Orion. Either he'd cloaked himself as well or he was finding his own way to the Visigoth king.

No matter. Without the bond, all Orion could do was follow. I angled my wings to soar toward the water.

Alaric was hurtling through the streets like a meteor, using magic to give himself speed. At least he wasn't sending the birds after me anymore.

With the marine wind whipping at my head, I soared after him—past the Abaddon Ward, the Luciferian Ward, the Tower of Baal. If he made it into the sea itself, I'd never catch him. A skilled witch like him would know spells for breathing underwater, and I didn't have the first clue there.

Licking the salt off my lips, I angled my wings to land, hoping to head him off before he made it to the ocean. Here, on the city's eastern shore, a few narrow alleys led to the sea. Once Alaric reached them, he could race down the ancient stone stairs, hiding in the depths.

My heart slammed against my chest as I glided downward.

I touched down hard in a little lane crowded with Tudor-style buildings, and I felt his momentum stop.

I turned to scan the little street, but I couldn't pick him out. I could *feel* him nearby, though, and I stared at the space before me as I caught my breath.

In my chest, I felt the pull of my connection to him, urging me forward just a little. Warm light beamed from behind leaded glass windows, illuminating old books and displays of sugared cakes. But in the center of the alley, the shadows looked unnaturally dark, sucking up the light from the shop windows. *There.*

Quietly, I began to chant the binding spell. I kept very still, whispering under my breath, trying not to spook him.

But unfortunately for me, I could hear someone else whispering a spell—and the disturbing sound of slithering behind me made goosebumps rise on my skin. A loud *hisss* turned my head, and my heart stuttered.

A serpent as large as an ancient oak bough snaked up the stone stairwell, scales gleaming with iridescent light. The monstrous thing opened its mouth, showing off fangs longer than my hand.

I exhaled sharply and called up my flames at my finger-tips, but the serpent darted for me, its teeth sinking into the flesh at my side.

"Rowan!" From a distance, Orion's voice called to me.

With the excruciating pain racing through my body, flames burst out of me—a white-hot instinct I hadn't quite thought about. The serpent didn't quite catch fire, but the heat must have hurt it, because the creature unlocked its jaw. The air smelled of burning flesh, and the snake's head swerved from side to side, mouth gaping. My blood dripped from its fangs.

From above, Orion landed on the serpent's back while it reared its head. Orion's silver claws shot out, and he plunged them into the back of the monster's neck, starting to sever the head.

I gripped my side, doing my best to block out the pain. I didn't think I could breathe correctly. Dizzy, I started swaying, staggering back.

Focus on the crown, Rowan. I whirled to scan the narrow road for the shadows again, but my vision seemed blurred.

I was pretty sure Alaric was gone already. Vaguely, I could feel him moving down the sea-slick stairwell. My wings burst out of my back, and I lifted into the air, above the serpent in its death throes.

With my thoughts on the crown, I soared above the stairs just in time to see Alaric waist-deep in the waves. I flew out after him, but I couldn't quite summon my magic. It sputtered and died in my chest.

In the ocean, Alaric's body shifted, turning sleek and dark, the blackthorn crown still resting on his head. As a seal, he dove under the dark surface.

A shock of pain rocked through my body where the serpent had bitten me, and I found myself losing control of my flight, careening down toward the water. My wings weren't working now, either.

Salty spray misted over me, and then I crashed hard into the sea, the agony blinding. Injured as I was, I hadn't managed to retract my wings in time before I hit the surface. The force of the fall plunged me under the waves, and pain splintered my bones.

I'd become so used to healing quickly, but that wasn't working out for me right now. In fact, I felt distinctly mortal. I felt like I wanted to vomit. Where the fuck was *up*? Where was down? My wings slowly slid back into my shoulder blades.

At last, my feet struck rough stone, helping to orient me. I pushed forward toward the shore until my head popped above the waves, and then I sucked in a furious breath.

I dragged myself from the sea, rasping for air. *Holy hell*, that serpent's venom had wrecked me, and the saltwater in the puncture wounds didn't feel amazing.

I trudged through the waves, my whole body shaking.

Orion stood on the rocky shore, knee deep in the water. His sleeves had been rolled up, and the sea spray had dampened his white shirt, making it translucent and leaving it clinging to his abs. "You okay?" he called.

I managed a smile as I trudged closer to him through the crashing waves. "I'll live, right?" I didn't want to puke in front of my rival but avoiding that wasn't the easiest thing right now.

As I moved nearer, he stepped forward, just in time to catch my arm as I started to fall. "I need to get the venom out of you."

I clutched my side, staring at up him. "We're competing."

He slid his arm around his waist, helping me to walk. "All we can do now is wait until old Alaric comes out of the sea, and I don't need you to be in pain that entire time. Alaric won't be able to stay transformed forever, but we might have a long night ahead of us."

I leaned into him, too agonized to refuse his help. Was his body shaking a little? I felt like his muscles were vibrating. "What *was* that creature?"

"A monster called a Ladon, with venom toxic even to demons." Even in the darkness, I could tell that Orion's face was drained of color. "Alaric must have called him from the sea. The venom won't kill you, but it'll hurt like hell and interfere with your magic."

I gritted my teeth as I sat on the stairs. "Legion thought taking a crown from a mortal would be easy."

"Legion has no idea what he's talking about." Orion knelt between my knees and lifted the soaking hem of my shirt. I grimaced at the sight of two deep puncture wounds. Dark poison flowed through my veins beneath my pale skin.

"How do you get it out?" At this point, I could hardly get the *words* out, and they mumbled forth as more of an incoherent moan than a question.

Without answering, he lowered his mouth to my skin just above my hip bone. He swirled his tongue once, and then he began to suck. The relief of pain was almost instantaneous, replaced by the warmth of Orion's magic— the fucking glorious healing power of an incubus. Heat spread from my hip bone outward, making my muscles go supple and relaxed. The feeling of relief quickly slid into something pleasurable that had me threading my fingers into his hair. Molten heat slid through my body.

Gods, I loved the way he healed me. Might as well admit it. His mouth moved above the hollow on my hips, and desire hummed through me, a hot vibration that made me want to pull him up over me. Except at any minute now, we'd probably have a whole crowd of onlookers, and I didn't want them to see their future queen in a compromising situation. I tried to keep my eyes on the sea as Orion worked his mouth over my skin, occasionally spitting venom onto the stones.

He really didn't *feel* like a rival right now. But of course he didn't—he was Orion, the last incubus. His sexual appeal burned with all the heat of a star.

My thighs clenched around him, and he looked up at me with a half-smile playing around his lips. "Seems like you'll be fine now."

I felt breathless as I released my grip from his hair, forcing my gaze from him to the dark sea. "You could have left the poison in me and won easily."

He shifted away and sat next to me on the stairs. When he turned to face me, his eyes were burning bright blue. "And you could have killed me instead of binding me. But the thought of you in pain makes me want to die. Or massacre people. And I'm doing my best to avoid both at the moment."

My chest flushed at that, but I tried not to dwell on it too long.

When I glanced at the seaside wall above us, I saw the first onlookers appear, bearing torches. "I'm afraid they might be in for a boring few hours."

Orion didn't answer. His shoulders looked rigid, his skin ghostly pale. His hands were tightened into fists.

"Did the serpent get you, too?" I asked. "You look a little ill."

He stared straight ahead, and silence filled the air between us. "I don't like snakes."

"I used to, but that fucker may have changed my mind."

He cast a quick glance up at the onlookers above us. "No, I mean I *really* don't like snakes," he whispered. "You asked what I was afraid of beside you. It's snakes. And that one scared the shit out of me." The moonlight sculpted the beautiful planes of his face.

"Why get a snake tattoo, then?"

"Just a reminder of things." His fists flexed again. Clearly, he was done with this conversion.

"But...all snakes? Even little garter snakes?"

His slid me a cool look, and his gaze bored into me. "I really didn't mean for this conversation to go on this long."

"Okay." I swallowed hard. "How long do you think we have until he changes back?"

"Could be hours. Maybe all night."

I rose from the stone, crossing back to the shoreline. My bond with Alaric was gone for now.

"I missed you when you were in Osborne," Orion said quietly.

My heart fluttered, and I turned back to look at him. "You knew where I was if you wanted to talk to me."

"I needed time. For centuries, Rowan, I teetered on the edge of sanity. And the single constant thread that kept me from descending into madness was my oath to Ashur. It's not something I could abandon overnight."

Cautiously, I slid my gaze to him. "And it's still the only thing keeping you from madness?"

From the steps, his eyes met mine. "You were the only person in centuries who cared for me. And when you were gone, I couldn't sleep. I felt like I'd returned to the prison cell. I needed you near me, Rowan. I needed time to I realize that we were twin stars. And that I'd always dreamt of you."

I stared at him, feeling like my heart was breaking and healing at the same time. But we were *mid*-trial right now. And how was I to know what was real? The entire kingdom was on the line. "Orion, we can't do this right now. I'm not going to speak to you during the trial. I'm concentrating."

I turned away from him, staring at the dark sea again. My gaze flicked up at the sky, my pulse racing as I caught sight of the spot where Gemini would rise.

❧ 23 ❧
ROWAN

By the time the first pale blush of dawn tinged the sky, Alaric still hadn't returned. Even so, the crowd of eager onlookers had waited up all night, watching us from the streets and buildings above. For the most part, I managed to keep my eyes locked on the sea.

I'd spent the night right here, watching, waiting. Orion lounged on the stairs just behind me.

A slight tug in my ribs had my muscles tensing. Faintly, the bond with Alaric was moving again, rushing toward the shore.

My fingers twitched with anticipation.

Orion must have sensed me tensing because he moved closer along the shoreline, quietly whispering a spell to himself.

After a night of standing vigil here, my legs ached, and my stomach felt like it was eating itself alive.

I glanced at Orion. "Hello, my shadow. What was that spell you were just chanting?"

He leaned in and whispered, "I thought we weren't speaking."

"Just wondering what you're up to."

"Not a spell, love. I was merely reciting the names of the Lilu dead. That is how I pray."

A ripple of cold magic spread over me from behind, like an arctic wind. A distraction, maybe. Orion playing a trick, getting me to take my eyes off the sea so he could steal the crown.

When a low growl rose from behind me, I glanced over my shoulder. A woman stood at the top of the stairs, her pale blonde curls radiating from her head. She wore a crown of spiked silver woven with ivy.

"Reciting the names of the Lilu dead or calling up a distraction?" I snapped.

But something about the glacial magic radiating from her body told me this was more than just a trick. The woman was eerily beautiful, with gray eyes and a wicked smile. She wore a blue velvet cape around her shoulders. Underneath, blood stained her white gown in great streaks of crimson.

My jaw tightened. This really wasn't the time for... whatever the hell this was.

Tightening my fingers into fists, I turned back to the sea once more. I had the sense that Alaric was barreling toward us under the waves, homing in.

Orion turned to face the newcomer, nodding at her. "Who the fuck are you?" Irritation laced his tone.

I rolled my eyes. Maybe he wasn't *always* charming. Maybe he saved that for special occasions, like trying to convince me we should murder everyone in Osborne.

From behind me, I heard her speak in a faintly French accent: "But, Your Majesty."

I glanced back again. Her breath frosted the air with a cold mist, and the sound of her wintry voice sent a chill down my spine.

"Your Majesty, you summoned me yourself. And here, in the City of Thorns, I will feast on demon blood." She turned her cold gaze to me, her smile vulpine. "And I will start with the *succube* who would be *la reine*. It is as we discussed."

"*La sorcière de Brocéliande,*" Orion murmured.

"You *summoned* her?" I hissed.

Turning back to the sea, I glimpsed Alaric rising from the waves—human once more, the sea pouring off him. And there was the blackthorn crown. My wings burst from my back. Just as my feet left the rocks, a clawed hand gripped my wings and threw me down hard to the rocky shoreline with shocking force.

Pain screamed through my wings, and I stared up at *la sorcière* as she leapt on top of me. She gripped me by the hair and smashed the back of my head into a sharp rock— once, twice—oh, *gods*, she was breaking my skull open.

I had to think...I had to think...

My head was broken, and I had no words to think with.

I moaned on the rocks.

Fangs bared above me. "*Les démons* murdered my family, and I have come to feast on your kind."

I stared dumbly as the witch drew a long, sharp silver blade. "Your lover and I share one thing—a lust for *la vengeance.*"

She raised her blade above my heart, and the world seemed to tilt beneath me.

As she started to bring it down, a blast of fire rolled across the horizon from the place where Orion had been standing. Searing flames engulfed me, but the fire didn't burn me. It gave me life, healing my broken skull like a salve of flames.

La sorcière de Brocéliande blazed above me, screeching with pain in the inferno. Her cries withered in the blaze as the fire consumed her.

But there was another figure here, burning in the inferno. Screaming to the heavens. Through the fire, I caught sight of the writhing figure of Alaric, his crown blazing like a torch.

No.

I pushed myself up, trying to reach for it. But the Visigoth king burned to cinders before me, and the crown crumbled in my fingertips.

A cloud of smoke and ash wafted above me, mixing with the sea spray. The flames started to die down, sputtering in the crashing waves.

I stood, stunned, on the hot rocks. Shaking, I tried to dust the ashes off myself, but I was so wet, they formed a sort of gray paste.

I swallowed hard. A gray paste composed of two witches...

My gaze flicked up to where the crowd had been, but they'd all fled. I could still hear them screaming in the distance. The stones around us had been blackened with the force of the blast.

I stared at Orion. "That was you, wasn't it? That was your fire."

"She nearly killed you," said Orion, sounding shocked. "I was waiting for you to fight her."

I touched the back of my head. It felt disturbingly *dented*, but there was definitely no longer a gaping wound. "I was having a hard time remembering how to summon magic with my head cracked open." I glanced at the rocks, sickened to see gore glistening on the stones. If I weren't a demon, I'd be dead. "She said you asked her to kill me. Is it just me, or is this a recurring theme, Orion?"

He'd gone completely pale again. "I didn't summon her. Of course I didn't. She loathes demons. She was lying."

"So everyone is lying but you?" I said sharply. "All your soldiers and *la sorcière de Brocéliande*?"

His expression darkened. "I just saved your life, Rowan. Again."

I clenched my jaw. True, he had. Several times. Right now, I couldn't figure out what was real and what was a lie.

I sighed. "You crisped Alaric."

Orion inhaled a deep breath. "Well, I didn't hold back."

I glanced out at the waves, which were stained claret under the rising sun. Disappointment coiled through me. "Okay. We need to raise him again, I guess, to start the trial over. Though I imagine he'll be a bit furious about being burned to death. And I need some Advil."

"Ah, Rowan." Orion's eyes twinkled as he crossed to me over the rocks, graceful as ever. "You don't remember what happens if the first trial is a draw?"

My throat tightened, and I narrowed my eyes at him. "You get to choose the next trial."

A lock of silver hair fell before his eyes, and he nodded. He leaned down, speaking quietly enough that only I could hear. "But when I win, love, you could be my queen. And we will protect the demons together."

I felt my cheeks heat again. Seductive bastard that he was, he made it sound so damned appealing, even as we stood here among the blood and the windblown ashes of two powerful witches.

W hen the trial ended, I'd returned to Orion's house. I'd changed into leggings and a T-shirt, then turned off my phone and closed the shutters.

In the darkness, I'd let a deep sleep wash over me. I'd dreamt of the green-eyed boy, crouching to watch ants on a sidewalk with his hands on his knees. I'd dreamt of him making cookies and eating the sugar off the table. I'd dreamt of him drawing a picture with vigorous scribbles and burbling narration about a battle between the demons and the mortals, blood staining the streets—speaking of things a child should never have seen...

By the time I woke, the sun was already setting, and rosy light slanted at an angle through the wooden slats. Disappointing, yes.

But I wasn't done yet. One more trial. I hoped.

As soon as Orion announced what it would be, I'd start preparing.

Sitting up in bed, I surveyed the darkened room, my

stomach rumbling sharply. I had no doubt my phone would be blowing up with text messages from Shai, but I didn't want to look at them. I didn't want to face the disappointment of my little team who'd been helping me all this time. And what could I say that they didn't already know? The news must have spilled through the streets as soon as the trial had ended.

I rose from the bed and opened the shutters.

The sun had dipped low and the sky darkened to indigo. The night's subtlety was much prettier than the garish daylight.

As much as I wanted to stay in here, hunger was compelling me out of my room. But to my delight, when I opened my door, I found that Amon had left a tray outside for me—slices of chicken breast, roasted baby carrots, and buttered cauliflower. A small flagon of wine and a glass stood on the tray next to the food.

Perfect.

I ate by the desk, staring out onto the dark garden. I had no idea what to make of everything—the fact that assassins kept reporting Orion wanted me dead, and then Orion would swoop in to save me. But if he were going to have me killed, surely, he'd make damn sure the assassins didn't keep telling me about it. Leaving a bunch of stupid loose ends wasn't his style.

I sipped my wine and drummed my fingertips on the desk. If you'd asked me a few weeks ago, I would have said that clearly, his incubus charm had scrambled my brain, that I was ignoring the obvious. That Occam's razor would say it was just Orion trying to take me down.

As I stared outside, I saw him cross into the garden

and sit on a stone bench, his shoulders slumped. The boughs of an apple tree arched over him. I watched him as he pulled out a handkerchief and started wiping blood off his hands, staining the white cloth red.

Cool. Yeah, not suspicious at all.

With dread crawling up my spine, I turned to head downstairs and into the salty night air. I'd drunk the wine quickly, but the buzz had worn off with the sight of blood. When I crossed into the garden, his head snapped up, the masculine beauty of his face cast in silver.

"Have you been...murdering people all day?" I asked.

He tossed down the bloodied rag on the bench next to him. "Have you been sleeping all day, Shadow Scion?"

"Hell, yes." I sat down on the bench next to him. "Whose blood is that?"

"Someone from our great city has been passing along information to the *Malleus Daemoniorum*, which is how the demon hunters know you're in here. I caught some hunters probing for weaknesses in our defenses, trying to find a way inside. Someone gave them a clue where to start. Someone with information about our magical signature."

"And if the demon hunters broke down our wards and walls?" I asked. "We could kill them before our magic faded."

"The mortals have missiles. If they obliterate our city walls and vaporize us with their weapons, we'd never have time to recover. We'd simply *die*."

A shudder rippled over me. "The demon hunters are very influential, unfortunately. They've been donating to politicians for ages, buying power."

He glanced at me, something sparking in his eyes. "Maybe not as influential as they once were. I've been working on weakening them." He looked down at his hands. "The blood is from two demon hunters. I wanted answers about who's trying to frame me, and who's working with the mortals."

I sucked in a deep breath. "Did you get any?"

"Not about those questions. But I learned something much more important." His pale eyes met mine. "I learned the location of something I want very much. The *Grimorium Verum*." A small smile curled his lips. "Finding that book will be our next trial."

A dark, unsettled feeling snaked up my neck. "Why is this book so important?"

He held my gaze for a long time. "According to the book of Demonic Trials, I'm not required to tell you anything about it, but I will because the book is more important to me than the crown. Because if I lose these trials, it will be your job to protect our city, and you will need this, Rowan. The grimoire is the very thing that keeps us locked in here. It contains the spell that makes our magic fade after a few days out of the city walls or trapped in the dungeons. The spell that sends us into the underworld if we stray too far. The *Grimorium Verum* will set us free. And it's locked in the demon hunters' headquarters in Sudbury."

Whoever controlled that grimoire would hold the fate of the mortal world in their hands.

Clearly, it would be safer in mine. "Why open the city gates when we know where to find the demon hunters now? They're the ones we need to kill, not the rest of the mortals. If we can take out the demon hunters, maybe we avert the war." I breathed in deeply. "You're reducing their influence? Maybe we could make them disappear."

"I need to unlock the curse with which the mortals saddled us."

"And without the curse, the demons could feed on mortals indiscriminately. Isn't that how it was in the old days? I think you were the person who told me that. Hunting them. Drinking their blood. Feeding off lust or sadness or gluttony."

He heaved a sigh. "I can't say I ever experienced that myself. But as king, I could order the demons not to hunt if it would keep the peace."

I swallowed hard. "But you're singularly dedicated to your revenge oath."

"Maybe, as you said, I could satisfy myself with killing the demon hunters. They were the mortals in charge when the Lilu were slaughtered." He cocked his head. "But we need the control in our hands, and not the mortals'. With the grimoire, we can turn back the clock to before it all happened." Sorrow shone in his blue eyes. "We could be safe again. And we could destroy the dungeons."

I got the sense that all this was his way of trying to find his way back to his family. "Turn back the clock," I repeated. "That sounds nice."

Silence spread between us, broken only by the rustling of the wind through the trees.

"What was life like for you before the mortals came?" I asked after a few moments.

He flashed me a sad smile. "When I was a boy? I just wanted to be Molor, my older brother. He looked like me,

but bigger. He was brilliant with a sword. Indestructible."
A line formed between his eyebrows. "Or so I thought. He
was only thirteen. But he seemed so much older. He could
play the lute, and he could draw monsters. He once shot a
stag out in the Elysian Wilderness. He was a real man. So I
wanted to be him because he could do anything. And I
also wanted to run a bakery with bread pudding because I
could never get enough of it, so I thought I might as well
control the whole supply."

I smiled at him. "Molor." I could imagine two beautiful
silver-haired boys, one a tiny version of the other.

"It's hard to imagine, but after a while in the dungeon,
I envied him. I felt like my brother died quickly, and I'd
died so slowly. I was a Lightbringer, so I was hard to kill.
But Molor died a hero, and I didn't. Not at all." He stared
down at his hands again. "I always think of him as fully
grown, but when I went home again, I saw how much I
was mistaken." When he looked up at me, his eyes were
shining. "And I don't feel as jealous anymore. Because I'm
here with you now, and he's not." A sad smile played over
his lips.

I felt my cheeks flushing, and I brushed a silver strand
from his eyes.

"What were you like as a child?" he asked.

"Dreamy. Always in a book, lost in thought. And as
soon as I learned what a psychologist was, that was what I
wanted to be. In my psychology classes, at the start of the
year, we would always go around the room and say why we
wanted to study it. Everyone, one after the other, said it
was because they wanted to help people. If I were a better
person, I'm sure I would have thought the same. But I

think I was just fucking nosy." I smiled. "I wanted to hear everyone's stories, and that's what psychologists do. You sit and listen to them talk about their lives. And my life always seemed so stifling at home. I wanted to know about everyone else's. Mom was..." I trailed off, my chest tight.

"What?"

"Chaotic. Unpredictable. I thought she was paranoid. She was always checking the windows, the locks, setting up traps, and she just seemed so unstable. I didn't realize there were actually people after her. She panicked a lot when I wasn't home, and sometimes, I caught her spying on me at school. None of it seemed normal. And she had no sense of what modern kids were like, or what they wore or did for fun, and we were these two strange outsiders in weird clothes...it seemed important at the time to fit in, to have a stable home. So I just became fascinated by other people's lives. I wanted to know what went on behind their doors, in their pretty houses." My breath had gone shallow. "I can see now she wasn't crazy. She was trying to keep me safe from my half brother. I just wish she'd told me what was happening."

"Why do you think she kept it from you?"

I looked at the beauty around me, the white flowers that bloomed in the night against the stone cottage. "Maybe she thought I would have wanted to come back here. This place feels like home. Especially at night." I found tears welling up in my eyes, and I didn't want to look at Orion. "It would have been hard to resist, even if it was dangerous."

"It is your home," he said softly, "and so is the wilderness. And the night. We are creatures of darkness—the incubi and succubi. In the old days, we were awake all night. We had festivals of starlight and shadows. We celebrated in the night sky, and we fed from mortal lust. Before the mortals caged us, we were free to race through the night, tearing over the forests and drinking from their dirtiest dreams." He leaned on his knees with his forearms, his gaze intent on me. "I think you can feel it. You're drawn to the dark, to the wilderness. You want to hunt like we once did. You feel that wildness trapped inside you, and you want to set it free. We may be Lightbringers, but we were born in the dark."

I hated how he could read me so easily. He could tell me things about myself I hadn't even put into words yet. Yes, I wanted to hunt and tear through the wilderness. "Lightbringers born in the dark. I'm not sure I understand."

He glanced at the sky, and I followed his gaze to Venus. "They say everything began with chaos. Then a light sprang from the darkness, and he was the god Astaroth. Every night, he would return to the shadows, and from the chaos, he'd rise again. They say Astaroth was a fallen god, beautiful as the dawn. His sons were Lucifer and Noctifer—the Lightbringer and the Nightbringer, order and chaos. And Noctifer's other name is Tammuz. My father."

"Beautiful as the dawn," I repeated. "A long day of beating the shit out of people brings out your poetic side."

"I should probably torture people more often so I'm in top form for the spoken word poetry night I'm starting on Tuesdays."

"It scares me that I can't tell if you're serious."

The corner of his lips curled. "Scares you, or excites you?"

"Oddly enough, I'm not turned on by brutal violence. Though I have maybe spent more time than I should have looking at the Wikipedia page about medieval torture devices."

"Of course you have," he murmured.

"Did you know there was something called the Pear of Anguish?"

"Rowan," he purred, "are you flirting with me?"

"Orion." I leaned closer, so our lips were almost touching. "Surely you know that if a succubus were flirting with you, you'd be on your knees between my thighs by now." The words just seemed to slip out of my mouth before I had the chance to consider them. My heart started to pick up its pace.

His eyes darkened, and his gaze slid slowly down my body, resting at the apex of my thighs. "Well, my Lightbringer, that is quite the image you've put in my mind." He met my eyes again, his gaze molten.

Tension charged the air between us, and I wanted to crawl into his lap so badly, I had to grip the bench to stop myself.

"What?" I asked at last.

"You're beautiful, that's all." His midnight voice wrapped around me.

"Beautiful." My stomach flipped. "I'm identical to your worst enemy."

"No, you're not. You look nothing like her now. The way you hold yourself, your expressions—you're completely different. The flush on your cheeks when something excites you or angers you. The way you look at me like you actually want to understand me, like you're trying to see into my soul. How you pull your gaze away every time your heart starts to race. The way you look like you're overwhelmed sometimes with the responsibility of trying to keep everyone safe, and you retreat into your own thoughts. You are nothing alike."

I let out a long, slow breath. "I wish you could have realized sooner."

He winced ever so slightly. "Somewhere, there's another world where you and I met before my soul died in the dungeon."

I turned to him, draping my elbow over the side of the bench. "This is going to blow your mind, Orion, but you're not actually dead."

His mouth ticked up at the corner. "It's a metaphor. Soulless. Dead."

"Hmm. But maybe you're not soulless. You've saved me over and over again, and you created a beautiful memorial, and so far, you only seem marginally psychotic. And that's mostly because I just saw you wiping blood off your hands."

He nodded sagely. "I always wondered what regal moniker would stick through the ages. 'King Orion the Only Marginally Psychotic' has a certain ring to it." His eyes sparkled with life, and he reached up, grazing the back of his knuckles lightly along my jawbone. "And what would tell you that I'm salvageable?"

The touch sent a hot thrill over my skin, and I desperately wanted to lean into his hand and close my eyes. "I need to see if you have a merciful side. If you can forgive the mortals."

He pulled his hand away. "Ah. But if they're trying to hurt you, love, I will never show mercy. I will make them suffer."

A sharp coil twisted in my chest. If what he was saying was true and the mortals were trying to break into the city to murder me, this had all become much more complicated.

All of this was starting to feel like a secret I was keeping from Shai, these late-night conversations with Orion. I'd been so certain coming in here that I understood him—that he was all charm and artifice, that I couldn't trust a word he said. But now, even though everyone kept saying he was trying to kill me, I wasn't sure of anything at all, except that Orion and I were trying to find our way back to the past.

✥ 25 ✥

ROWAN

No matter how much we had in common, I still needed to win the trial.

I rose from the bench. "Thanks for telling me about the grimoire. I'm going for a little walk since I won't be sleeping for a while."

He stood and peered down at me, then reached into his pocket and pulled out a strange little misshapen piece of wood. "Wait, I have a gift for you."

My first instinct was to make some kind of a joke—maybe *Got wood for me?*—but then I realized it was such a strange gesture from him that I should keep my mouth shut until he explained. When I took it from his hand, I saw that it had been whittled roughly in the shape of a woman in a dress with a spiky head. "What is it?"

"She's a queen. It was a birthday present for my mother. Somehow, I thought she hadn't noticed me whittling it in the same cell. But her birthday didn't come in time. Or maybe she lied, because she knew I was excited about the birthday, so she wanted to keep giving me something to look forward to. Anyway, it's a Lilu queen, and I never got to give it to her. So it's yours. Because you are the last succubus, and you are queen of the Lilu." He met my gaze. "And as queen, you will need the grimoire. Learn everything you can about the Noyes Mansion in Sudbury. That's where we'll find it."

"Thanks, Orion." I was still staring at the little queen, my eyes going blurry. It really did break my heart to think of a tiny Orion looking forward to giving this to his mom, then never getting the chance. "Well, she would have loved it. But I'll love it instead." I turned away from him, because for some reason, I didn't want him to see the tears that were about to start rolling down my cheeks.

As I walked away, I clutched the wooden queen, thinking of his mom and little Molor.

Was it insane to think that Orion and I could actually work together? We were the last of our kind, trying to find our places in the world again after we'd lost everything.

Everything hinged on what form he wanted his revenge to take.

As I crossed out of the garden gate, I already knew Orion would order guards to follow me—that is, if he wasn't going to follow me himself.

Until I found myself heading toward the river, I wasn't entirely sure where I was going,

I was heading for the dungeons.

Maybe I wanted to see the cells for myself, the place where Orion had been for all that time.

As I reached the tunnel's riverside opening, I slid the little wooden queen into my pocket. The Acheron flowed past, glittering under the moon. Carefully, I lowered myself into the tunnel, and my feet dropped hard on the wet stone. As soon as I was in its depths, I felt a subtle weakening of my magic.

Because of the grimoire's spell that depleted our magic outside the city walls, Orion's magic had no longer worked in the dungeons. If it had, he'd have blown the entire fucking place apart and ripped off the king's head centuries ago.

Down here, I was in the liminal space between the world of the mortals and that of the demons—a place where magic would fade after a few days. In the dungeons, Orion had been as vulnerable as a mortal but deprived of the mercy of death. If he got his fingers on the grimoire to reverse the spell, he'd never have to fear that kind of helplessness again.

It took me about twenty minutes of wandering aimlessly with a little fire burning in my palm before I found the dungeon itself. It was the scent of burnt flesh that eventually led me to the right place, a miasma of death pulling me forward.

The iron gate was open to the row of cells. When I stepped inside, the orange light from my hand wavered back and forth over rows of cells lining either side of a dark stone corridor. I hadn't seen most of this dungeon when I'd first come into the City of Thorns.

But as I walked further, I saw a large hall jutting off from the central corridor. Firelight wavered over, blackened with time and glistening with moisture. Here in the hall, an old, threadbare noose hung from a gallows. It swung gently back and forth—which was very eerie, considering there was no wind in here. The sight of it made my heart clench. I could almost feel the sadness emanating from it.

This was the execution room. The Puritans loved a good public execution, but no one knew the Lilu were kept alive down here, so they were killed in secret.

It didn't take me long to find the fresh bodies whose scent had drawn me here—or rather, the two piles of ash on the floor. The smell of blood faintly lingered in the air, too.

In the light of my flames, something metallic flashed on one of the piles of ash. I leaned down to brush some of the cinders away. When I did, I found a silver pin shaped like a hammer. The symbol of the *Malleus Daemoniorum*.

Orion had incinerated them, but I'd done the same when the congressman threatened my life. We all did what we had to in order to protect those we loved. Sometimes, it meant killing. And sometimes—in my mom's case—it meant dying.

With the light wavering over dark stone walls, I found my way back to the cell at the end of the row. This was the place where I'd first woken up in the City of Thorns, where I'd stood when Orion had tasted my blood.

The cell's walls crawled with ivy, and my throat tightened with emotion as I thought of Orion in here as a little silver-haired, blue-eyed boy. Holding up my palm of light, I found the carving in the wall. I leaned down, brushing aside the vines. Before, I'd only had my fingertips to feel the contours, but now, I could very faintly see the full text.

Luciferi— The *i was* faded and worn at the end. I ripped aside the rest of the vines to reveal the rest: —*urbem spinarum liberabunt.*

Just like Orion had said: *The Lightbringers will set free the City of Thorns.*

My chest warmed as I thought of his mom carving this. I felt an overwhelming urge to protect the boy who'd once been in here, carving the little queen in my pocket, but he was long gone.

A heavy sense of sadness hung in the air, a chilled mist that clung to the stones.

Right before she was killed, the guards moved me to a different cell by myself.

I crossed into the corridor again, sorrow twining with curiosity. From cell to cell, I scanned the stones, looking for something that would show me where he'd lived for all that time. On a few of the other walls, I found carvings, but nothing that could clearly be connected to him. Disturbingly, some of the carvings looked like claw marks.

About halfway down the row of cells, I went still. Through a tiny crack in the stone wall, a pinprick of light shone near the ceiling. It looked familiar somehow, the exact image of it seared on my heart. I'd seen that little crack before.

Under it, the warm light of my fire illuminated elaborate carvings in the dark stone walls.

My breath went still when I saw what he'd marked in the stone—three queens with spiked heads like crowns. He'd carved them three times, the markings violent and desperate, like the little Orion was trying to bring her back to life through the rock.

After the three queens, some of the carvings became more sophisticated. He'd rendered the Asmodean clock-tower, frozen in time at six, the way it looked now. He'd carved a snake that seemed to writhe back and forth in the guttering light of my fire. Odd, given his terror of snakes.

There was the word *Vindicta*—revenge—carved with what looked like thorns jutting from the letters' curls. And next to that, the carvings reminded me of the old Puritan gravestones—the skulls and crossbones, the words *Memento Mori—Fugit Hora*.

Remember death—time flies. I was sure that down here, time didn't exactly fly, especially for an immortal. But that phrase wasn't about Orion, was it? Even as he was trapped in here, he was reminding himself that the mortals who'd crushed the Lilu would be dying in Osborne. A comfort to him, maybe.

And above it all, he'd carved stars—the shape of Orion's constellation. Beyond the tiny pinprick, he had no real light in here, so the stone stars were all he had.

I didn't want to stay in here a moment longer. But as I turned to leave, the real horror of this place hit me. His cell stood directly across from the execution room, where the noose still hung from the ceiling.

Right before she was killed...

Orion had been locked in here with a perfect view of his mother's death. And that was where he'd stayed, trapped for centuries right across from the gallows. No wonder he felt like his soul had died. They'd wanted to crush his spirit completely.

As I took another step, a vision slammed into my mind—the same one I'd seen when Orion and I had first agreed to a blood oath, and we'd pressed our bleeding palms together.

In my mind's eye, I saw a crystal-clear vision: stone walls, cracked to expose a bit of the stars. Then a shadow swinging over the stone—the bloodied, swaying feet of a hanged body. Wood creaked above, and a pain pierced my heart to the core.

The vision cleared again, and I pressed my hand to the stone, steadying myself as I caught my breath. My heart pounded against my ribs.

Holy hell, how had he managed to stay sane at all in here?

I rushed out of the corridor, sick to my stomach. Desperate to be free, I hurried out of the dungeon, back into the tunnel.

And there, I discovered I wasn't alone.

One of the shadow figures cleared his throat, and I summoned a burst of fire to get a better look.

The flame in my hand illuminated the smiling face of Amon, his hands raised to placate me.

"Sorry," he said. "The king wished me to ensure your safety." If I had to guess, Amon was just about one of the only people Orion trusted now.

"I'm fine, Amon, thanks." Physically, I was. Emotionally? Not really. But Amon didn't need to know that. "I was just heading back."

But what I really wanted to do was find Orion and help him forget everything that had happened down here.

My throat constricted.

So much for my determination to keep him at arm's length.

26

ROWAN

By about three a.m., I gave up on lying in bed, because every time I rolled over and closed my eyes, I saw that noose swinging. And those three carved queens...

Maybe it was because I was a Lilu, or maybe it was the nightmarish visions I'd seen in the dungeon, but trying to sleep tonight was like trying to catch fog in my hands.

Orion was just on the other side of the door, fast asleep, and I couldn't keep my mind off him.

From my window, I stared out at the garden, watching the wind rustle the apple blossoms. My eyes locked on the bench where Orion had given me the wooden queen—the birthday present that never made it to the birthday. I plucked the figurine off the desk and ran my fingertips over it. My heart gave a sharp flutter.

Tomorrow, I'd be meeting with my team of teachers, and I needed them to help me stay focused on the trial. I had nothing to lose by having the crown on my head, the decisions in my hands.

But I glanced at the door, feeling claustrophobic, like part of me was still trapped in the cell. Restless, I opened the window, then climbed back into bed, curling up under the sheets and breathing the scent of the sea.

With the sultry night wind floating in my room, I managed to sleep, dreaming of the stars.

                                        ☙❦❧

I WOKE TO THE ROOM ON FIRE. FLAMES SURROUNDED ME, engulfing everything.

Oh, *fuck,* I was going to burn alive...

From the confused haze of sleep, fear had a tight grip on my heart. It took me several terrified moments to remember that fire could no longer burn me, and by the time I'd recalled that very important fact, my brain was still lagging behind.

So when a cloaked man jumped from the fire onto my bed, I reacted more slowly than I should have.

I stared at him, stunned to catch a glimpse of silver hair and pale blue eyes. The beautiful face of the king. "Orion? What the hell—"

He raised his hand, and ivory claws shot out.

Panic stole my breath. Had he lost his mind?

I reached out and grabbed his wrist, twisting it to the side so he lost his balance. I shot up and headbutted him, his bone cracking as my forehead slammed into his nose. My claws extended, and I swiped wildly, slashing across his face. He let out a strangled growl as he staggered away from me.

I jumped from the bed, my body glowing with golden

light. Heat simmered through my blood. As I lunged for him again, he leapt out the window into the garden below. Fleeing on foot, he trampled through the garden and disappeared into the shadows.

"What the *fuck?*" I shouted.

A second later, the door to Orion's room burst open. Shirtless, he stood on the threshold, raking a hand through his hair. "What's wrong?"

"You're just waking up now?" I asked. "Your house is literally on fire. Why don't you have alarms?"

Orion's gaze slid across the room, a line between his eyebrows. "What are you talking about?"

I started to gesture at the burning room, but not only was the fire gone, it had left no signs of damage whatsoever. No smoke, no ashes or char.

I glanced back at the window, confusion whirling in my mind. Everything looked just as it had been—still and dark under the night sky, white flowers blooming in the shadows.

I turned, staring at the unburnt room. "Maybe it was a nightmare."

"We *are* the nightmares, love." He nodded at the window. "But was the window open? The protection wards depend on having the gates and windows locked. Was someone in here, Rowan?"

Outside, the sky was just starting to turn pink and gold. I searched my bedsheets, and when I spotted the crimson streak of blood on them, I felt a strange sort of relief.

I wasn't losing my mind.

"Yeah, someone was in here. I raked my claws across

his face, and his blood is on my sheets. I thought he had silver hair. I thought it was you for a minute. He *really* looked like you."

Orion crossed to the window and slammed it shut, then scooped me up and carried me into his perfectly tidy bedroom.

"What are you doing?" I asked.

"Not letting you out of my sight," he whispered against my ear. "We have two more hours before it's reasonable to wake, and I still have no idea who wants you dead. But I do know that two Lightbringers are stronger than one."

He dropped me down on his bed, and I slid between his sheets, which smelled so beautifully of him. He lay down next to me and wrapped me in his powerful arms. I nestled my head into the crook of his neck, feeling far more comfortable than I should have.

As he relaxed, I listened to the slowing of his breath, and I felt the gentle rise and fall of his chest.

I loved the sound of his heart beating.

Fuck.

Why not just admit that I loved being near him?

✿ 27 ✿

ROWAN

In Kas's kitchen, I sat before a bowl of freshly made *spaghetti aglio e olio* as he filled our glasses with Syrah. My mouth watered as I twisted the pasta around my fork. Night had fallen, and a lantern swung outside his little house, casting swaying shadows on the Tudor buildings.

Shai held her wineglass in her right hand, not touching her food. "You two first, Rowan. Did you and Legion check out the Noyes Mansion?"

"Yep," I said. "We spent the day in Sudbury. The mansion is completely cloaked with magic, but it was easy to find. There was a group of demon hunters patrolling the woods, giving the game away. So Legion turned invisible and moved close enough to learn the magical signatures of the protection spells." I took a big bite of the spicy, garlicky pasta, hoping no one was going to ask me to elaborate, because right now, I really needed to eat this.

Legion nodded. "There's the spell that cloaks, and another that will kill any demons who pass by the wards.

I'll be able to disable the demon-killing spell on the day of the trial without them even realizing. We'll leave it cloaked so as not to alert them. They don't need to know that Rowan is going in."

Shai looked even more exhausted than I was, and she rubbed her eyes. "Only problem is that this all benefits Orion, too."

I sipped my wine. "Well, Orion, unlike me, won't have a whole team to help him. He won't know where the book is in the headquarters."

Kas was already refilling my wine glasses. "Why do you two lovely women look so exhausted?"

I picked up my glass, feeling a sharp pang of protectiveness for Orion. If I told them about the assassination attempt—a silver-haired, blue-eyed assassin who looked a lot like the king—I could only imagine how they'd respond: *That's because Orion is trying to kill you.*

"Just insomnia," I said.

"Same." Shai's eyes darted away from me as she spoke, and I had the feeling she wasn't giving the whole story, either.

Interesting. If I had to guess, she and Legion were keeping each other company late into the night.

"Okay," Legion said. "Kas, what did you learn today?"

He stood, pushing back his chair. "Hang on." A minute later, he returned to the room with a large, rolled-up piece of paper. He spread it out between glasses and plates, and I found myself staring at the blueprint of a building.

"Blueprints for the Noyes Mansion," Kas declared. "Now owned by the Corwin family."

"It was built in secret by a creepy religious fanatic

named Reverend Nicholas Noyes in 1690," Shai said. "He used to operate a grist mill nearby. The demon hunters built their headquarters near the site of a battle the English lost to the Wampanoag. It's a sacred place to them. Something about the blood of the righteous feeding the soil."

My ears perked up. "Reverend Nicholas Noyes from the Salem Witch Trials? He's the guy one of the victims cursed with, 'God will give you blood to drink.'" A shudder rippled over me. "I'm pretty sure he hanged me in the underworld."

Silence fell over the room, as no one knew exactly how to respond to that.

I waved a hand. "Okay. Never mind. Back to the blueprints."

"Our American demon hunters come from a long tradition of English witchfinders," said Kas.

"The *Malleus Maleficarum*," added Shai. "Hammer of the Witches. They published their manual by the same name in the late fifteenth century. And the demon-specific sect is *the Malleus Daemoniorum*."

"Of course, what they never admitted in their texts," Kas went on, "was that they also used magic. They realized they were no match for demons or witches without the use of spellcraft."

I stared at the mansion's blueprint before us. "Where did you get this?"

Kas's cheeks dimpled as he smiled. "Mortal librarians are truly amazing. I just had to flirt with a young woman at the library in Lexington. She showed me to a locked room where they'd collected historical documents about the

Malleus Daemoniorum. As soon as she left us alone, we hunted through every document until we found a locked safe."

My eyebrows crept up. "You stole it from a locked safe. Any chance the demon hunters are aware we're coming?"

Kas glanced at Shai. "Shai helped with that."

"I learned a spell for erasing memories," she said.

My jaw dropped open. "Holy shit. You can do that?"

"I can now." Her smile faded, and her dark eyes bored into me. "But don't you think it's weird that Orion would tell you where the book is held if the trial rules don't require it? Is there any chance this is a trap?"

I shook my head. "I believe him. I can't really explain why, but I just do." I breathed in deeply. "I think he's more invested in finding the grimoire than he is in being king. He views it as crucial to keeping the demons safe. That's always been his main goal: protecting demons in some ongoing war with the mortals."

Legion scrubbed a hand over his jaw. "And he's not wrong. Mortal warfare isn't the same as it was centuries ago."

I stared at the blueprint—a stately building with three separate wings, forming a sort of angular U shape.

Legion pointed at a room labelled *chancery*. "In old buildings, this is where official documents would be kept and handwritten. I already identified this as the most likely location for the grimoire."

I leaned back in my chair, narrowing my eyes at Legion. "What if..." I lifted a finger to my lips. "What if you did a trial run? Tomorrow? Go invisible, sneak past the magical defenses. Get into the building and search the chancery. You can find out if the book is actually in that safe before I go in. Do you know a spell for unlocking safes?"

Shai pointed at the map. "That's how we got this blueprint. Which, by the way, is like three hundred years old, so maybe we shouldn't be getting garlic pasta all over it?"

Legion nodded. "I can do that. But you should all be there, hiding, in case I need your help. I'll find a spell that will allow me to communicate with you, even when we're separated."

I stared at him. "Sweetie, that's what cell phones are for."

He glanced at Shai. "*Right*."

"Shai can teach you how to text," I said. "Like, this is a really important skill."

No matter how emphatically Kas had said not to trust anyone, trust was an element of nearly everything I was doing here. It was quite simply part of working with other people.

28

ROWAN

Day of the second trial.

I awoke in Orion's arms again, my legs wrapped tightly around him. I could tell I'd been moving against him in my sleep and that he'd liked it.

For the past three nights, I'd been fighting the sexual torment of being in bed with him but unable to kiss him.

But wrapping my arms around his abs—that was allowed.

We hadn't spoken about the trial, even if it hung over us like a shadow. This morning, however, there was no way to ignore it.

He turned to me and brushed the hair from my eyes. "Today's the day we set the city free."

"We'll see about that." My heart kicked up a notch. Over the past few days, I'd done an amazing job of staying focused and compartmentalizing, but now that we were out of time, a million new worries spiraled through my brain. After all, I was Rowan Morgenstern, and whether I was mortal or demon, my brain would offer up the worst-case scenarios on a platter. Without fail.

I looked up at him. "Orion, what if somehow, we fuck this up and lose our chance to get the grimoire? Or what if the demon hunters report us to the federal government, and the feds just bomb the City of Thorns before we get a chance to unlock the spell?" I swallowed hard. "What if our actions kill all the demons? And aren't you worried I'm going to fuck it all up, and you'll miss your chance at getting the book?"

He stroked his hand down my spine, slowly. Heat shivered in the wake of his fingertips, making my muscles melt into him all over again. "First of all, I have complete faith in you not fucking it up." His face was close to mine, our cheeks nearly brushing. "Second of all, the protection spells will hold the City for now. And I don't think the hunters have enough influence to attack us."

"Why?"

"Since I took the throne, I've been working on isolating the demon hunters from powerful figures. Human politicians are remarkably susceptible to blackmail and various forms of bribery. Money rules the world of mortal power brokers. Campaign donations, threats to fund their opponents. Managing them is honestly much easier than I expected. For now, at least, the demon hunters are on their own. They have no political capital whatsoever."

My eyes widened. "For an ancient, marginally psychotic demon, you're surprisingly savvy about the modern world."

"I love it when you say sweet things about me." His hand slid up and cupped the back of my neck, and he pressed his forehead against mine. "If you ever decide you trust me, I'm going to fuck you until you beg for mercy. Until you forget your name."

My core coiled tight, and I fought the urge to kiss him. "Only in you, Orion, is that kind of confidence not misplaced."

The corner of his mouth twitched—not with a smile, but with something like uncertainty. He was looking at me with an expression I'd hardly seen on him before: vulnerability. His chest rose and fell faster, his heartbeat racing. Orion—the big bad Lord of Chaos—was nervous. "But you're going to need to know what I did. You're going to need to know the real me."

I stared at him and the dark sweep of lashes framing his blue eyes.

My chest ached. "What do you mean? What did you do?" It came out a bit sharper than I'd meant it to. I just wasn't sure I could handle any more horrific surprises from him.

His gaze shuttered, and he rolled away from me. He rose from the bed, and I found myself staring at his muscular back. "The trial is today, but I will tell you later."

As I stared at him, I felt like ice was spreading between us, chilling the air.

And something else was bothering me. Something I'd avoided talking about in the past few days. "He really looked like you, you know. The person who came in through the window."

He turned back to me, one eyebrow raised. "You were half asleep, weren't you?"

I swallowed hard. "I had a doppelgänger. Sort of. What

if someone else looks like you?"

"Doppelgängers are mortal. They don't have claws." He turned to me with a frown. "And you exist because Mortana died. I'm not actually dead, as you pointed out."

I didn't want to say it, but I had to ask. "It's just... everyone thought my parents were dead. And they weren't. You said your brother looked exactly like you—"

"Rowan," he said sharply. The temperature plummeted. "I saw him die. I will never forget it."

I let out a long breath. *And I saw you attack me.*

A new set of worries had now taken root in my brain, thorny vines that pierced every other thought. But I didn't say a word as I found my way to the shower in my room. I turned on the water and stripped, letting the steam fill the bathroom. His words from a month ago echoed in my mind.

Consider it an accident if it makes you feel better. My hands slipped, and I accidentally ripped off Carl's head and shoved his remains under the desk.

Orion felt guilty for some terrible secret. What would someone like him feel guilty about?

As I stepped into the shower, I closed my eyes, trying to visualize that conversation—the entire mental image of his room—boxed up and locked away. Everything hinged on how today went, and I needed my mind to be one hundred percent focused. In the next half hour, my goal was to stop thinking about Orion's promise to fuck me until I forgot my name and everything else he'd just said to me.

Mentally, I started reviewing the plan I'd made with my team. Chant the invisibility spell as I flew, and race to

Sudbury. I'd touch down near the mansion. Kas and Legion would be sheltering nearby to disrupt the mansion's wards and protective spells. I knew how to find the entrance by a little stone marker, even when the house remained cloaked.

With a spell for invisibility, I'd slip past the three or four guards—or their dead bodies if Orion got there first. I'd use a spell to open the front door and the safe. I could waltz right in. Unnoticed.

I'd head straight for the chancery.

If the hunters detected us, the mansion's automatic locks would trap us inside, with great iron bars that would slide across the doors. The mansion would become a sort of prison for us, with hunters hell-bent on killing us.

But the doors could be opened from the outside, so Shai would be waiting for me by the southern exit with an unlocking spell. I'd knock four times, letting her know she needed to open the iron bars.

I could be back here by sunset, grimoire in hand, ready to be crowned.

In theory.

ORION AND I STOOD ACROSS FROM EACH OTHER BENEATH a cloudy sky. Although my muscles were rigid with tension, he was simply relaxing against the stone wall, his hands in his pockets. He wore a dark gray T-shirt that stretched over his large shoulders, and my gaze slid down to his serpentine tattoo. My mind flicked back to the feel of his fingertips stroking down my spine this morning...

I ripped my gaze away from him. I was keeping that mental lock on my thoughts.

The rules of the Demon Trials required that we start in the City of Thorns itself. From here, we'd be racing to Sudbury.

Turning from the wall, I glanced at the crowd around us. I recognized Lydia, the duchess who'd once tried to murder me. Apart from Amon, I didn't know most of the other demons yet.

To spare us from any leaks that could alert the demon hunters, no one in the crowd had any idea exactly where Orion and I were going today, only that I could be queen by tonight.

Mistress Blacknettle pushed her way from the crowd, draped in silver robes that matched her hair. "Today, you leave from the City of Thorns. The first of you to return with the grimoire wins the trial and the crown. While none of us know where you are headed, we eagerly await your return from this journey. May the gods bless you both."

I nodded at her. My blood pounded in my veins, a steady war drum of nerves. As soon as the clock struck with the ringing of bells, we'd be racing through the skies.

I stole another quick look at Orion. A sly smile curled his lips as he looked back at me, like we shared some kind of secret.

I took a deep breath, and my body jolted as the bells began to peal, signaling the start of the trial.

My wings burst from my shoulder blades, and I shot into the air, soaring beneath the cloudy sky. The sea wind tore through my hair as I headed southwest toward

Sudbury. As I flew, I chanted the cloaking spell, and magic hummed over my body as it took effect. Adrenaline raced through me.

When I reached my hand out before my face and saw nothing, I had a dizzying sense of madness. It took me a few minutes to get comfortable with not being able to see myself.

Scanning the skies, I searched for Orion, but all I could see was a faint twisting of shadows under the clouds. Good—the *Malleus Daemoniorum* wouldn't see either of us coming.

Orion had been right. I'd been craving this kind of wild flight, spiraling free through the air above the earth, the way a succubus was meant to be. His intoxicating scent floated on the wind, wrapping around me like a caress.

But as I flew, my phone buzzed in my pocket, jolting me out of my exhilaration. *Really?* Now?

Immediately, my pulse started to race. Only Kas, Legion, and Shai had this number. I'd been very clear that they were only supposed to text me if something had gone very wrong.

I pulled my phone from my pocket and stared in horror at—nothing. The fucking phone was invisible, too.

With frustration mounting, I pushed the side button and yelled at Siri to call Shai.

I pressed it to my ear, and my blood pounded when it went straight to voicemail.

Fortunately, Legion picked up immediately, barking, "This is Legion," into the phone.

Breathless, I shouted at him. "What's happening? I can't read the text. I'm falling behind, Legion."

"Something is wrong, Rowan. I think the hunters knew you were coming."

My blood turned to ice. "The demon hunters? How? No one except us knows where we're headed."

"I have no idea. Someone tipped them off. Because it's not just the three or four guards—there's a whole army out there."

I scanned the clouds, but I saw no trace of Orion's shadowy presence. "Where's Shai? She didn't pick up."

"She's fine. She told me she'd be waiting for you at the southern wing if you need help getting out. I just can't see her because she's invisible."

"Legion, it's too late for me to stop this. I've lost Orion, and I won't get the chance to tell him before we arrive. This is happening, no matter what. All we can do is fight our way in and out."

I shoved the phone back into my pocket and focused on my flight, trying to pick up speed.

My heart pounded hard as I raced further west and the land beneath me grew greener. Drawing closer to Sudbury, I swept closer to the ground, my eyes sharp on the earth beneath me. If I overshot the mark, I'd find myself in the underworld again, and the last thing I needed was another angry Puritan mob...though I supposed I was heading for an angry Puritan mob either way.

And there it was—the outer edges of the Great Meadows conservation land stretched beneath me. In the cool autumn air, the trees had turned the color of flames.

As I homed in on the Noyes Mansion, the metallic scent of blood hung heavy in the air.

29

ROWAN

My stomach turned at the sight of the slain mortals—some of them decapitated, others burned. Blood pooled over the earth, staining the grass. Feeding the soil, just as the Puritans had done.

And for a moment there, I'd almost been worried for Orion's safety.

I swallowed hard, ignoring the shaking in my legs as I found the stone slab that marked the entrance to the invisible mansion. I pressed my hand against the spot where the door should be for the unlocking spell, but Orion had left it open for me.

Inside the mansion, distant shouts rang across the building. This place was far grander than I'd ever imagined, with towering arched windows that let the forest's light spill onto an old stone floor. Oil paintings of demon hunters festooned white walls above mahogany wainscoting. At either side of the hall, sweeping stone stairwells led upstairs.

But the chancery was on this lower floor.

Demon hunters were racing around the large halls, shouting orders at each other. They passed by me, completely unaware of my presence. One of them slammed the door shut behind me, and the sound echoed off the stone.

Quietly as I could, I raced toward the chancery. I sprinted through the eastern wing, counting four doors on my right. Then I slipped into a stone room with stained glass windows that let in flecks of colored light. A wooden cabinet stood in one corner. Legion had found the safe—and the grimoire—in there.

But as I approached the cabinet, a loud bell started ringing.

"Lockdown procedures in place," a voice boomed over the intercom. "Demons have been identified in the building. We are initiating lockdown procedures."

Breathing hard, I knelt before the safe to whisper the unlocking spell. A thrill rippled through me as the lock spun and the door clicked open. Relief loosened my breath as I pulled out the leather-bound grimoire—though it was much smaller than I'd expected. And much *newer*, too.

When I cracked it open, I found that it was not a grimoire at all, but a list of ordinary names and addresses.

My stomach clenched. *Fuck.* Had Orion already found the grimoire, then? Or had the demon hunters known to move it?

My gaze snagged on one of the names in the book, my heart hammering.

Giuseppe Esposito, 8 Gallows Hill Road, Osborne MA. Missing since September. Believed to use glamour to appear older. Likely dangerous. Missing.

I flipped to the start of the book, my hand shaking as I read the handwritten inscription: *Suspected Lilu Fugitives.*

The book had about a dozen names and addresses spread all over the world. Holy shit.

There were more of us out there. Suddenly, this felt like a bigger find than the grimoire. Maybe Orion and I weren't the last Lilu after all.

My heart hammered. I stood and sniffed the air. Faintly, I smelled cedar, the scent that had become like home to me. I was now starting to understand what Orion had meant about demon senses being heightened—and overwhelming. Because along with Orion's smell, there was a whole lot of blood and burnt hair and skin, pungent human sweat, and other things I absolutely did not need to think about.

I tried to tune out the clanging of alarm bells, just focusing on Orion's smell to lead me to him. Still completely invisible, I crept down the hall. In the wide corridor, mortals rushed past, armed with long rifles. Did they think they could stop us with bullets?

And only now did I listen to catch some of what the mortals were saying to each other.

"One of those Lilu fucks is leaving a trail of bodies behind."

"The grimoire is gone," someone bellowed.

"How are we supposed to find them if they're invisible?"

My blood roared. How did they know we were *Lilu,* specifically? The only people who knew exactly what was happening today were Orion and my three friends—and yet, the mortals had known *exactly* who to expect today. So who the fuck had passed along this information?

I had no idea where to look now, so I simply followed Orion's scent—until an arm shot out and pulled me into a small library. The door slammed behind me, and I whirled to see the shadows unwrapping from Orion.

Despite my perfectly laid plans, someone had fucked this up. I felt more stunned than angry, unable to accept that one of my friends could have been so careless with this secret.

A smile played about his lips as he lifted the grimoire— a faded, deep green book with chipped gold text. "Looking for this?"

A sharp tendril of disappointment coiled through me. "Do you *want* me to fight you for that? Because I will." I glanced behind me at the closed door. "But why are you still here? Why didn't you leave with it?"

His expression grew serious as he held out the book to me. "I want you to trust me." He wasn't quite meeting my eyes, because I was still invisible, but he was looking in my general direction. "It's yours, Rowan. The book. The crown. You can have them."

I felt like my heart was about to burst. I didn't know what to say, so I just took the book from him, and I watched as my cloaking spell made it disappear. "I can't believe you're giving it to me."

"I trust you to make the right decision."

I inhaled a shaky breath, hardly believing this was real. "How did you know where to get it?"

"The same way I always learn things. I found a demon

hunter and started breaking his bones until he gave me the answers I wanted."

Maybe it would've been better if I hadn't asked. "I have something for you, too, Orion." I handed him the book of Lilu names, watching it materialize as I handed it to him. "I think there are more of us out there. The demon hunters have been tracking some of the Lilu."

He flipped through the pages, his body glowing. "Holy hells, Rowan. Do you think this is real?"

"I recognized one of the names, Mr. Esposito. And yeah, I think he could be a demon. He's the one who told me about the trials. He was friends with my mom."

He stared at me with a kind of awe. "Maybe revenge doesn't have to be a massacre. Maybe it can be the return of the Lilu that these fuckers tried to exterminate." His forehead furrowed, and a wicked smile curled the corners of his lips. "But I'm still going to kill the demon hunters, and I'm going to enjoy it."

"Can we at least get the books out of here before you incinerate everyone? We can get out quickly at the southern exit. Shai's waiting for us there to unbolt the door in case of a lockdown."

I watched his perfect features disappear as shadows enveloped him.

"Let's go, love," he whispered. "I'll come back for the demon hunters later."

❧ 30 ❧
ROWAN

We pulled open the door, finding the hall mostly empty.

Hand in hand, we walked unseen through the corridor, and I used my mental map of the building to lead him. The southern exit was just ahead of us—a great wooden door, crisscrossed and studded with iron. I glanced behind me, making sure no one was around. Holding my breath, I leaned forward to knock—*One. Two. Three. Four.*

I waited for the door to open.

"Shai's not there," a deep male voice said from behind me.

My muscles froze at the sound of a voice I recognized.

"Seems like your friend didn't really want you to leave," the voice added.

I turned to see two men holding rifles. And one of them was Jack Corwin.

Now, *here* was a question—how the fuck did they know

I was standing there when they couldn't see me? Seems my friend had told them that, too.

Pain ripped through my stomach. When I looked down, I saw that I hadn't been hit with bullets, but rather darts. One had slammed into my ribs; the other caught me in the gut. I plucked them out, but as the poison from the darts spread through my veins, it seemed to be eating away at the magic protecting me. My body was becoming *visible*.

I fell to my knees, turning to look at Orion. He'd been hit too, but he was still standing. He rushed the hunters like a wild animal, flinging one of them against the wall. Jack turned to run, screaming for help.

Blocking out the pain, I scrambled to pull my phone from my pocket. I pressed the button on the side, frantically screaming into it. "Siri. Call Legion!"

The phone started ringing, but I could tell by its crackle that we didn't have a good connection. I glanced up to see Orion trying to chase down Jack, but he was stumbling now with the poison in his body.

"Legion here!" My friend's staticky voice came through the phone.

"We're trapped! Can you get to the south exit?"

I couldn't hear his reply, but my skin was growing hot from behind, and smoke billowed through the air. Tears stung my eyes.

I whirled to see flames consuming part of the door behind me, climbing up and blacking the wood and iron. This should be a good thing. Fire could burn us out of here. But the heat was making me feel sick, the heated air searing my face. And when I swiped my hand across the flame, pain screamed through my fingertips.

Fire *hurt*. The poison was fucking up our magic.

"Orion," I shouted.

I turned to see him staggering back to me. Jack must have sensed Orion's growing weakness, because he turned to walk after us—cautiously this time. I wondered if we could die out here without our magic. Ordinary demons, yes. Lightbringers? I had no idea.

Mentally, I reviewed the map of the place. There was a stairwell just to our left, and two more floors upstairs that would probably have fewer hunters.

I shouted at Orion to follow me and tried to ignore the searing pain of the poison moving through my body. In the stairwell, I glanced behind me, relieved to see Orion was on my heels. Pain etched his features, and I wondered how much extra energy he'd expended trying to chase down Jack.

I didn't love the idea of running *up* into a burning building, but we were low on options. And as we climbed the stairs, a sprinkler system started going off, and cold water rained down on us. I shoved the grimoire under my shirt to keep it dry.

Orion pushed ahead of me, opening the door for me on the top floor. When I caught a view of an empty hall, I exhaled with relief. The sprinklers hadn't set off in here, and I pulled the book from my damp shirt.

"We can't rest, Rowan," said Orion. "We have to find a way out."

"I know." My body burned with the toxins. I dragged myself through the hall, still clutching the grimoire.

I just no longer had any idea how we were going to get out.

I pulled out my phone again, ordering Siri to call Legion. This time, the ringtone was clear, and he picked up immediately.

"Where are you?" he shouted into the phone.

I didn't have time to waste on elaborate explanations. "We need you to open the front door for us. Not yet! I'll knock. Just wait for me there, okay?"

We'd nearly reached the end of the corridor, so I pushed myself as hard as I could, and Orion ran at the same speed.

We finally made it to the wooden stairwell at the front of the building and staggered down as fast as our broken bodies would take us.

As we reached the lowest level, my heart thundered.

Jack Corwin stood there, aiming his gun at us.

If I'd had the ability to summon my magic, I'd have turned the mansion to ash to keep Orion safe.

Jack's face was red, and sweat dripped down his forehead. "Did you just think you could kill my dad and get away with it?" His shouts sounded ragged, crazed.

Orion turned and started to pull me back up the stairs, his arm around my back like he was shielding me. But I felt the sharp sting of pain as the darts ripped through my skin from behind.

"Hawthorn berries and Ladon venom," shouted Jack. "Doesn't feel so good, does it, my friends?"

Orion whirled. "You stay the fuck away from her." His voice boomed off the walls, like the knelling of a dark god. "If you harm her again, I'll make you wish you'd never been born. I am a nightmare the likes of which you cannot even comprehend. I will burn this place to the ground and make you choke on the smoke, and then I'll rip out your lungs, Jack."

"Not with the venom in you," he shot back. I could tell he was attempting mockery, but his voice was shaking, ruining the effect.

I fell to my knees, horrified to hear the sound of footfalls upstairs. We were about to be trapped in here between Jack and the rest of the demon hunters.

With a wild snarl, Orion barreled toward Jack and pushed him against the wall. He pressed his forearm against Jack's throat, pinning him hard. Jack's face turned as red as the leaves outside.

"Stay away from my queen," Orion growled.

Jack dropped the gun, and his legs kicked at the air.

I had no idea how Orion had found the strength for that, as the Ladon venom felt like it was corroding me from the inside out.

"Go, Rowan!" Orion was shouting, but it sounded hazy to me. "I'm right behind you. Get it out of here!"

I staggered past the two of them, my mind whirling as I reached for the door.

Orion had trusted me with this grimoire, and I was going to get it to safety. Distantly, I heard Orion and Jack shouting at each other, but my senses seemed muddled, like the poison was eating at my brain. I narrowed my focus to getting the book outside. I leaned against the door, then knocked four times until it gave way.

I fell to the ground outside in the blinding sunlight, where the air smelled of death. I clung to the book as I felt a pair of strong arms scoop me up, and then the wind rushed over me.

I leaned into Orion's chest, and every bone in my body sang with agony.

Now, there was only the feel of my nerves splitting open, and the rest of the world faded away.

❧

MALE VOICES PIERCED THE AIR AROUND ME. I WAS GOING to be sick. I rolled onto my hands and knees, and vomited onto the dirt.

"Rowan!"

I looked up to see Legion's face before me, blurred like the world was smeared with Vaseline.

"Rowan," he shouted again, crouching beside me. "I need to know what they poisoned you with."

I fought the urge to throw up a second time and tried to cast my mind back. Jack had told us what it was...

"Ladon," I muttered, leaning back on my heels. Gripping my stomach, I lay on my side. But no position was relieving the pain, no matter how much I shifted around. "Ladon venom. And hawthorn." I fell onto my back in the dirt. "Where's Orion?"

❧

AN ARM CURLED UNDER MY NECK, AND I LOOKED UP into Legion's face looming above me. He was holding a cup to my lips, one that smelled of pine needles and berries.

"Open, Rowan," he said gently, cupping the back of my head. "This will help."

The scent of it nauseated me, and I wanted to puke again. My mouth felt dry, fiery.

"Open, Rowan," said Kas. "It's medicine. It will make you feel better."

He reminded me so much of my mom right then that I only wanted to please him, so I took a sip of the viscous, earthy liquid, and drank it down. It tasted like dirt and leaves—but the effect was almost immediate.

Whatever it was, it washed away the corrosive pain, soothing my muscles. Slowly, my vision started to clear, and the nausea settled in my stomach. My limbs shook, but they didn't hurt.

I looked up into the concerned faces of Legion and Kas. At last, I was strong enough to sit up, and I wiped the back of my hand across my mouth.

But something still felt wrong, and my heart thumped wildly with panic. Fear still gripped every muscle in my body.

I looked around me as I realized the source of the fear. "Where's Orion?"

Legion shot a confused glance at Kas. "I don't know. We were trying to get you to safety as quickly as possible."

"We weren't waiting around for him," said Kas.

"You got the book, Rowan!" Legion passed the grimoire to me. "You won."

"Wait." I was scrambling to keep up with their conversation. "Orion's still there?"

"When you said you were trapped," Kas went on, "I thought it would help to light a fire, because the two of you would survive it, but—"

"Kas," I shouted. "I need to go back for Orion!"

Kas looked startled, then frowned. "Of course. But shouldn't you bring the grimoire back to the City of Thorns first? He'll be fine. He's Orion."

"He's survived worse than a few mortals," added Legion.

I gripped the book tight against me. "No. Our magic wasn't working with that poison. I won't let the mortals break him again."

I was already rushing to my feet when Legion touched my arm. "Wait. Shouldn't you leave the book with us?"

My gaze slid between the two of them, and the thought still nagged at the back of my thoughts—someone had tipped off the demon hunters. "Shai never showed up at the south entrance. Where is she?"

Legion shook his head. "She's not answering her phone. We couldn't find her. But you don't think she would..." His sentence trailed off. "She wouldn't have left you there on purpose, Rowan."

Kas scrubbed his hands over his mouth. "Sadly, no one is above mistrust. Not even our dearest friends."

"And that's exactly why I'll be keeping the book with me." I pulled the glass from Legion, the one filled with the antidote. "Thank you both for getting me to safety. I'll see you in the City of Thorns."

They were shouting after me to leave the book with them for safety. As long as I brought it back to Orion, he could still win.

But the fact was, at this point, I trusted Orion more than I trusted them.

31

ROWAN

I felt it for the first time—the unrestrained panic of knowing Orion was in danger. My twin star. Even if he didn't realize his soul was calling to me, it was. He *needed* me now, and nothing would stop me from getting to him.

Our separation was a sharp physical pain in my chest.

What if he thought I'd abandoned him on purpose?

The thought made my heart slam against my ribs. He'd sacrificed himself to the demon hunters so I'd have a chance to escape, giving up the book, the crown, his life—

I wouldn't let them break him again.

Racing west, I soared over autumn leaves the color of hellfire under a cool blue sky.

I'd rip Jack's head from his body if he killed Orion. I'd leave nothing behind of that mansion but a dusty miasma of blood and bone. Darkness unfurled inside me—shadows that I'd always kept wrapped up tightly. The demon in me that craved blood, vengeance.

I swooped down on the clearing where the mansion

stood, and the scent of mortal blood filled the air around me.

I crossed to the stone marking the door and kicked it open. The door slammed off its hinges, and I stepped inside. I tucked the book under one arm and gripped the antidote with the same hand. If any mortals showed up with dart guns again, I'd be ready to unleash flames from my fingertips.

Apart from the portraits of demon hunters above the wainscoting, I found the hall empty.

I sniffed the air, inhaling blood, burnt wood, and the scent of fear.

I wasn't just Rowan now, but a demon who hunted by scent. And when I heard footfalls behind me, I reacted immediately. I had no time for coherent thoughts, just my hands gripping a mortal throat and slamming his head against the wall. I hit him hard enough to make him panic, not enough to knock him out. His eyes snapped wide open so I could see the whites, like a frightened horse.

"Where is your prisoner?" I hissed. "The incubus."

His mouth opened and closed soundlessly, so I drew out my claws against his neck. He let out a whimper as I drew blood.

"If you scream," I whispered, "I'll kill you. Now tell me, is there a dungeon? A jail?"

I'd be killing him either way. Were these Orion's methods? Yes. But I was a demon now, and it seemed I needed the ruthless efficiency of violence to protect those I loved. I'd keep him safe, and I knew he'd do the same for me.

"Where is he?" I demanded.

"O-on this floor." he stammered. "The northern wing.

We don't have a dungeon or anything like that. We're not the monsters. He's chained to a chair in the drawing room."

"He's just in an open room?"

He shook his head. "There are bars, like a prison cell."

"Tell me exactly how I get in, mortal, or when I come back to find you, I'll slowly drag your entrails from your body."

"The code is...it's 1486," he stammered.

The year the *Malleus Maleficarum* was written.

For an instant, I released my hold, and then I slashed my silver claws against his throat. His blood arced from his neck as he fell to the floor. I couldn't risk him pulling the alarms as soon as I left.

With the air rushing over me, I raced to the northern wing, tracking Orion by his scent. Shouts echoed through the corridor as Jack barked questions at him.

Fury snapped through me, so sharp and hot I had to take care to temper it with cooler emotions. If I gave in to my rage, this place would turn to dust, and the grimoire along with it.

I was closing in on the drawing room, where iron bars blocked off a stately chamber. Pressing my back against the wall, I had a glimpse only of an antique rug and a stone fireplace, but I could smell Orion here. I desperately wanted to curl around him and keep him safe.

I could easily melt the iron if I had to, but I didn't want to give them advanced warning. If they had their dart guns ready, this wouldn't go well.

"Tell us how to get into the City of Thorns!" It was Jack's voice, teetering on the edge of hysteria.

"I think we need to stop." An unfamiliar voice. "If he dies, we won't learn anything from him. A demon corpse is no good to us."

I tried to block out the particular horror of that comment. Hidden from view, I clutched the book and the antidote tight, and I punched in the code: 1-4-8-6.

The iron gate slid up, and I shifted into the room. For a fraction of a breath, my brain registered what was happening.

Everything in the space looked expensive and luxurious —the antique furniture, the Persian carpet. Everything except the chains and the rickety wooden chair they kept Orion in.

To my left—my Orion, shirtless, pinned down. Jack had carved his body with symbols all over, and Orion's blood streamed to the floor, pooling red.

Three hunters stood to my right, blood covering all of them.

A fraction of a breath later, I loosed a stream of fire that engulfed those three men, setting them ablaze.

Jack was too close to Orion to risk the flames, and he started running as soon as he caught sight of my fire. The pungent stench of Jack's fear filled the air.

I'd be going after him, but I'd be healing Orion first. What was better than one ferocious Lilu hell-bent on vengeance?

Two Lilu hell-bent on vengeance.

But when I looked back at Orion, sadness welled in me, along with panic. They'd ripped him apart.

Was he even breathing? I rushed over to him, shaking

with horror. They'd carved the word *matricide* into his chest in vicious slashes. What the *fuck?*

And it was a merciful thing that my sorrow for him dampened my fury at Jack, or everything around me would be tiny flecks of ash.

They'd carved swirls that looked like snakes...

I cupped the back of his head, and when his eyes fluttered open, relief swelled in my chest. Oh, thank the *gods*.

"Rowan," he murmured. "You need to go."

"Fuck, no." I lifted the antidote to his lips. "Drink this."

He'd lost so much blood, he was struggling to keep his head up, and he looked like he was going to be sick. But he managed to close his lips on the edge of the cup. I tipped it, and the earthy liquid slid onto his tongue.

At first, he nearly choked on it. He was barely swallowing, but then he closed his mouth, and I watched his Adam's apple bob.

"Open, love," I whispered. "It will make you feel better." Mirroring Mom's words, and Kas's.

One tiny sip at a time, I let the potion slide into his open mouth. And when his eyes started widening to that ethereal blue—almost focused on me—joy lit me up.

"Orion," I whispered. "Come back to me."

I tilted the rest of the antidote into his mouth, and he swallowed it, stronger now. His eyes closed as he drank it down, and my gaze swept over his skin. As he finished the potion, his body was already starting to heal. The brutal carvings were disappearing as his demon strength and magic returned to him.

His head tilted down, and he stared at me, a fierce look in his eyes. "You came back for me."

"Of course I did. I always will." I slipped behind him. Gritting my teeth, I ripped through the chains that bound him. He slumped forward a little, resting his forearms on his knees. Blood still dripped from his arms onto the floor.

I knelt in front of him, peering up at his face. I'd never seen him look so exhausted. "Orion, I need to know this now." I gripped his thighs. "If we can bring the Lilu back into the City of Thorns, do you promise that will be enough for you? Or at least that you won't launch any preemptive attacks on the mortals to satisfy a centuries-old blood oath?"

He looked up at me, weary, a smile flickering over his lips. "I think I like your interrogation better than theirs, although you're somehow more terrifying."

"Do you promise?" I pressed.

"Yes, Rowan. I can restrain myself from launching preemptive attacks. I never promised Ashur specifics about how I'd get revenge. And the return of the Lilu is certainly revenge." He cocked his head, raising an eyebrow. "If we can't find them, we could always *make* more Lilu."

I ignored the flush of heat in my cheeks at his comment, trying to stay focused before I lost my chance to hunt down Jack.

I shoved the grimoire at him. "Good. Take this home."

He rose, handing it back to me. "You take it home. You return and take the crown."

I gripped him by the elbow, and helped him to his feet. "I'm going after Jack to see what he knows about Shai. She never showed up where she was supposed to be, and I don't know if she was the leak, or if she's locked in here, or what the fuck happened. And I want the book of names back."

I breathed in deeply, smelling the air for sweat, listening for heartbeats. My heightened senses told me the whole place was empty. Jack—and every other hunter—had fled.

I touched the side of Orion's face. "I need to go. Take the grimoire. Bring it back to the City of Thorns."

He leaned down, resting his forehead on mine. "I think this means you trust me now."

"I do. And when I get back, you and I will figure out how to rule together." I turned to run for Jack, but Orion grabbed my bicep.

When I turned to him, his eyes were burning with a strange intensity. "Wait, *wait*. You need to know what I did before you decide that you trust me."

I cupped his face. "Tell me now, then. Quickly."

His face was so close to mine, and he pulled my hands from cheeks. Pain etched his face, and his shoulders slumped.

"I condemned my mother to death," he said quietly.

That wasn't what I'd expected, and my gaze slid down to the words carved on his chest, now healed over into angry scars. *Matricide.*

"I don't understand," I said. "How is that possible?"

"Molor died defending her, Rowan. Molor was a hero. But only a few months after they locked me in prison with her, I was brought to another cell. She was highborn, and they wanted a crime on the record books. So they asked me to say she wanted to kill the king, and I did. All they had to do was scare me, and I told them whatever they wanted to hear."

His sorrow seemed to fill me, a well of pain so deep, I'd never reach the bottom.

He met my gaze again, his expression ravaged with pain. "I did that because that is what I am deep down. I'm someone who will always save himself. I'm not Molor. He died because he was better than me. I always thought the ones who live are the worst ones. There is something twisted inside me, Rowan."

Something in his words struck a chord in me because we were the same—the ones who lived. But he was wrong.

I wrapped my arms around his neck, pulling him close to me so I could hear his beating heart. "You didn't condemn your mom because you're an abomination, my love. You condemned her because you were five—or six? You were a young child, and any other young child would do the same." I stood on my tiptoes to nestle into his neck.

Tentatively, his arm slid around my lower back. "A hero should protect people," he said, and the sentiment was strangely childish, like that part of him had stopped at five.

I kissed his neck. "But a little boy shouldn't be a hero. And the abominations were the people who tried to break you, because that wasn't just about getting a confession on the books. They were trying to break the Lightbringer. Orion, I know your mom would have wanted to go to her death instead of you. My mom ran into actual fire for me, and I know yours loved you just as much. How could she not? You weren't born twisted somehow. You were just a boy who loved his family, and they used it against you. You have some scars, inside and out, but we all do." I stared up into his eyes. "How many times have you saved my life? You went through torture today to keep me safe. You're protecting me."

His hand slid up, and he cupped the back of my head.

I traced my fingers over his scarred skin, finding it already more healed, the ridges nearly gone. "You're my Lightbringer—the shining one who fell into the shadows."

Ferocity gleamed in his pale eyes. He leaned down and kissed me deeply, pulling me up by my lower back so my heels lifted off the floor. I felt all my anger melting away, and my fears too, as his warm magic vibrated around me.

He withdrew from the kiss, looking at me from under his dark eyelashes. "Rowan Morgenstern, Queen of the City of Thorns."

I pressed the grimoire to him again. "Bring it home, Orion."

✿ 32 ✿

ROWAN

It was a good thing that I'd left Orion when I did, because I was pretty sure Jack was getting close to the boundary—the magical turnpike that kept demons trapped.

I found him by an old stone grist mill. The trees around it burst with crimson, the colors enflamed with scarlet, marigold, and ochre. But since blood covered Jack's clothes, it was easy to hunt him by scent. And by the time I reached him, he'd run out of energy. Jack was limping along below me, red-faced. Orion's blood soaked him, and another hot rush of rage burst through me. I landed before him, my wings spread out.

I savored the look of fear seizing Jack's body as he took me in and stumbled back. "Rowan. Just remember, we were friends once."

I took a step closer. "Except we were never friends, Jack."

"You're not like these demons. I *know* you, Rowan. We grew up together." He lifted his hands. "Remember the talent show? You did a magic show! In high school." A wild laugh escaped him. "It was...it was...it wasn't even *good,* Rowan. *You fell off the stage.* And now you can fly? You can incinerate people? This isn't the Rowan I knew growing up."

My lip curled. "Even when you're begging for your life, you can't stop yourself from reminding me what an asshole you are. You took a video of me falling off the stage, and you uploaded it to Instagram. Remember that?"

He looked like he was about to cry. "But you're not like them. That's my point. You're just...you know. Rowan. You're harmless."

My hand shot out, and I lifted him by the throat, squeezing. "You hurt someone I loved. And it turns out, when that happens, I am *very* much like a demon. I'm not harmless anymore."

I dropped him on the ground. He started scrambling to get away from me, and I reached for him again. This time, I let my claws out a little, piercing his skin when I lifted him above me. "I have a few questions for you. First, I want to know where the book is. The one with the Lilu names. When I release you again, I'm going to find a way to make you tell me."

I dropped him a second time, then slammed my heel into his knee. He screamed, grabbing the broken bone. I had to wait until his cries subsided, and then he managed to choke out, "Burned."

My teeth clenched. "You burned it?"

I brought my heel down hard into the same knee. His screams ripped through the air.

"We didn't need it." He rolled over, looking like was about to be sick. "It's digitized now."

Such a banal statement in the midst of all the carnage, but it was useful.

"Where is Shai?" I demanded. "Was she the one who turned me in?"

Even as he was shaking, he managed to smile at me. "She's not exactly who you think she is. Even now, you don't have any real friends, Rowan. The demons don't care about you. I could be your friend if you let me live."

"Where is she?"

"Back in Osborne." He cradled his knee, tears running down his face, his features contorted. "You killed my father. You killed my brothers. And now you're going to end me. This is why we hunt you," he shouted. "Because you're monsters!"

I knelt next to him. "You and me both. You nearly tortured Orion to death. What's Shai doing in Osborne?"

"Orion isn't who you think he is, either. He's forever stained by his sins. Did you know he killed his mom?" Streaked with dirt and blood, Jack looked up at me from the ground. "All they had to do was put snakes in his cell, let them slide all over him until he shrieked for mercy, and he sent his mom to her own death." A wild laugh escaped him. "Your big bad demon was scared of snakes."

"He was *five,* you fucking maniac."

"Only the blood of demons will cleanse the world of all your sins. It's the sacred duty of the Hunters to spill it."

I gritted my teeth. "Except you'll all be dead soon, Jack. We'll hunt down and wipe out every last one of you.

And when that's done, we'll have peace between mortals and demons. Too bad you won't be here to enjoy it."

Jack was shaking. "You grew up among us, Rowan. What if you joined us again? No one needs to know. Your friends betrayed you. And Orion will, too. Demons aren't loyal. They only look after themselves, like animals." He was desperate now, white as milk. "You can't trust the Lord of Chaos. The man is *insane*, Rowan. Of course he is. He condemned his own mom, and then he spent the rest of his life staring at the scene of his crime, staring at the noose that killed her. Dwelling on his sins, on how rotten he is underneath, because that's what demons are. Abominations." He yelled at me. "And when we carved his chest, we marked him for his sins, we spilled his blood to force him to atone, the way Cain was marked as a murderer!"

As he was speaking, my body had been growing hotter, brighter. They'd done this to him—tried to break him. They'd branded him with the guilt of condemning his mom when he was no more than a little boy. Jack was both a physical and mental sadist.

I heard myself say, "You're wrong, Jack. I'm not like you. Maybe I'm an abomination, but I'm a demon, not mortal. And I'm loyal down to my bones. I'll keep those I love safe."

"Then show some loyalty to the mortals you grew up with!"

Fire raged in my mind, and my voice echoed off the stone of the grist mill. "I'll keep the *innocent* mortals safe. But that's not you."

Starlight spilled around me as my wrath lit up the world. It was a strange sort of ecstasy to let myself go.

I was the light descending into darkness. Lady Lucifer, the fallen.

Jack's screams spiraled into the air, and traces of blood and bone, earth and rock drifted upward, swirling around me as I took him apart, a maelstrom of destruction. I was the nightmare, and I would take the wicked down with me. I let the light flow out of me, and I opened myself to the darkness.

Empty inside, I devoured the world. "I am Chaos, the eater of worlds," I heard myself whisper. "I was the first to exist, and I will be the last."

33

ROWAN

Shadowy nightmares flooded my mind. Now I lived in a palace of ice, of crushing solitude.

I am the nightmare.

Thoughts spiraled in the darkness of my mind, tiny whirling galaxies in darkness. Heat did not exist here.

I wasn't sure if *I* existed...

I died, I think...my body consumed itself in its fury, and my soul along with it.

Order and chaos...a light falling into the underworld.

Shadows consumed my light.

I am infinite. The alpha and omega.

I ached for warmth again. For him. A beautiful, fallen god—so perfect that the shadows desired him for their own. I among them wanted to devour his beauty.

A craving split me open, and I was grasping for him.

I could feel again. I needed to consume that light...

If I could feel, I was alive.

Someone I loved kissed my throat and jaw. What was his name?

My nostrils flared as I smelled him on me. And along with his scent, the faint perfume of lavender soap was bringing me back into my body.

I *craved*. I hungered. The chaos inside me demanded to be fed.

My muscles were warm, slick, and limp, and water dripped down my body. I wanted to be naked, to feel the fallen god's bare skin against mine.

He wasn't giving me what I wanted.

Cotton covered me, damp with warm water. Muscled arms wrapped around me, then laid me down in a bed of cool, clean sheets. The sensation of the sheets against my skin, that smooth and light friction, was an erotic torment that made me feel as if I were swelling with need.

He tried to pull away from me, but I wrapped my arms around him. My fingernails were in the bare skin of his back, pulling him closer. Distantly, I heard myself moaning for him. The fallen god was what I needed, and I knew he was the one who could fill me with light again. I licked his neck, tasting him. My skin felt sensitive, desperate for his touch. I couldn't decide if I wanted to bite him or fuck him. Both? I needed to devour.

"Rowan?"

I opened my eyes, looking up at perfection. Blue eyes, golden skin, angular jaw—a god of masculine beauty.

His darkening eyes burned with ferocity. "You're coming back to me." He kissed me lightly on my lips, but it wasn't enough.

Strength poured into me. I pushed him onto his back, delighted to find that I wasn't wearing underwear. Because

I wanted to feel myself right on his bare skin, and I wrapped my thighs around his abs.

I ran my hands over pure, sun-kissed muscle. When I looked into his obsidian eyes, he seemed on the edge of losing control, his expression fierce. His fingers were on my thighs, clenching tight. I ached for him.

"Rowan, careful," he said. "We can't have too much."

I wanted too much.

And I knew if I took off these damp clothes, he would give me what I needed. So I tugged at the hem and lifted it off in one smooth motion. I watched his eyes slide down to my breasts and the apex of my thighs, naked on his body. This is where I should be—on top of my fallen god.

Conquering him.

His hot, silky magic twined around us, making my skin glow.

I watched his throat bob, and I moved down to his pants to unbutton them.

"Rowan, no!"

And then something happened that I didn't like at all. It was those magical bindings, snaking around my wrists and ankles, pulling me off him. Completely naked, I was bound to the bed, unable to get what I needed.

And worst of all, the fallen god threw a blanket over me again. I ached for him, and the faint friction of the sheet was nothing but torture.

He lay next to me, his head slumped against my shoulder "A little at a time, love."

Love.

With that word, his name dropped through the darkness in my mind like a falling star. "Orion." The memory of the word filled me with a little light.

A faint smile curled his lips. His eyes were still that coal black, telling me that he wanted to fuck me.

Under the blanket, he traced his fingertips over the curve of my hips. "I didn't want to leave you alone, Rowan. Even though you told me not to. I flew back, following you. And I saw the flash of light, and I've never felt more terrified."

His hand traced down my thighs, making me shudder at the contact.

❧

I DREAMED CARNAL, FEVERED DREAMS...THAT WE WERE in the Temple of Ishtar, the night after my initiation. I was sitting in his lap, and he toyed with me, touching me where I was wet. Hunger ripped through me, and my thighs opened wider, shamelessly demanding more. I didn't care that everyone was watching as long as I could come...

I dreamed that he bent me over a desk and ran his finger down my spine. He slid his hand into my hair and forced my skirt up, my underwear down to my thighs. Gripping my hair, he took me hard and fast, filling me while I screamed his name.

When I woke, the restraints were gone, but he was still next to me. Darkness filled the room. I was clothed again, which was annoying, but I twined my body around his. He stirred in his sleep, moving his arms around me. I could feel his hard length through my nightgown. Turning toward him, I searched for his lips, and when I found them, I kissed him deeply.

He moaned into my mouth, hips moving against me. But he pulled away with an agonized sigh, his eyes dark with shadows. "Not yet, love."

I needed more contact. *More.* "Orion."

There was something important I needed to tell him, and it was just at the edge of my consciousness. Where my mind had been whirling with chaos before, clear images started to flit through my thoughts...

A silver-haired boy covered in snakes.

"You didn't mention the snakes." The words startled me, and I wasn't yet sure what I was talking about. Then the memories began to flood me, flickering in my thoughts like an old film reel. "They covered you in snakes in the dungeon until you broke down. You didn't tell me."

He pulled away from me, staring at the ceiling. Another, worse memory burned in my thoughts—I'd made *fun* of him for his fear of snakes. I touched the side of his face and angled it toward me. Exhaustion shaded his sensual features, his eyes half-closed. He stroked his thumb over my cheek, and I felt myself lighting up from the inside out.

"Do you know what happened to the book?" he asked quietly. "The Lilu names?"

That's what it was—the thing I needed to tell him. I closed my eyes, trying to remember the specifics. "He burned it, but they're still there."

"Still where?"

What was the word he'd used? "In the Puritan building."

"The Puritan building," he repeated, brushing his thumb over my skin.

The darkness inside me wanted him to lick me and kiss me, for us to be a tangle of limbs and tongues, but I knew this was important, so I tried to focus and picture the face of the demon hunter...the one I'd destroyed. Images burst in my mind like fireworks. His sneering, freckled face. A maroon sweatshirt with Greek letters. A silver hammer pin, a knife dripping with blood. *Matricide.* He'd been my tormentor for years, and tears ran down his cheeks, streaking through the dirt on his face—

He'd carved words into my fallen god.

I inhaled sharply. "Digitized. That's what he said. It's in their files."

A smile creased his face. "Nice work, love." He traced his thumb over my lower lip.

With the important task completed, I felt I deserved a reward. And the way he was looking at me with that intense heat, that love—it was almost enough of a reward. But not quite.

My hunger for him would never be satiated. When I ran my hand down his hard, muscled body, the look in his eyes told me he was at war with himself, too.

I kissed him, taking his lower lip between mine. His fingers slid down, tightening on my ass. He pushed my hips against his length and groaned, a desperate sound that made my nipples tight. I needed my clothes off, our bodies sliding against each other.

I'd become a monster, turned the world into ashes around me. I'd made people burn. And I needed primal, animalistic sex to forget it all.

Agonizingly, he pulled away, his muscles tense as he lay flat on his back.

"You're not ready, my queen. Slow and steady, love. Almost there."

Orion kept denying me what I needed. I was about to rip off my clothes again, but I felt him curling into me, his hand cupping my face. My eyes were growing heavy, my body limp. He was using magic on me—a different kind of Lilu magic. We were creatures of the night, of sex—and sleep.

Erotic dreams filled my mind before I could say another word.

Soon, I knew, I'd be getting everything I wanted from him.

34

ROWAN

I woke by myself, to a room streaming with light. Orion's room.

For the first time in days, my muscles felt imbued with energy, my thoughts clear. I jumped out of bed and looked down at myself. Orion had dressed me fully in sweatpants and a long-sleeved shirt, which made me smile. This outfit was for him, not for me—so he could restrain himself.

I crossed to the window and opened the shutters to look out at the garden. Immediately, sharp hunger gripped my stomach. I was starving. When I sniffed the air, my mouth watered. Was that baking bread? And something with cream? Potatoes? Butter?

Gods, I needed to eat, or I'd lose my mind.

I pushed the door open and raced downstairs. Before I reached the bottom, Orion swung around the corner from the kitchen into the stairwell. He grinned up at me. "You've returned to us."

"I've never been this hungry," I said, salivating at the scent of food.

I glanced hopefully at Amon, who was cooking something in front of an expansive stone hearth. He nodded at the table. "Clam chowder?" he asked.

"Oh, God, yes." I sat at the wood table, and Orion slid bread and butter across to me, then filled a glass of water.

My throat was dry as sand, and I drank it down. As Amon ladled chowder into a bowl for me, I attacked the fresh bread, slathering it in butter. Curls of steam rose from the bread, and the butter melted immediately. Salt and fat melted on my tongue...

Orion sat across from me at the table, his eyes glinting with amusement. "Take it easy, Rowan. You haven't eaten in almost a week."

The bread was gone.

The chowder—thick with cream, potatoes. Heavenly. More bread.

Orion touched my hand. "If you eat too much too quickly, you'll make yourself sick." It felt very much like something he'd been saying, something that had annoyed me *very* much over the past week.

"Always with the restraint," I muttered.

Sunlight streamed in through the kitchen windows, over clean white walls and a terracotta tiled floor. Slowly, the memories from Sudbury started trickling back to me.

I leaned back in my chair. "I was out for a week?"

A smile ghosted over Orion's lips. "We've been waiting for you to recover. I have something planned for the moment you're better."

I shook my head, my brain scrambling to keep up. "Wait. How did the trial end?"

He inhaled deeply. "I returned with the grimoire and you in my arms. The crowd was waiting for us, and they saw us return with the grimoire at the same time."

So he was still king.

As if hearing my thoughts, he added, "I announced that we would rule together. A king and queen in the City of Thorns. And if you're feeling well enough, tonight, you can address your subjects at the festival."

"What festival?"

He beamed at me from across the table. "A Lilu celebration to commemorate the triumphant return of our people."

My eyes widened. "You found them? Already?"

"It only took a few days," said Amon.

"Traditionally," said Orion, "the Lilu celebrations involve a human sacrifice, usually a prisoner dressed up as a mock king, and we tear him to pieces with our hands and consume his flesh."

I gaped at him. "Can we just do, like...a taco truck, maybe?"

"But since we've already killed all the demon hunters," he added quickly, "we can consider the spilling of mortal blood already completed."

I had a feeling he was trying to placate me, and that if I weren't here, he'd just go with the original plan. "Sounds like a fun festival."

The afternoon light gilded his beautiful face, bathing him in warmth. "Also, traditionally, the king publicly mates with his lover during the celebration," he murmured. "It symbolizes the primordial coupling of light and dark."

This was all a far cry from the two college parties I'd been invited to, with keg stands and red Solo cups.

Wait a minute—*was* I more like the mortals than the Lilu? My mind was churning, roiling, trying to keep up with everything. The world seemed to be moving in fast motion suddenly, and there was still so much I didn't know about Lilu culture.

"Yeah, we're not doing that in public," I said. "Though if you'd asked me a few days ago, when I was writhing in the depths of chaos and lust, I'd have been up for any kind of fucking with any kind of crowd. As it is, the Lilu will have to be happy with light and dark coupling away from their prying eyes."

Orion nodded. "The rest is fairly normal for a festival. Dancing, eating, a reenactment of Astaroth's descent into chaos, and the ritual slaughter of a bull so the Lilu leaders can bathe in its blood."

I cleared my throat. "I might skip that part?" He looked so freaking happy, though, I almost wanted to do the bull blood.

If it weren't for Orion, I would absolutely stay inside and read a book for a few weeks. But after all this time, he had his people back, and he wanted to celebrate—so I'd try out things the Lilu way for tonight.

"The Lilu are already in the Asmodean Ward." His unguarded smile was a thing of beauty. "We've been repairing the windows, cleaning out the dust. And at night, they've been swooping through the air, circling the city." Orion stood. "Come with me. I have a dress for you."

Gods, I loved seeing him like this. He took me by the hand, leading me back upstairs and into the room that I'd first stayed in. There, he'd laid out a dress for me—one both stunning and daring at the same time. It was a sheer material of midnight blue, beaded with tiny pearls in the shape of a constellation. A little slip under the dress would hit me below the hips, and it would just about cover my breasts and tummy, but the rest of me would pretty much be on display through the transparent material.

Still—I was a Lilu, and this was normal for them.

Not to mention, I was fairly certain that everyone had already seen me completely naked when Orion had returned with me in his arms from Sudbury.

"It's gorgeous," I said honestly. And alongside the dress was a necklace—silver that curled and twisted like delicate vines—and a crown to match, the silver vines dappled with pearls. "All of it is gorgeous."

The idea of Orion picking these things out for me, thinking of what he'd like to see me in, was beyond delightful. I slid my hands around his waist, pressing my head against his chest. I loved listening to his heart beating.

But a worry still nagged at the back of my mind.

I pulled away from Orion and looked up into his face. "Did you hear anything about Shai?"

He shook his head. "I don't know what she was thinking, Rowan."

I slumped down on the bed next to my dress. "But you killed all the demon hunters. And she wasn't with them?"

"She's just gone, love. She ran away. But we'll find her eventually."

I was ruining his joy over the festival and the return of the Lilu after all this time, so I smiled at him as I sat on the bed. We would find her.

Kas had told me not to trust anyone—not even him. Not even Shai. But I *knew* her, and she'd never disappear on me without a very good reason.

Hadn't I just discovered that people would do terrible things when survival depended on it?

I'd turned into a chaos god to keep Orion safe.

If Shai had turned on me, she must have been desperate.

☙❧

WHEN I CROSSED INTO THE ASMODEAN WARD FOR THE festival, I felt like a goddess in the dress. The sheer material caressed my legs, and the silk covering my breasts and hips was heaven on my skin. But even if I felt like a goddess, I was perfectly happy to stand on the edges of it all, watching the festival unfold.

Music from stringed instruments filled the air, melodies that were both new and familiar at the same time. I had the unnerving sense that I'd carried these melodies in a part of my soul. A drum beat steadily, and a lilting song rose above it all—a man with a beautiful countertenor voice. Tonight, the air was perfumed with jasmine, and incubi and succubi swooped through the air overhead, wings spread under the moonlight. The joy here was palpable, infectious. I found myself laughing for no reason.

After hundreds of years, the Lilu had their magic back,

and the gift of flight. Once dark, the Lilu quarter had come to life again, and it thrummed with happiness. A star rising from the darkness.

Demons of all kinds danced wildly around the clock tower, and the golden hands moved once more, marking the time now as seven past nine at night. By Orion's side, I sipped an exotic Lilu beer, spiced with orange peel and safflower, and sweetened with honey.

Orion's face shone with joy as he looked out onto the festival, the dancers who moved in graceful arcs like the whorls of a solar system. He leaned down to kiss me on the lips.

When we pulled away from the kiss, the crowd was chanting for us both. *Long live Queen Rowan! Long Live King Orion!*

Technically, I wasn't queen yet. But they seemed to accept me as one already, and Orion slid his arm around my waist and leaned down to kiss me on my temple. Warmth flickered through me, and I wanted nothing more than to get him away into the Elysian Wilderness so we could reenact the primordial coupling of light and dark. Just—in private.

As if hearing my thoughts, Orion warmed the shell of my ear as he whispered, "I'm dying to get you alone, my queen." Heat flared across my chest, and I wanted to wrap myself around my demon king and drag him into the wilderness before anyone made us bathe in bull blood.

"Rowan!" A drunken, familiar voice rose above the music, and I turned to see Legion and Kas staggering toward me, shirts opened at the collar, buttons undone.

Kas lifted his beer. "Queen! Queen Rowan. Teamwork!" He held out a hand for a high-five, and I slapped his palm.

I smiled at them, but my throat tightened at the painful absence of the fourth member of our team. No wonder they were already trashed to forget that missing piece of the puzzle. And I had to wonder if they were a little disappointed that Orion was still on the throne, since they'd worked so hard to get rid of him.

Kas's beer sloshed out of his glass as he leaned over in a deep bow. "Your Majesty," he slurred. "My queen. May I have this dance?"

Already, I could hear the low, possessive growl emanating from Orion's chest. I was perfectly fine ignoring that, but another demon male was approaching, smiling at me like he knew me.

"Rowan!" The beautiful stranger beamed at me, opening his arms. He was nearly as tall as Orion, but with bright red hair that hung around his chin, his eyes deep brown. Abstract, curling tattoos curved over his thickly corded forearms. He was Lilu, his dark wings stretched proudly behind him.

I stared at his grinning face, unwilling to go in for a hug. "Have we met?"

His smile fell. "Of course. Yes." He looked down at himself and straightened his deep green shirt. "But I didn't look like this when you knew me." He met my gaze, waiting for me to catch on. "Your mother did fine without magic, but my body didn't do as well. It withered and aged outside of the city walls."

Understanding started to dawn. "Hang on..."

"I was the weak and doddering old man you played

chess with every week." He ran a hand through his hair. "I brought you the book, and then I ran. Or at least tottered away as fast as my walker could take me. The fucking hunters found me."

I could hardly contain my shock. "*Mr. Esposito?*"

"That was not my real name." His wings spread out behind him, resplendent in the moonlight. "Your first cousin, Sabazios, on your father's side. I was at your house all the time when you were a baby, helping your mom."

"Sabazios!" I beamed at him. "You wrote the inscription in the demon trials book."

"I did!" He looked around at the dancers. "God, it feels good to be back. When are we bringing out the bull? I've been desperate to scent bull blood. One of the things you really miss, you know?"

I laughed at the absurdity of it all, then threw myself against Orion's muscled chest, wrapping my arms around his waist.

He looked down at me with a wicked glint in his eye, a sensual curl of his lips. "We have another ceremony to enact now, but that one will be out of view."

Heat slid through me, and everyone around me seemed to fall away, so it was just Orion and me. "Come with me, *now*."

We were heading for the place that demons belonged —the wilderness.

35

ORION

I *could* walk by Rowan's side into the Elysian Wilderness, but I preferred to watch her walk. I was entranced by the sway of her hips through the forest before me. The material of her dress was so thin, I could see her legs from the thigh down. It would be hard not to rip through that beautiful dress and take her like an animal.

For the first time since I'd thrown Rowan out of the kingdom, my body actually started to relax. I was comfortable in my own skin again, apart from the increasing tightness in my trousers as I watched Rowan walk.

I'd been holding back for so long now, driven out of my mind by temptation. Tonight, our lust magic would entwine, and I felt like the power of it would shake the earth and harrow the hells.

Rowan turned to face me, a curl of red hair falling before her face. A sly smile crossed her lips. "We're alone, finally."

My gaze slid down her body, and I breathed in her

scent. I pulled her close to me, purring, "Rowan, you perfect creature. You brought the Lilu back."

She looked up into my eyes and responded with her own dazzling smile. "We both did."

I locked eyes with her and let the back of my hand slide down her cheek. Energy crackled where I touched her. "You're not going to bite me again, are you?"

"I might." Her voice held a seductive promise, and I can't say I hated the idea of it.

This cocky, succubus version of Rowan was nothing like the Rowan I'd first met—and I loved them both.

"I swore I wouldn't kiss you until you trusted me," I said. Our mouths were inches apart.

"And you understand that I trust you now?" Rowan's lips looked plump and red, ready for mine.

"You gave me the book," I said, my index finger on her chin, tilting her face to meet my kiss.

Instead of her sweet mouth, however, my lips found the first two fingers of her left hand, raised to block me.

My brow furrowed with an unspoken question. Who refused a kiss to an incubus?

I wanted her. She wanted me. But she intended to toy with me tonight—and I can't say I minded that, either.

With unexpected force, she shoved me flat on my back and leapt onto me like a wild creature—which she was. In the moonlight, I could see the flush of her cheeks, the untamed light in her eyes.

She straddled me, the hem of her dress riding up, and leaned closer. "Remember when you told me I didn't have it in me to take you down?"

I smoothed my palms over her thighs. "You haven't entirely forgiven some of the things I've said, have you?

She unbuttoned the top of my shirt and pressed her palms on my skin. A wicked smile curled her red lips. Her fingernails raked over the top of my chest, ripping the shirt open more. "I may exact my revenge little by little. You belong to me now."

Desire flared in me, and sparks ignited in the darkness at every point where our bodies made contact. "I do."

But even with Rowan, it was nearly impossible to suppress my instinct to dominate. A demonic impulse snapped through me, and in the next moment, I'd shifted her off me until she was facedown on the mossy earth, her dress hitched up from behind. Her gasp made me stir with lust.

I pinned her wrists to the ground, then pressed over her, drinking in her delicious scent—ripe fruit. I wanted to mark Rowan's body and soul as mine. I fought the urge to rip through her underwear and take her right now. I *had* to savor this.

I lowered my face to hers. "I want you to never again think of another man like you think of me."

She turned to look at me and licked her lips. I hardened even more as I watched the movement of her tongue sliding over her lower lip. "Still jealous, are you? I thought you were supposed to be a god or something."

I yanked her dress up higher, exposing her arse in tiny lace underwear that nearly made me forget how to speak. "The gods are all jealous," I snarled. "It's why they get so angry when you worship other ones."

"I never should have told you about Tammuz."

"Let's not talk about my dad right now." With one hand pinning her wrists, I used the other to trace over the dark silk between her thighs. She moaned, shifting her hips upward with my touch. Just under the silk, I could already feel how much she wanted me. I fought the urge to pull the silk aside and dive in because I delighted in tormenting her.

"Orion," she moaned my name. And I could hardly take it anymore.

I found myself covering her with my body, my erection pressing against her through my trousers. "Yes, love?"

Unexpectedly, she shifted her hips upward and elbowed me in the chest. This was more strength than I could possibly imagine from someone so small, and I was flat on my back again, the wind knocked out of me.

Holy hells.

One of her perfect thighs slid over me once more, and her hair was a wild tangle around her head, embedded with a few leaves from the forest floor. She looked like a gorgeous wood nymph with her thighs spread over my hips. Her dress had hitched up, and I had a view of that little triangle of silky underwear again, where I'd just been stroking her. I already knew how much she needed me, but she was determined to be in control—for now.

This time, I let her pin my wrists down—welcomed it, even. And when she leaned over to lick my neck, the heat shuddering through me told me I'd made the right choice. Gods, she was divine.

"Do you remember me begging you to fuck me when you healed me?" she murmured into my neck. "Let's see how you like it."

My muscles coiled tightly, and all the blood had rushed from my head. "An incubus never begs, love."

"Just pray to Lucifer that you beg well enough that I give you what you need."

With that, she let go of my wrists and ripped the rest of the buttons off my shirt. Then she moved further down, stripping off my trousers. With the fingernail of her index finger, she traced my length from the tip to the base. Every muscle in my body tensed, and I throbbed at her touch.

I was at her mercy.

There was nowhere I'd rather be.

✥ 36 ✥
ROWAN

lready, I wanted him inside me. Like an animal in heat, my body had immediately responded to the way he'd pushed me down and yanked up my dress. To the way he'd dominated me and pinned me. What I really wanted was for him to take me hard right now.

But I was going to draw this out anyway. I wanted him to feel a little of the erotic torment he'd blessed me with so many times.

I kissed his neck, tasting the faintest hint of salt—from the sea, or the heat. With my thighs spread over his hips, I rocked against him and heard him catch his breath. He reached up, threading his fingers into my hair, gripping it hard and pulled me in for a kiss, his tongue sweeping against mine. This was it—the kiss he'd withheld from me. With this kiss, I claimed him as mine, and he claimed me as his. A kiss of such overpowering sexual pleasure, it could *almost* be enough to kiss all night...but not quite, because the rising ache between my thighs demanded more. More friction, more fullness between my legs.

I moaned into his mouth as he gripped my hair, holding me in place. One of his hands was on my hips, pinning me over his length. He nipped my lower lip, pulling away from me to look into my eyes. Desire hummed through every inch of my body.

His thumb stroked my cheek, then brushed my lower lip. "I loved you the first time I saw you, but I refused to let myself believe it. Not just because you looked like her, but because I never wanted to feel the maddening grief of loss again."

My lips hovered above his, and I breathed in the perfect scent of Orion. "What made you change your mind?"

His unwavering gaze locked on me. "Because being without you was the same maddening grief of loss. I realized that in the weeks after I kicked you out. I need you. I wasn't really free of the dungeon until you brought me out. You set me free. And I had to take the risk to see if you'd still accept me, all of me."

"And I do."

He pulled me in for another sensual kiss, and I felt my magic twining with his, vibrating over our bodies. My body was shaking with need for him. But I'd promised to draw this out, hadn't I? Like he'd done with me so many times...

I moved down to his chin, brushing kisses over his jaw, down his throat. I felt each of his muscles tense as I moved down over his abs, then lower as he moaned my name like a prayer. I ran my hands over his glorious body, kissing, licking, nipping. His skin was a soft gold, his body gloriously muscled. A perfect warrior.

My mouth hovered over his shaft. His length stood tall and proud, an obelisk below his carved abs. I licked him once, twice. I kissed him, swirling my tongue.

His inhale was sharp and loud, fingers tightening in my hair. "Are you trying to make me snap?"

I pulled back, staring at him. "What were you saying about being an incubus?"

Orion was all done playing, and with a wild growl, he sat up, his hand cupped around the back of my neck. "I was saying that I need you naked now, succubus."

I was straddling him, moving my hips against him. "But a succubus needs to be worshipped, love."

"And worship you is exactly what I'm about to do." He leaned in, his midnight voice heating my skin. "With my mouth, my hands, my cock."

The king—my king—reached up and pulled my dress from my shoulders, exposing my breasts. Savoring the view, his gaze caressed me. "I know you want to be in control, love, but my instincts drive me to dominate you."

My nipples were already painfully hard, and when Orion palmed them, his control seemed to fracture. My beautiful, delicately beaded dress was gone with it—ripped off, tossed onto the soil and rocks. A cool breeze slid over my naked skin.

But demons were creatures of the wild, and the dress was a thing of civilization. It had no place here between two Lilu. Our bed was the moss, and the king wanted me naked and spread out before him.

Orion's hungry gaze slid over my body, wild with his

desire. The forest air began to shift, growing heated now as the lust magic crackled between us.

The corners of his lips curled. "I must see all of my queen." He slowly slid my underwear down my thighs, my calves. The cool forest air whispered over me, and wild need coiled tightly within me.

He was kissing me now, his mouth on my shoulders, my breasts. His lips closed over my nipples, making my back arch. His tongue swirled, his kiss devotional. With every brush of his lips and tongue, he claimed me. His mouth moved down to the hollow of my hips, and my body was on fire for him. A moan threatened to escape my lips.

When Orion spread my thighs, my body flushed. I was ready to cry out for him, my body ripe with desire.

I gripped his hair and lowered his mouth. Not a kiss this time. He raked his fangs across my inner thigh, the touch making my breath hitch. Teasing me. I wanted his mouth on me so desperately, his tongue inside me. I nearly crushed his head between my thighs.

"*Now,* Orion." Not a plea this time. An order.

❧ 37 ❧

ORION

I dipped my tongue into the warmth between her perfect legs.

Locked in prison as I'd been for all those years, the number of women I'd actually seduced could be counted on one hand. I'd desperately needed to feed from their lust when I escaped, but those experiences had been nothing like this. That was merely feeding, satiating a need.

This was an act of devotion, and the woman lying before me was a goddess.

I greedily inhaled the perfume of her arousal, and it enflamed me. Wisps of heated magic rose from her body, stroking me as I kissed her. Holy hells, the hellfire within threatened to consume me. Rowan's hips circled slowly once she made contact with my face, seeking the key to unlock her climax. But I wanted to keep her on the edge for just a little while because the air was aflame, and her power surged through my veins. I pulled back for a moment, and she barked another order for more, sounding more desperate this time.

She was mine, exactly as I needed her to be.

I pulled her tighter against me, allowing me even deeper access. My tongue swirled, licked, explored while her fingers ran through my hair. Her hips bucked as she moved against me, but I held on to the top of her thighs.

"You'll be doing this..." she hissed, "every day." She gasped, her hips moving up and down.

If I could have spoken, I would have agreed. Magic shimmered around her, lavender and gold, hot to the touch. She was right on the brink of release...

She tilted forward so I could reach her exactly where she needed me. I slid one finger into her heat, and she clenched around it, her muscles tight. A second finger glided in. As I moved my fingers in and out, I heard her shuddering cry. The orgasm ripped through her, and I felt as if the earth were shaking beneath us, and the air sparked with heat.

Her thighs tightened around me so hard that if I'd required breathing the way mortals do, I'd have been in real trouble. Rowan held me in place, undulating in her afterglow as I kissed and kissed.

But of course, I wasn't yet done with my queen.

❧ 38 ❧

ROWAN

The reverent strokes of his tongue had left me dizzy, limp-limbed. Every one of my muscles had gone supple.

But he'd kept kissing at the apex of my thighs, and that molten need had built again. Orion, naked and glorious, moved up my body, his mouth on my skin. My hips, my breasts. Worshipful, indeed.

With each brush of his lips, liquid heat slid through me, and an ache coiled more tightly in me all over. Gentle and reverent though he was, I could feel the tension vibrating through him. His careful control could snap at any moment. My gaze slid down over his strong arms, the shadows carving his muscles. I gripped him by the shoulders and pulled him up higher over me. "More."

"More," he repeated.

My body was slick from lust and the humid air, ready for him.

His coal black eyes bored into me, letting me know he'd taken control. I raked my hands over his back, urging him into me. I brought my thighs up on either side of him and slid my hands toward his hips to move him closer. He paused at my entrance, teasing me, and my arousal unfurled in me. "I need you now, Orion."

This time, he wasn't making me beg. Rock hard, he slowly pushed into me, filling me. He stretched me just to the edge of discomfort. Oh, *gods*...

My head tilted back as the erotic charge hummed through my core. I whispered his name, raking my fingernails deeper into his flesh.

"Look into my eyes, love," he murmured.

I met his gaze, my breath catching at his unreal beauty as I adjusted to his size. My thighs wrapped around him.

The temperature in the forest had climbed so high that some of the leaves had begun to burn like candle flames—but that was a problem for later.

With his enormous body, he pinned me to the moss. Slowly, he started to move in and out of me, taking me, stoking my arousal. Not Rowan anymore...just a succubus, a creature of the wild.

Ecstasy spiraled through me, primal and overwhelming.

He thrust in again, slowly, his eyes locked on mine. "You're mine, Rowan," he breathed. "I love you."

I felt I should return the sentiment, but a plea for *more* was all I could manage as his powerful strokes had me coiling with sexual pleasure.

He covered my mouth with his, moving faster in me. Making the ground shake beneath us and the air glow with the gold of the sun. The world was on fire, and we were creatures of the light.

I shuddered as my orgasm tore through me. My cries must have reached the forest's canopy, the city across the river—a scream only a banshee could appreciate.

Orion growled as my clenching muscles gripped him.

Just when I thought it was over, everything started again, the dip only the marker to begin another climb. I rocked my hips at a blinding speed, and before I knew it, my mind was fracturing again, my body shuddering.

With Orion's release, his mouth opened wide enough that I could see golden flames licking at the back of his throat from deep within his core.

In that moment, I had no words anymore, only the heat and the light, and the perfect ecstasy of a wild beast set free.

I CURLED UP INTO HIS ARMS, LISTENING TO HIM breathe, as rain slid down our naked bodies. Once my mind had cleared again from the mist of arousal, I'd managed to remember the words for the storm spell and doused the flames.

Orion stroked his hand down my damp hair and nestled me further into him. Goosebumps had risen on my skin in the cool air.

"Rowan," he said softly, "I ripped your dress. Again."

"Either you're going to need to take up sewing, or I need to start wearing things that are much easier to take off around you."

He kissed the top of my head. "You could just stay

naked. Around me," he clarified. "Not around anyone else. I don't need Kas and Legion getting an eyeful."

"I'm genuinely not at risk of becoming a nudist."

"Rowan." He propped up on his elbow. The shockingly pale blue of his eyes gleamed in the darkness. "When are we getting married?"

I stared at him. "Is this…a proposal?"

He traced a fingertip over my collarbone. "A proposal?"

I fought the urge to smile. After seeing Orion uncharacteristically vulnerable so many times recently, I found myself relieved that his wild confidence had returned. Also, he really had no idea whatsoever how normal social conventions worked.

"Usually, it's a question," I said. "You ask someone if they want to marry you before assuming. And there's kneeling and a ring."

"Ah." He nodded slowly. "Shall I get a ring?"

"Yes." I ran my fingers through his hair. "Orion, do you think we have everything we need now? We have the grimoire and the Lilu."

We'd both rule the City of Thorns. But what I was really asking was, *You're not hell-bent on revenge anymore, right?*

His fingers stilled on my collarbone, and he took a breath before answering.

My nerves fluttered with dread at his silence until at last, he said, "Yes. We have everything."

I lay flat on my back on the damp earth, staring up at the star-flecked sky through the boughs. I was perfectly satiated and happy, and his hand trailed down my body, following the curve of my waist, my hips.

But as I stared up at the heavens, a vision bloomed in my mind:

Stone walls, cracked to expose a bit of the stars. Then a shadow swinging over the stone—the bloodied, swaying feet of a hanged body. Wood creaking above, and pain piercing my heart to the core.

Why did I have a nagging feeling that I was still missing a piece of the puzzle, that even Orion didn't yet fully understand himself?

❧ 39 ❧

ROWAN

The morning after the festival, I woke alone in Orion's bed. I stretched like a cat until I had the energy to get dressed and search for coffee.

As I was pulling on a pair of jeans, my gaze caught on a handwritten note left on top of the bed: *Meet me by the clocktower, love.*

I cocked my head, staring at it.

What did my incubus king have in store for me today?

I smiled to myself. The ring. He'd probably found a ring.

I CROSSED INTO THE ASMODEAN WARD WITH A COFFEE in my hand, shocked to find that the entire city had turned out, thronging the square like they had last night. This time, however, there was no music, no dancing—just a silent crowd, and Orion standing in the glaring sunlight on top of a stone pedestal by the clocktower. All eyes were on him, waiting.

Oh, gods. Was he about to propose in public?

But that was so unlike him, and so unlike me. I didn't want that happening in front of a crowd.

And then dread started to slither up my nape when I caught a glimpse of something tucked under his arm. The grimoire.

What was he doing with the grimoire out here in public? In the wrong hands, that thing was dangerous as hell.

A horde of Orion's soldiers stood around the dais, protecting him. I couldn't even get to him.

Orion's blue eyes locked on me. His expression was cold as ice, sending a flutter of unease through my veins. "Our former shadow scion." His voice boomed across the courtyard, dripping with disdain. "Is a traitor. And when I called her queen last night, I was merely under the spell of a succubus."

Icy dread danced up my spine. What the *fuck?*

The crowd parted around me as everyone stepped back. Where was he going with this?

Yes, technically, I was a former shadow scion. Someone who'd tried and failed to take the crown from the king. *Technically,* I was someone who'd committed treason, and that usually came with a death penalty.

But Orion and I loved each other, so none of that mattered right now.

Right?

My throat went dry as I stared at him, waiting to see if

this was leading to something less terrifying. But if it was, I wasn't a fan of this kind of surprise.

"I cannot in good conscience rule over you and keep you caged," Orion's voice echoed off the clocktower, his eyes locked on me. He lifted the grimoire above his head.

Darkness started to rise in me.

"But I have the key to unlocking my people." His eyes held the crazed light of a fanatic as he held up the book. "Here. The grimoire. I am the one who can set you free once more. I am the Lightbringer prophesied to set you free. We must not live in fear of mortals any longer. We cannot allow another massacre to happen in our city walls. And we cannot allow traitors among us to keep us living in danger. Traitors like the disgraced shadow scion."

Everyone edged away from me—keeping their distance, like I was suddenly emitting a toxin that could bring them all down.

Frantically, I searched the crowd. Was anyone else baffled by this sharp change of personality?

I saw only Mr. Esposito—newly hot—catching my eye. He looked like he was panicking as much as I was, sweat running down his furrowed brow.

Orion had lost his fucking mind, and I needed to speak to him alone before he made this any worse. "Orion," I shouted. "You—"

My words were cut off by a hand gripping me by the throat, then a sharp needle piercing my neck. The effect was instant, a corrosive poison flooding me. I knew the feel of it anywhere—Ladon venom mixed with hawthorn. The poison screamed through my veins, weakening me.

My heart started to pound out of control as I realized I

was all out of magic now. The only person here moving toward me was Legion, who was fighting his way through the crowd to get to me.

The world seemed to be tilting beneath me.

This was a nightmare come to life.

Orion's eyes were on me as he held the book over his head. "Three days from now, I will open the City gates. We will feast again. We will hunt again. We will drink mortal blood once more. Never again will we make a contract with the faithless mortals that will put us at risk. And what do we do with traitors?"

A soldier gripped my arm, ready to drag me up to the dais along with Orion. For one moment, my heart went still.

He couldn't possibly...

My heart shattered. I should have seen this coming.

I'd missed something. I'd been too trusting.

A powerful arm gripped me by the bicep, and I felt the air go arctic around me. Frozen wind rolled through the square, powerful as a hurricane. Legion's magic ripped through the crowd as he scooped me up, and I did my best to wrap my arms around his neck. He was moving with me. Racing. Getting me away from the danger.

I looked up into his face as he carried me swiftly through the streets of the City of Thorns. I dug my nails into him as he ran, trying to manage the blinding pain.

Three days from now.

I closed my eyes against the brutal heartbreak and leaned into Legion's icy chest. Shai was gone. Orion had lost his fucking mind...

They all said he was too crazy to trust. The snakes had ended him...

I swallowed hard, tears stinging my eyes. It couldn't be, though. He'd saved me too many times. He'd sacrificed himself for me at the headquarters.

Hadn't he?

Maybe he'd just snapped. The shadows had consumed him, the chaos taken over.

In the City of Thorns, things aren't always what they seem.

I was vibrating from rage and confusion, unable to put it all together. But all I knew was that right now, Legion was the one taking care of me.

Fleeing with me from the man I'd thought loved me to the ends of the earth.

❧ 40 ❧
ROWAN

I was on my hands and knees in an abandoned garage, my body shaking with the exquisite agony of the poison. When I looked up through blurred eyes, I saw three forms. One of them was Kas, rushing over to me with a glass of that sludgy antidote, which was exactly what I fucking needed.

He knelt by my side and helped me shift back off my knees. I leaned into the curve of his arm, and he tilted the cup to my lips. "That's it, Rowan."

I sniffled, covered in snot and tears—hardly regal. But as the antidote filled my throat, some of my shaking subsided, and the pain seeped out of my bones. I collapsed against Kas and let him wrap an arm around me.

My vision was filmed from tears when I looked up at the other two. With a twinge of disappointment, I realized I'd been hoping for Shai and Legion, but the third figure was Mr. Esposito, also known as Sabazios. Ginger and hot as fuck, but also very much related to me, so I needed to stop thinking of him as *hot as fuck*.

"Are you okay, Rowan?" Sabazios asked.

I nodded. "Physically, I'm recovering." I shifted away from Kas and sat cross-legged on a concrete floor. "Do you all realize you're committing treason with me right now?"

"Yes," they answered, all at once.

Sabazios lifted a leather bag. "But at least this time, before fleeing, I was able to get my things."

"And we're not leaving you," said Kas. "This was why we wanted you to rule in the first place."

"Of course I'm not leaving you," said Sabazios. "You and your mom were literally the only friends I've had in the past several centuries."

I couldn't stop my tears. "We have to warn the mortals. We need to evacuate..."

"Rowan," said Legion, "you're still the only one who can stop Ashur."

I stared at him with the strange disorientation of feeling like the world was tilting beneath me. "Ashur?"

"Or whatever he calls himself now." Kas scrubbed a hand over his jaw. "Orion."

I shook my head, trying to understand what he was saying. "Ashur was someone else." My heart started beating faster. "That was who he made a blood oath to. Ashur."

Sabazios shook his head. "His parents named him Ashur. I remember him. They were part of our social set, and the little silver-haired boys were Molor and Ashur." His eyes took on a haunted look. "I had no idea he'd survived. We didn't know that anyone lived in the dungeon, or that it existed at all."

I staggered to my feet, my blood roaring in my ears.

My mouth had gone dry, and I tried to swallow. "Maybe Ashur is his dark side, then. The part that wants blood."

Kas stood and rested his large hands on my shoulders. "It's okay if you love him, Rowan. But we always knew he wasn't coming back from what happened to him. And you're the only one who can stop him from starting an apocalyptic war."

I shook my head. "I'm not going to kill him."

Kas breathed in deeply, his amber eyes gleaming. "Only an heir to the throne can kill a king."

I threaded my fingers into my hair, and memories of Orion's midnight voice whispered through my thoughts.

Because being without you was the same maddening grief of loss...I wasn't really free of the dungeon until you brought me out.

My breath was coming too quickly, my heart beating out of control. I couldn't explain what was happening, only that deep in my soul, I felt he didn't need killing. He needed saving.

And in the meantime, I needed the mortals to evacuate every town around here.

"I have to go to the police," I muttered.

I didn't wait to hear the others' response because I knew what they wanted from me. Something I wasn't ready to give them—the death of a king.

I knew this town like the back of my hand, and I started sprinting for the police station, a one-woman rampage along Gallows Hill Road. My powers hadn't quite returned to me yet after that poison, but they were slowly trickling back. With the wind in my hair, I picked up speed, hurtling up the hill. It was cold out here, the November chill biting at my skin.

But by the time I realized my destination, I was out of steam and breathless, my legs burning. I'd used up most of my energy.

I slammed through the door into the police station anyway, finding a guard working at the desk. She rose, alarmed, and put up her hands, asking me to stop. "Can I help you with something?"

I rested my hands on my knees, trying to catch my breath. "We need to evacuate the city." I pointed toward the City of Thorns. "They're coming. In three days, the demons are coming to feast. To hunt. They're going to try to kill everyone."

"Okay, ma'am? I'm going to need you to calm down. Have you ingested any substances today that could be affecting your mental state? Any alcohol? Drugs?"

I was shaking, vaguely aware that my hair was wild and that it might have vomit in it. "No, but I *have* been poisoned." Some part of me was aware that I wasn't communicating in a way that suggested I was sane. "I'm a demon. I'm supposed to be the queen."

"Ma'am, you appear to be under the effect of a substance of some kind. If you have a care coordinator—"

"I'm not on drugs," I shouted. "I'm telling you about a real threat." I pointed back at the City of Thorns. "I'm a demon. I know the king personally..." *Fuck.* "Look, demons from the City of Thorns are planning an attack on Osborne. It's revenge for something that happened several hundred years ago. I need you to get me in touch with someone who can help."

She nodded at me slowly, then drummed her fingers on the desk. She stood before a locked door, and I wasn't getting through it without her permission. Or violence, which I was trying to avoid. "We haven't had any reports of threats from the City of Thorns' leadership." She narrowed her eyes. "Are you with the demon hunters?"

Of course. Orion had already bought as much influence as he needed.

"Is there someone else I can speak to?" I asked desperately. "A detective? The police chief?"

"Ma'am, I'm going to ask you to step outside now, okay?" She started moving from behind the desk.

A little strength was crackling back into my body, and I raised my hand, summoning enough magic that fire flickered from my fingertips. "See? I'm trying to let you know about a credible threat—"

The officer drew her gun, and my stomach dropped as she started barking for backup. I turned and fled out the door again.

❦

I HUDDLED ON THE SOFA OF SHAI'S AUNT'S HOUSE WITH my new mobile phone. With shaking hands, I called one person after another to report the need for an immediate evacuation. A senator's office. Homeland Security hotlines. The FBI.

I opened the window, screaming at the mortals to leave.

But demons and mortals hadn't been at war in centuries, and most people had forgotten it was a possibility. None of them knew anything about a grimoire, or that the magical boundaries placed on demons could be dissolved.

And every one of them thought I was insane.

My phone buzzed—a message from Kas.

Where are you? I'm going to help you, Sunshine. I promise xo

I shoved the phone back in my pocket, choking down my ragged sense of loss. I wasn't giving up on Orion this easily.

I lay flat on the sofa, trying to clear my head. Everyone in the City of Thorns had been telling me all along that things weren't always what they seemed. That I couldn't trust anyone, not even my own senses.

So what did I believe deep down? What did my instincts say? I covered my eyes with my arm, and my mind looped back to the night I'd been attacked in Orion's house. Someone fled out the window, and Orion came out of his room.

My instincts told me my assailant hadn't been Orion. Someone, somehow, had been impersonating the king, convincing others that he was trying to kill me.

Deep down in my soul, I knew he wasn't responsible for this. We were the twin stars, and I knew him as well as he knew himself. His fear of snakes. His crushing guilt. The lacerating loneliness of all those years, so indescribable that he'd imagined a friend in the next cell. And the way all that pain had finally started to heal when someone finally showed him he was worth saving.

I didn't have a doubt in my mind. The person who'd stood before the clocktower and declared me a traitor— that wasn't Orion.

An incessant ringing was interrupting my thoughts, and I bolted upright on the sofa, irritated.

Was that...a landline?

The phone kept ringing as the call came in again, and I followed the sound into the kitchen. When I peered down at the phone, I read the caller ID displayed on the back.

A 508 area code—all the way down near the country-side of Sudbury. My heart sped up.

Were there some remaining hunters trying to get in touch with Shai?

I picked up the phone, staying silent.

"You have a collect call from"—a robotic voice cut off, and I heard my old friend's voice say, "*Shai Morton,*" before the recording continued—"at the Massachusetts Correctional Institution in Concord. Do you accept the charges?"

My heart hammered as I cleared my throat. "Yes."

The phone line clicked. "Hello? Camille?" I'd recognize my friend's voice anywhere.

"*Shai?*"

A long pause. "Wait. Rowan? Oh, thank the gods. What happened? Fuck. Did Orion win? I haven't been able to get any demon news in here."

My mind whirled at her barrage of questions. "Shai. Why are you *in prison?*"

"I was arrested in Sudbury when I was waiting for you by the southern entrance. Even though I was invisible. I can't really go into the specifics here on the phone. But is there any chance you can bail me out? I've been desperately calling my aunt and my mom to get me out of here so I could get to you. There are things I need to explain.

Someone screwed us over, Rowan. We just...can't talk about it on the phone. But I *really* need to warn you."

Yeah, I supposed we couldn't mention murdering an entire cadre of demon hunters on the jail phone. "Why didn't you call me?" I practically shouted.

"They took my phone when they arrested me. These are the only numbers I have memorized."

"It wouldn't have mattered anyway, I guess," I muttered. "My other phone evaporated."

"What?"

"Never mind." I gripped the phone tightly. "So...that's why you disappeared? You've been in jail this whole time? How much is the bail?"

She cleared her throat. "Can you get a hundred thousand dollars? I know it's a lot."

Fuck.

Orion could easily get a hundred thousand, but it's not like I could hit him up for that right now. Or really anyone I could think of. "I've been kicked out of the City of Thorns. That's why I'm hiding here. Something's happened to Orion. I'll try to get the money, though—"

"So he won the trial and just kicked you out?" Anger laced her voice.

I closed my eyes, trying to understand how to explain this to her without sounding like an absolute fucking moron. "That's what it looks like on the surface," I said carefully. "But like you said, we need to talk in person."

"Hang on." I heard the sound of her muffling the phone and talking to someone behind her. "Shit. Rowan, I've got to go. I'm going to try to call back soon."

Shouting echoed in the background, and then she hung up. I needed to talk to her *now,* though.

I crossed to the window, staring at the exact spot where I'd seen the boy with his cotton-candy fingers in my dream. Now, casually sitting on a bench outside, sipping a coffee, was my disturbingly hot cousin.

Sabazios—Mr. Esposito—had a habit of turning up when I needed him. I remembered him. He'd come to our house for tea and biscuits and bring my mom books he liked. He'd given me warnings when the hunters were coming for me. Sabazios was the one who'd given me the demon trials book. He'd been there on the fringes, helping me the whole time, without ever being intrusive or pushy.

I turned and ran down the stairs to find him.

ROWAN

The wind whipped at Sabazios's red hair as he drove away from the Concord prison, the windows down in his new convertible. Chilly October air stung my cheeks.

The setting sun tinged the sky with honey and lavender, warming our faces as we drove toward Osborne.

From the back seat, Shai leaned forward. "How did you get the money?" she shouted over the wind. "And the Porsche?"

"The first thing I did when I got back into the City of Thorns was find my family's buried gold," Sabazios replied. "So if I'm stuck in Osborne again, at least I can do it in style." He coughed. "Or as much style as an old man can have. My magic is already fading. I hate it. But at least I'll be rich, and I can buy a fancier walker."

"We're going to get you home," said Shai. "This is just a temporary setback. But Rowan, here's what I need you to know. Someone fucked us over. Someone told the state police where I was the day we went to the demon hunters' headquarters. They were waiting for me right at the southern entrance, and even though I was completely invisible, they were able to find me."

"But why were you arrested, Shai?" I asked.

She let out a long sigh. "Either Legion or Kas screwed us. Or both of them."

I swallowed hard and turned around to face her. "Explain."

"Okay, so...a few weeks ago, Legion and Kas were helping me learn a spell to control the weather. It was just the three of us. That's it. And I lost control of the spell. I have no idea how it happened, but it was too much all at once, and I caused a storm in the Atlantic. Or someone I was *with* caused it, because I didn't feel like I was losing control at all."

My mind flicked back to the night of thunder booms and a churning sea, when Jasper had attacked me. "Yeah, I remember the storm."

"I didn't tell you about it because you had so much stress already. But either Kas or Legion reported to the mortal police that it was my fault. No one was killed, but it wrecked a ship and caused a bunch of property damage. Then the cops knew exactly where to find me. I've been freaking out this entire time because I had no idea what happened to you."

My veins buzzed with anger. "Do you think it was both of them?"

She stared at me for a long time before answering. "I think it was Kas. I don't have a rational explanation, but I just don't think Legion would do that to me. I think he actually cares about me. Like, I *know* him. Does that sound stupid?"

I shook my head. "That's how I feel about Orion, even when I watched him call me a traitor and kick me out of the City of Thorns. I know him, and that wasn't him. Orion technically won the trial, but he *gave* me the book in Sudbury. He left himself behind just to save me. He sacrificed himself to torture, and he only won because I went back for him and exploded with magic. *That* was the real Orion. I know the real Orion. And the person who kicked me out? That wasn't him."

"Okay," she said tentatively. "Magic can create so many illusions, Rowan."

"Kas told me not to trust anyone, not even him. He said a demon never lets you know all the kinds of magic they've mastered because it's an advantage to keep their weapons hidden."

She swallowed hard. "Yeah, well, he was right about not trusting him. But what do we do now?"

My phone buzzed again, and my hands shook as I read another message from Kas.

"What is it?" The wind whipped at Shai's dark curls.

I took a deep breath, staring at the text. "Kas says he managed to trap Orion in the dungeon, and he can break the wards to let me in there. He says I can't trust anyone, and I shouldn't speak to anyone, and it's time for me to take matters into my own hands."

"He's desperate to end Orion's life," said Shai. "This isn't even subtle."

I swallowed hard. "He's panicking."

As the Porsche hurled northeast on Route 128, I felt sick.

"What, exactly, are we doing?" asked Sabazios. "For your mother's sake and yours, I'll do anything in my power to protect you, but please just clue me in."

"Thank you, Sabazios." I pulled out my phone and flicked to Legion's number. "Before we get too close to the city walls, let's start by trying to find out whether Legion is working with Kas. As subtly as we can."

"He isn't," said Shai from the back seat.

"Okay, but let me prove it, Shai." I dialed Legion's number, and he picked up after just one ring.

"Rowan?" he asked in a loud whisper. "What's happening?"

"Legion, have you been back into the City of Thorns, by any chance?"

"Yeah," he said, sounding surprised. "I'm here now. Invisible, of course. I wanted to see what Orion was doing. He's been making speeches throughout the day at the Tower of Baal. He has a crowd there thoroughly worked up. Seems completely unhinged."

I closed my eyes. "When was the last time you saw him?"

"I just left one of his rants fifteen minutes ago. He's talking about enslaving mortals and seeking revenge on them. He's lost his mind."

I took a deep breath. "I'm a bit confused because Kas sent me a text saying Orion was locked in the dungeons right now."

"*What*? No. Kas told you that?" he asked, baffled. "I

haven't been able to find him since you ran off. Are you sure it was him?"

It would appear Kas hadn't filled in Legion on his latest lies. "What do you know about Kas's magical abilities?"

A long pause met me on the other line. "Why don't you ask him?"

"Why don't I ask him?" I replied. "Because I'm trying to figure out who the fuck to trust, and—"

Shai grabbed the phone from my hand and turned on the speaker. "Legion, it's Shai. Someone turned me in to the mortal police in Sudbury. Now that someone was either you or Kas. We all know someone from our team gave advanced warning to the hunters, the cops. So if you have any knowledge of Kas's abilities, now is the time to tell us. How good is he at creating illusions? Can he glamour himself to look like another person?"

Legion waited so long to answer, I almost thought he'd hung up. "Shai," he said softly, at last. "Are you all right?"

"Yeah, it's me. Straight from the Massachusetts Correctional Institution in Concord. Can you answer my question?"

"Kas is extremely powerful, yes," he said at last. "He's an artist. You've seen his work. His illusions are as skilled as his drawings. Yes. He can appear as another person. He really loathes the entire concept of the monarchy. But I have a hard time believing—"

"Legion," she interrupted, cutting him off. "Sorry, but that's all we needed to know."

"It's not Orion," I shouted. "It's *Kas*, Legion! Pretending to be him. He created the illusion. I'm going to guess you haven't seen the two of them in the same place at the same time today."

"I haven't," he admitted.

"Meet us outside the City of Thorns," said Shai. "Where the secret entrance leads underground. Stay away from Kas and King Orion. We're going to need to work together."

"And Legion?" I shouted. "I'm going to need more of that antidote."

✣ 42 ✣
ORION

I lay on the cold stone floor of my own cell, my hands bound behind my back. The caustic poison slid through my veins. In a few days, the poison wouldn't matter. In the dungeons, outside the city walls, my magic would ebb from me.

I'd be locked in here once more—my old home.

Kas had bound my wrists behind my back and gagged my mouth. I'd left my cottage before dawn because I'd wanted to bring Rowan back my favorite fresh bread. I didn't need guards—at least, that's what I'd thought.

But all it had taken was a few darts fired from a distance, and I'd fallen to my knees.

I remembered Kasyade, all those years ago. When the mortals had taken me from my home and marched me past Molor's severed head on my way out, Kasyade had been standing there, watching it all. An older boy, a friend of Molor's, he'd watched it unfold. I'd screamed at him for help, and he'd done nothing. Hadn't even looked upset. He'd just watched.

He'd always been competitive with Molor, resentful of his aristocratic background. I remember thinking that Kasyade was delighted to see his friend's head ripped off.

Kasyade must think I was going to end his life at some point for that.

And he was probably right.

The cloth in my mouth smelled of some kind of oil, and I wanted to vomit, but that would make the situation considerably worse. The effect of the Ladon venom and hawthorn was only getting more painful, and I wasn't sure how much longer I'd be conscious here, or if I'd ever wake again.

The worst fucking thing was that Kas had probably learned about this particular poison from the demon hunters after Rowan had been captured.

A tiny light burned in my chest. Would Rowan know the truth?

Kas said she wouldn't. He said she'd come to rip out my heart, that she didn't really trust me anymore.

From the damp floor, my gaze slid over the carvings in the walls. It had always been so quiet in here during the decades when they didn't even bring us food.

It had just been Ashur and me, starving together in cells side by side.

My gaze flicked to the noose hanging across from my cell, where I'd last seen my mother. They'd left her there so long...

Ashur had shown up right after she'd died, I think. Mom and I had been the last ones, then Ashur. My thoughts were growing foggy, and I couldn't remember where he'd been before she'd died.

And his face—I couldn't remember that, either. He'd been strong, and then he'd grown weak. He'd lost his mind. But every time I tried to remember his expression as he was dragged away to his death, I only saw my own—an agonized, ravaged visage. My own.

The poison must be confusing me.

On the stone floor, my body shook. I loathed feeling weak. My gaze slid over those carvings of the queen with her spiky crowns. Even as a little boy, I'd hated feeling weak, so the slashes in the stone had been vicious, brutal.

My eyes started to drift closed, and I could hear my mom saying my name in her soothing voice, like she was right there.

"Ashur."

A jolt of recognition ripped through me.

The crack of stone, the noose swinging in the gallows. The heartbreak that tore me in two.

Ashur had arrived. Someone older, stronger.

Someone who'd taught me to be angry instead of scared, to stay sane by marinating in wrath instead of sorrow. Someone I'd promised to avenge.

Someone who'd never existed at all.

Ashur.

The name Kasyade had called me when he'd dumped my limp body here in the dark, because he remembered me better than I remembered myself.

But all those thoughts drifted away from me as the venom started to seep into my brain, and all that was left was her—

Rowan.

My light in the darkness.

❧ 43 ❧
ROWAN

Shadows thickened around Osborne as night fell, and an autumn chill nipped at our skin.

In an alley around the corner from the gates to the City of Thorns, I stood in the shadows. Here was my new team—Shai, Legion, and Sabazios. Fallen autumn leaves spread out beneath us.

Every time you put trust in someone, it was a risk. But all the same, I didn't think I could do this without them.

"Okay," I said, "let's lay our cards on the table. I know it's not part of demon culture, but we have to be honest right now."

Sabazios's green eyes locked on me. "I always have been. Especially after you gave me those elasticated pants to protect my dignity. And do you know that I gave you that bear you always had with the red sweater you chewed on until it ripped..."

My eyes misted. "Mr. Huggins?"

He nodded.

Legion stood with his arms folded, eyes averted from me.

"Legion!" I grabbed his arm. "I need to know if you're with us or not."

His eyes slid to me. "I've known Kas for centuries. Since before the City of Thorns was built." He glanced at Shai, his features softening. "But he's always kept secrets. He's always had an angry side that he hid from the rest of the world. Without the Lightbringers, he'd be the most powerful demon in the city. He's never told me he had anything planned, or that he was going to call the police on Shai. It was all behind my back, using me for information. I knew there was something about that storm that night...I didn't think Shai lost control of it. Someone was causing it." His eyes were still locked on Shai. "And you are where my heart lies now, Shai. So yes, I'm on your side."

She beamed at him, her eyes twinkling. "Good."

He turned to me again. "And yours. Kas wants Orion off the throne for good, and I did, too. I wanted to replace him. But unlike Kas, I have limits to what I'll do to stop him. It's no good getting rid of an unstable maniac if we just replace him with another one."

I nodded. "Okay. Not the most ringing endorsement of Orion, but I'll take it. Now we lay our cards on the table about what powers we actually have."

"Fuck knows anymore," said Sabazios. "But I can tell you what I used to be able to do."

"And Legion?" Shai brushed her hand over his bicep, and that was all it took to make his eyes darken. "We're gonna need to know exactly what Kas can do."

MY MUSCLES HAD GONE TENSE, AND A QUIET RAGE coursed through my blood.

The last time I'd trod this path, it had been on a mission to beat Orion in the first trial. Now my body hummed with fury at the thought that Kas had laid a finger on him.

So as I approached the old stone overpass—the one that shielded a secret door into the city—I focused on masking my true emotions.

I stood before the vine-covered door under the bridge and knocked on it four times. Our signal.

A little flicker of magic crackled over the door, and Kas pushed it open. He looked exhausted, his eyes shadowed. His blond hair was wild.

I swallowed hard as I stared at him, schooling my features. "Kas. I'm so glad you're here to help me." The words tasted like acid on my tongue.

He ran a hand through his hair, feigning anxiety as we walked through the dark tunnel. We were both wearing masks here.

"He wanted to execute you as a traitor, Rowan. I had to do something. Even if it was dangerous. Orion would destroy our city, and he'd hunt you down. I couldn't accept either."

Acting cool when my mind was racing at a million miles a minute has never been my thing. Months before, I could barely handle the pressure of giving a psychology presentation. And now here I was, strolling next to a powerful enemy, on the way to break a demon king out of jail.

Even if *I* wasn't good at acting cool, Mortana was. My sister, my dark shadow. I let my hips sway a little, pure composure, as Kas led me into the dungeons.

"I feel stupid for letting him fool me again," I said, my voice steady. "I actually thought he'd changed. But he's just the same Orion who threw me out before. How did you capture him?"

"It wasn't easy, but I used the venom. The demon hunters taught me that, I guess. I imagine this is an old secret of theirs, the way they stopped the Lilu from fighting back all those years ago."

Underneath my placid smile lurked a deep well of fury. "Thank you for looking out for me, Kas."

We crossed into the dungeons themselves. In here, a haunted sense of pain thickened the air. It slid into my lungs and settled in my bones as Kas led me to Orion's cell and pulled out an old iron skeleton key to unlock the door.

My heart was ready to shatter as I looked at Orion, who lay unconscious on the floor. Kas had locked him up in his old cell with his arms bound. His dark eyelashes swept over his cheeks, still beautiful as ever, even now.

Legion's warnings played in the back of my mind: *The moment Kas realizes something is wrong, his claws will be in your chest, ripping out your heart.*

"I know this will be hard for you, Rowan," said Kas, his voice dripping with feigned sympathy. "But I also know you're a survivor. And a protector. You won't let him destroy you or our kingdom."

I stepped into the cell and glanced back at Kas. Behind him, the noose swayed in a phantom breeze.

"Could you give me a minute alone with him?" I asked.

A muscle twitched in his square jaw, but then the bland smile returned. "Of course."

He stepped back into the shadows, and I crossed into the cell.

I reached into my pocket, and my fingers tightened around the syringe filled with the antidote. But as soon as I started to pull it out, I could already feel the burst of Kas's smooth magic wrapping around me, tendrils of silk that slid around my neck, cutting off my air.

That was when I understood exactly how powerful Kas could be—even down here, where magic started to fade.

✦ 44 ✦

ORION

It was her scent that made my eyes flutter open, and the warmth of skin bathed in light.

For a moment, I wondered if I'd died. Of course *she'd* be the first person I'd think about in the afterworld—her presence. And it was as if I could feel, that deliciously warm magic like the glow of summer. The scent of ripe fruit...

My heart went still. I couldn't feel her now. A dreadful silence hung over me.

I opened my eyes, and my blurry gaze swept over my cell walls. With a hazy sense of dread, I wondered if this would be my afterworld. Just—here. Forever.

Rowan.

I felt her soul calling to mine. My fingers flexed behind my back.

Maybe I wasn't dead, then.

My heart still beat. And tiny rivulets of strength were flowing through me once more, from my thigh upward.

I glanced down to see an emptied syringe jutting from

my upper thigh, and from that syringe, strength was coursing through my body. The antidote.

Where was Rowan, then?

Fear snapped through my nerves, making my muscles go rigid.

Someone was screaming nearby. A male voice I hated...

"You think you're the hero?" he was bellowing. "A leader chosen by finding a magic crown? Or a book? Fucking trinkets and games? A twenty-two-year-old with no magical knowledge. What the fuck do you think you deserve?"

I strained my gaze upward again. And that was when I saw her—

She swiped her claws across Kas's face, drawing blood. But his retaliation was swift and brutal. Spidery tendrils of his magic bound her arms. He lifted her by the throat, his claws springing from his fingertips—

My blood roared.

I would end him. I would tear him apart, piece by piece. I would feed these old stones with his blood.

I hardly had any strength in my body. But for her, it was enough to rip through the ropes binding my wrists.

My world went silent apart from the sound of my heart beating, a war drum in my chest. As I rushed to my feet, I tore the gag from my mouth, and my fangs lengthened.

Rowan was just breaking out of the bindings, her claws ready. She struck Kas across the chest, and blood arced through the air. When he spun, facing me, I drew my own claws, ready to eviscerate him.

But where I'd just been staring at Kas, Rowan now stood before me, looking terrified.

Two Rowans, both soaked in blood. I staggered back, trying to work out what the fuck was real here.

And while I was making that calculation, one of the Rowans disappeared into shadows.

The other stumbled forward, clutching her neck. Blood poured from her throat, and I caught her around the waist. By her scent and the way she folded into me, I knew it was her.

I pulled her in close to me. "You're still losing blood. We need to get you out of the tunnels."

"He can shapeshift," she rasped.

"I just about put that together."

She turned to me, one hand around her bleeding neck. "Get to safety. I've got this under control."

She must be fucking joking. As if I'd leave her to fight an ancient demon alone.

Rowan was already off, racing after Kas, blood trailing behind her. I ignored the ache in my muscles as I ran after her, trying to keep up. She was a blur of speed through the tunnels, like smoke disappearing between my fingers. But as soon as we burst into the City of Thorns, my magic would be restored.

I watched her shimmy up the side of the tunnel and disappear through the opening. Fatigue corroded my bones as I forced myself forward and up the tunnel wall.

At last, under the canopy of the stars, my magic surged through me. First, Rowan brought my soul out of the dungeon, then my body.

I roared as my wings burst from my back, and I followed my love into the clear night sky.

❧ 45 ❧

ROWAN

As soon as I'd hoisted myself into the City of Thorns, my magic had slammed into me with the force of the ocean. I took to the skies, swooping under the stars to search for Kas.

Orion's warm magic beamed over my body as I felt him soaring near me. The wind rushed over my wings, whipping at my hair as I raced above the trees. This was the old Lilu way—washed in silvery moonlight, hungry for blood. Hunting from the skies while our prey scuttled around on foot.

My heart slammed against my ribs at the strange thrill, and I turned to catch Orion's gaze. His pale eyes gleamed at me, and his demon mark, the star of Lucifer, beamed from his forehead. Divine.

We were Lightbringers. And when the shadows consumed us, we'd rise again.

I just hoped Orion wasn't going to unleash his power until the right time, because I wanted to leave this city standing.

I breathed deeply, catching Kas's perfumed scent. He'd cloaked himself, of course, so I couldn't see him. But it didn't matter. In the old days, we hadn't used vision to hunt, and I could sense him moving toward the Tower of Baal—which was exactly what I'd feared. Kas was calculating that as long as he was around enough other demons, we wouldn't use our Lightbringer powers. We wouldn't want to destroy the whole city, after all, and everyone in it. Who wants to rule a city of dust?

But unlike the Lilu of the old days, I had a cell phone to coordinate. So as I swooped through the air, I pulled it from my pocket and called Legion.

"Yes," Legion whispered. "What's happening?"

"Can you clear the area before the Tower of Baal? I'm closing in on Kas, but we can't have anyone around. And make sure you get to safety when you need to, got it?"

I shoved the phone back in my pocket and circled above the esplanade. A throng of demons stood before the tower.

Storm clouds churned above, and an icy wind began sweeping across the stones. The temperature in the air plummeted so quickly, my teeth started chattering, and my breath misted around me in the dark.

Lightning speared the sky, and a maelstrom of ice spun from the center of the square, forcing the crowd away. Screams rose as people started to flee. A crack of Shai's lightning touched down on the stones—and another, scorching the rocks beneath us. The glacial storm lashed at us, and I fought to keep control as I flew. Snow and hail whipped at me. Legion's magical storm sent a chill right down to my marrow, and the gale battered at my wings, my feathers. Shivering, I touched down in the cleared space.

Orion landed by my side, his coal-dark eyes scanning for signs of our prey. Legion seemed to have cleared a space for us, an eye in the storm. My muscles started to soften again, and my breathing slowed.

We could hunt for Kas, or we could get him to come to us. A man like him might be powerful, but his ego would get in the way. That's really what all this was about, wasn't it? His mortally offended ego.

A twenty-two-year-old with no magical knowledge. What the fuck do you think you deserve?

Kas might hate Orion, but that wasn't what really lit the fire beneath him. He thought *he* should be on the throne.

An icy squall swept the air around me, but I rooted my feet to the ground and stood in the center of the stones to address the crowd. "Kasyade has deceived you," I shouted above the winds, hoping the crowds could hear. "He used his magical glamor to take the form of your king. But he's a poor substitute, a shadow of your true king. Kas was not blessed by the gods as we were. He's an illusion, a commoner, and nothing more than a charlatan."

"Blessed by the gods?" Kas's voice boomed, but I couldn't see him yet. "The gods are insane. Let the people choose! Let the demons see who deserves to rule! Let he who possesses the most skill take the throne!"

"You want the people to choose—the same people you're willfully deceiving?" Orion snarled. "The same people you've been lying to?"

"I was protecting them," came Kas's voice. "Neither of you are fit to rule. I studied magic for centuries. While you were locked in a prison losing your mind, Ashur, I was dedicated to the craft. To our history. To understanding what a demon truly is. And Rowan, long before you were born, I'd memorized every spell book in the city's libraries. Suddenly, you stumble in, ignorant of our world, and think you deserve the crown? Because of an accident of birth?"

"Why don't you show yourself?" shouted Orion. "Since you're so confident of your skills. Let's see who survives, shall we?"

They burst into silvery light before us—six versions of Kas. All tattooed, muscular, and glowing with pale light. A demon mark shaped like a crescent moon glowed on their foreheads, and their eyes were dark as pitch. Orion's claws shot from his fingertips, and he slashed at one of them, then another. He was moving at the speed of lightning, but every time he struck one, a new one appeared.

Silky threads whipped around me, ripping me from the earth, high into the sky. They slammed me back down again, breaking me hard on the stones. The agony splintered me, and for a moment, I felt each of my bones shatter before they started to heal again.

From the ground, I looked up at the sky, where inky shadows spread above us all—a shield of ice and shadow, trapping us inside.

There it was—Sabazios and Legion, working together. Exactly as planned.

Good.

Darkness wrapped over us.

The tendrils of silky magic spiraled around me again, lifting me high into the crushing darkness—

But it didn't matter anymore because I was summoning my light.

❦ 46 ❧

ORION

Do not mistake me for a hero. I'd destroy the entire world to save the person I loved the most.

Shadows slid over us, and I could no longer see Rowan.

The terror of losing her unmoored me until I hardly knew which way was up and which was down. If I lost Rowan now, the world would stop again—a frozen clock-tower, a stilled heart. A world of silence.

Once, I'd failed to protect those I loved. This time, I'd burn my enemies to cinders, even if I had to take the rest of the city down with them.

Because I only loved her—Rowan. She was the beginning and the end for me. And when someone was hurting her, I'd tear the stars from the skies and hurtle them like spears.

Rowan and I would be the last ones standing, and that would have to be enough.

Ice and shadows enveloped me, and my thoughts began to spin wildly into little pinpricks of light. A queen with a spiked crown. Molor teaching me to play chess. My mother telling me her birthday would be next week—always next week. A beautiful woman with red hair sleeping in my arms, someone who meant the world to me now. A soft hand against my face bringing me to life again. Leading me from the dungeons to the world beneath the stars.

Order and chaos...a light falling into the underworld.

Shadows consumed my light.

I am Chaos. I am the beginning and the end.

I will consume.

🦋 47 🦋

ROWAN

The light bloomed in the darkness, pale gold and blinding. It swelled to fill the shadows under the shield, burning away each illusion of Kas until all I could see was light. I hadn't even finished summoning my own before Orion's exploded under the shield like a dying star.

Hot magic rushed over me, into my blood and bones, healing my broken body. Orion's infernal light was a baptism of pure flame, and it gave me strength.

Kas was now nothing more than particles drifting around in a glittering mist.

Slowly, the light started to fade, leaving behind a world of shimmering dust—and only one other person remained.

Orion lay naked on the ground, surrounded by glittering motes of light and the darkness sweeping over us. Warmth flooded my chest as I looked at him.

I pushed myself up from where I'd landed and hurried over to him, resting his head in the crook of my arm. His dark eyelashes fluttered, and he opened his eyes. Pale blue eyes, flecked with silver, stared back at me. He was in there, but dazed, unfocused.

A faint smile curled his lips, and he reached up to touch my cheek. "You're here."

I smiled down at him, brushing his hair from his eyes. "You saw the shield."

His brow furrowed. "Shield?"

My eyebrows rose.

So maybe Orion was fine with destroying the entire city with his Lightbringer power. I supposed it was a good thing he'd have me to rein him in, because I wasn't leaving him.

I glanced up at the haze of light and shadow until the stars began to appear in the sky again and the shield slid away. The shimmering mist around us drifted into the night, whirls of gold that floated toward the moon. Orion still looked delirious from the burst of his light, but I slid my arm around his back and lifted him to his feet. He leaned into me, nuzzling me, as I surveyed the damage.

A large circle surrounded us, and the stones beneath us had been destroyed. On the edges of that circle, where the shield had been protecting us, a crowd stood gaping. The Tower of Baal loomed behind them, nearly obscured by the haze of dust.

I caught Legion's eye, finding him standing by Shai and Sabazios.

It was at this point I thought about the fact that Orion and I were completely naked, because the blast had destroyed our clothes.

I stood tall anyway. We were Lilu, and we weren't ashamed of our bodies.

"This is your king, Orion," I shouted. "And I am your queen! We will protect you, but we will not start a war with the mortals to do it. And we will never sacrifice you like Nergal once did. We will not bend to unreasonable demands. Our city will be a beacon of light in the darkness."

I heard them chanting my name and Orion's as I supported his waist. I was taking him home.

I STRADDLED ORION AND BRUSHED MY THUMB OVER HIS lower lip. He nipped at it, then tugged at his magical restraints.

I leaned down and kissed his throat, feeling the muscles in his shoulder jump.

"Rowan," he growled, "it's been a week. You can let me free now. I'm fully healed."

I kissed his chest. "I can't be sure."

When I looked up, I caught an indulgent smile on his lips. "I already presided over your coronation. I've proven myself healed."

I pressed a finger over his lips. "That's too much talking from you. You'll wear yourself out."

I nibbled at his lower lip. As I did, the sound of voices rose up through the stone floor.

"I think Amon has company," I said. My ears perked at the sound of a female voice. "Is that Shai?"

"Perhaps some clothes are in order, then," said Orion.

I frowned and released the magical restraints. "What day is it?"

"I have absolutely no idea."

We'd hardly left Orion's room in the past week, and dates no longer had meaning.

I jumped off him and pulled open a drawer, yanking out underwear and a long black dress. "I think Shai's birthday is this week."

"Ah! I'll get the sacrificial altar ready. Perhaps there's a criminal we could slaughter in her honor..."

I turned to him as I slipped into my underwear. "You know, Orion, I still can't quite tell when you're joking, but I think drinks and music will be sufficient for Shai."

I pulled a dress over my head, and it hung to my ankles.

When I went downstairs, I found a little crew sitting around the table, sipping wine with Amon.

Shai was sitting on Legion's lap. Sabazios was extravagantly dressed in a maroon velvet suit with a black shirt underneath. "Rowan!" He beamed. "Your Majesty."

"Let's go with Rowan."

"Come on," said Shai, lifting her glass. "It's my birthday. And it's two-for-one cocktail night at *Cirque de la Mer*."

My eyes widened. "Ooh, I need a flatbread. And mojitos. And now that I'm queen, I'm buying."

Barefoot and shirtless, Orion entered the kitchen wearing only a dark pair of jeans. He ruffled his hair. "You're going to spend the night among mortals?"

I blinked at him. "And you're coming. I've never seen you dance to Daft Punk."

"And you never will, my queen. But I'll join you anyway."

"Good," said Shai. "Because I want to help plan the

wedding. And I guess you might have some thoughts about it, but, like, what if the ceremony was in the old disused temple of Asmodeus? Ceremonies are usually so boring, so maybe there could also be a cocktail bar for that part. Then we could have the party in the wilderness, but we'd turn part of it into a garden. Total 'whimsical enchanted forest' vibe, with the food on wooden discs like tree trunks, and—"

"Shai?" Orion interrupted. He pulled on a shirt and started buttoning it. "I'm not sure about whimsy. There are the ancient Lilu wedding customs: the oils and perfumes, the consummation before the guests, the augury with the entrails of a slaughtered pigeon—"

I cleared my throat. "Let's just go out for drinks, maybe?"

"Fine." Orion slipped into his shoes. "If I'm going to hang out with mortals, I will be flying there." He turned back to Shai. "What do you want for your birthday?"

"For you to have a whimsical themed wedding?" she said.

Orion turned away, heading out into the night. Sabazios followed after him—no doubt lured by the inexorable tug of an incubus to the skies.

I turned to Amon. "Come with us! When was the last time you went out in Osborne?"

He frowned, his scar deepening. "I've literally never gone out in Osborne. Mortals and demons don't mix."

I looped my arm through his as I walked to the door. "That changes tonight, Amon."

The more time demons and mortals spent around each

other, the more they'd realize that apart from lifespan, they had plenty in common.

Outside, I unhooked my arm from Amon's. I glanced up at the starry sky, where Orion and Sabazios were already circling overhead, their outlines lit with silvery moonlight. Breathtaking.

I turned to see Shai and Legion stepping outside, hand in hand. "Meet you guys there in twenty."

My wings burst from my back, and I raced into the sky, tasting the salty air. Exhilaration lit me from inside as I arced higher with the two incubi. It was so thrilling, all I could do was laugh wildly, and I could hear Sabazios and Orion doing the same. We'd all been missing this from our lives, and now that it was back, the thrill gave me life.

High up, I peered down at the City of Thorns, and it seemed to glow with gold in the night. The Lilu were free once more.

Maybe there'd come a time when we really did need to open the grimoire and free the demons completely. But for now, we had everything we needed here—and our little city was a light rising from the darkness again.

❧ 48 ❧

THIRTEEN YEARS LATER

I sensed him in the room, and when I opened my eyes, I saw him there—my little green-eyed boy, his eyes wide. I should be annoyed that he was waking me from the dead of sleep, but he was so ridiculously cute that it was hard to resent him here, even at this hour. Moonlight washed over him, and his auburn hair stuck up in all directions.

I glanced at Orion, who slept as still and immobile as a statue, not waking for any of this.

My little boy held one arm up. The other clutched his stuffed wolf, imaginatively named Wolfie. "I want snuggles," he said in his small voice, waiting to be picked up.

He was wearing his pajamas with the cartoon octopus that said, "More arms for hugs."

As I stared at him blearily, he reached out for the sheets and gripped them hard as he tried to pull himself up. Already, his bum was in the air, and he grunted with the effort.

I scooped under his bum to help him onto the bed. "Come on up here, sweet boy."

He nestled in tightly, trying to get the covers over himself. He was getting as close as he possibly could, like he wanted to crawl back into the space in which he'd once lived.

I wrapped him in a hug and pulled him close against my enormous, round stomach. "Be careful, baby. Remember, Mommy has a baby in here."

"Sorry, Mama," Nico said as he nuzzled into me. "And sorry, baby," he added as he reached down to pet my belly.

Nicodemus shoved the collar of his shirt in his mouth to chew on it, his favorite habit since we got rid of his pacifiers.

"The baby is fine," I assured him, rubbing his head. "Just too big."

"Hey, Nico." Orion reached over me, touching Nico's hair with sleepy fingers.

"Hi, Daddy," Nico replied. "I need to be in the middle." He climbed over me, carefully trying to avoid my stomach and stepping on my boobs instead. He settled in the gap, delighted to be between his two favorite people. "I'm the middle of the sandwich," he declared in a voice too loud for the hour.

Given the size of my belly, rolling over wasn't easy. But I flopped onto my back first until the lack of air from the baby made me shift again, and then I hoisted my large stomach over the other way. You'd *think* being a pregnant demon would be easier than being a pregnant mortal, but while I'd never experienced pregnancy as a mortal, I had a sneaking suspicion that this wasn't really a better deal.

When the gods had cursed women with this discomfort, it had applied to us all, demon and mortal alike.

My body finally relaxed when I was facing Nico and Orion, and I could breathe a little easier again. I slid my arm over Nico's toddler belly. "Go back to sleep, sweetie."

He furrowed his brow in deep thought before producing the question we'd come to expect on a nightly basis: "Are ghosts real?"

No need to ask what the bad dream was about. It was always the same.

And even though Orion and I knew firsthand that ghosts *were* real, and that they haunted the Asmodean Ward, I didn't see any reason to fill Nico in just yet. If we did, we'd be sharing our bed with him until he was at least a teenager.

"I don't believe they are," said Orion. "And even if they were, so what? They can't do anything. They're just like fog. Maybe the fog is a little sad sometimes, but the fog can't hurt us."

Nico nodded.

"And let's pretend," Orion added, "just for fun, since none of this is real anyway, that a ghost managed to get past the magical wards and then somehow got into our palace. What do you suppose would happen to that ghost when Mommy got a hold of it?"

"No more ghost?" Nico asked.

"That's right." My eyes started to drift shut. "No more ghost."

Of all the scary things in the world, especially in *our* world, my baby had, for some reason, glommed on to ghosts as being the worst kind of nightmare fuel. While I was no fan of hauntings, they posed no threat to any of us. Ghosts were insubstantial as smoke.

In any case, when it came to threats, our little Nico didn't have much to worry about.

Not once we learned what the gods had bestowed upon him.

ॐ

WITH A SMILE, I CRACKED ANOTHER ANZU EGG INTO THE bowl and whipped it. The scent of coffee filled the air, and sunlight streamed into our kitchen. Amon still came over for dinner in the evenings, but the mornings we had all to ourselves. At some point in the night, Orion had carried little Nico back to his room after he'd kicked us too many times in our sleep. Now Nico was slumbering away upstairs after an exhausting night of thinking about ghosts.

We'd moved into a new palace—larger than Orion's cottage, but smaller than the Tower of Baal. A palace of golden stone, filled from top to bottom with libraries, right across from the clock tower in the Asmodean Ward.

While we had several cooks, I liked making breakfast for my two boys, Orion and Nico. Granted, I also liked it when I slept in and Orion woke me with hot coffee and fruit.

I pulled out a loaf of fresh bread and started cutting slices to toast in the oven. I'd be slathering them in butter before piling them with the anzu eggs. We hadn't had any anzu eggs since before Nico was born, but now our son had developed a taste for scrambled eggs. An anzu was like nothing else, so I was already smiling at the thought of him tasting it for the first time.

There were only about three anzu in the Elysian Wilderness, demonic birds three times the size of condors, each one with the head of a lion. When they were hungry, they thought nothing of taking a horse or a cow for lunch. They loved to eat pigs. Demons weren't generally on the menu, but if the anzu were hungry enough, mortals would be advised to take cover.

Anzu eggs fetched a premium when they came to market, as harvesting them was a nasty, bloody business. If a group of hunters found a nest with a clutch of eggs inside and managed to spirit them away before the mother tore them all to pieces, they could live for a year or more on the profits.

As I was popping the bread in the oven, warm magic slid over me. I turned to see Orion crossing into the kitchen, shirtless, his silver hair ruffled. Even now, every time I looked at him, my breath caught.

His gaze swept down my body, and I heard his appreciative growl. "You're wearing my favorite silky green robe. Are you trying to tempt me?"

I rested a hand on my bump and felt the *thump thump* of little hands as the baby made his presence known. "I can barely move. I'm not trying to tempt anyone."

He quirked an eyebrow at the bright red eggshells. "Where did you get the anzu egg?"

"A gift from the Duchess of the Luciferian Ward herself, also known as Lydia."

Orion ran a hand through his hair. "Which means she

wants something from us for the next meeting of the Council."

I arched an eyebrow. "Apart from extra financing for Shalem Square, she's always wanted you."

"Of course." He slipped the green robe off my shoulder and started covering my bared skin in kisses. Heat tingled along every point of contact. "But she can't have me. Not for all the anzu eggs in the world."

I cupped my hand around the back of his neck. "Let me make breakfast, love, before Nico wakes up starving." The little guy didn't handle hunger well.

Orion checked his watch and frowned. "He's never slept until nine."

My heart started to beat faster. Was it nine already? Nico was normally up at seven or earlier. I supposed I shouldn't look a gift horse in the mouth.

I heard the distant sound of Orion's weight creaking on the stairs as I cracked another egg and added a dollop of cream to the mixture.

"Rowan!" Orion's voice pierced the silence, booming through the palace and echoing off the stone stairwell. "Where is Nico?"

I froze, and my heart slammed into my ribs.

As fast as my pregnant body would take me, I ran up the sweeping stone stairs into Nico's room. Orion stood in the center, clutching our boy's crimson blanket.

But Nico wasn't in the room.

All the air left my lungs. This shouldn't be a big deal. He was four and probably hiding somewhere. But Orion and I felt the same thing—the terrifying absence of Nico. We couldn't feel his magic now or hear his little heartbeat.

"Nico?" I shouted, my eyes scanning Nico's bed, bookshelf, and pile of toys.

Blue-uniformed soldiers began rushing to hall, their bodies tense, awaiting orders.

Orion's eyes darkened to night. "I can't sense him anywhere."

This palace exterior was protected with the most powerful wards and a horde of demon soldiers. We had layers of magical protection as well as the old-fashioned brute force of hellhounds patrolling the thorny gardens around it. If an intruder had come in, the hellhounds would have let us know.

I closed my eyes and concentrated. Orion and I shared a bond with Nicodemus that allowed us to always monitor his whereabouts psychically, no matter where he was.

I gasped for air. Right now, I felt nothing.

Orion raked a hand thorough his hair. "Search the house," he barked at the soldiers. Then, more quietly, he said, "He's probably in a closet or something."

Like all parents, we had been eager for our son to start walking. And like all parents, once he did, we wished he would stop. He wanted to climb everything, to know what was behind every locked door, in every cabinet and drawer. His curiosity and energy were boundless.

And now he was missing.

"I'm going to check the grounds outside," Orion said.

I went from room to room carrying Nico's blanket, calling his name, then quietly listening for a reply. Our soldiers were searching now, too, tearing the place apart piece by piece.

Silence met our calls, but I couldn't believe he was

gone—it just wasn't possible. I was furious at someone, but I couldn't quite pinpoint who it was. The soldiers who should be patrolling this place? Nico?

Myself, I thought.

In his bedroom, decorated with octopus imagery (his favorite), I started ripping the place apart with a growing sense of urgency—flinging blankets, pulling open the closet. The windows were closed, so he hadn't jumped out or been abducted. How could no one have seen him?

Exhausted, I sat down on his little bed.

What we needed was some magical help. I grabbed my phone and called the City of Thorns' best mortal oracle, Isabeau. There were magical ways to contact her, but she preferred text.

I wasn't waiting for a text now, though. I was calling her.

Midway through the first ring, she answered. "Good morning, Your Majesty," she greeted me. "Nico, is it? Missing?"

"Yes, thank you." Already, I was reassured that she knew what was happening. "We can't find him. I haven't seen him."

"Curious," the oracle replied. "Your sigils and glyphs are all in place. The wards continue to function."

"Yes, I believe so..."

"That wasn't a question." Her abilities allowed her some leeway when it came to snark, but I wasn't in the mood for her games.

"If they're in place, then where is Nico?" I demanded. "How could the spells have been bypassed? Who took him, and how are they shielding him from us?"

"So many questions," she answered slowly. "But no answers. If he were on this plane, I would know. If he'd left this plane, I would know that as well, even if I couldn't follow. He'd have left a trace behind."

Panic snapped through my body. "Is he in Osborne? With mortals?"

As I listened to her reply, Orion rushed into the room, all color drained from his face. He shrugged and turned both palms up in resignation.

"There are those with the talent to hide things from you," Isabeau observed. "And a very small number with the ability to conceal things from me. But none of them would have reason to harm your son. The person you need...the person who can help you...a duchess from the House of Shalem."

Orion motioned for me to hand him the phone.

"Lydia delivered anzu eggs to our cottage this morning," Orion informed the oracle. "I don't believe in coincidences." I watched him nod as he listened to Isabeau. "Find him. Do you understand?" He handed the phone back to me.

I nodded and stared at Nico's blanket in my hands. I considered a thought too awful to contemplate, and nausea rose in my gut. "Orion, if neither of us can sense him, and neither can the oracle, can it mean he's...he couldn't be..."

I had to keep a distance from that terrible thought, and Orion only shook his head. When he glanced over my shoulder at the soldiers, his eyes had turned the color of ink.

"Bring the Luciferian Duchess to me," he said, a deathly chill in his voice.

W E SAT ON THRONES. I DIDN'T WANT TO SIT ON A throne—I wanted to be running around, tearing the city apart for Nico. But apparently, the thrones were a show of power that could strike fear into someone and convince them to tell the truth. I gripped the edge of the throne, staring at her.

Lydia of the House of Shalem crossed into the marble hall before us with a grace that made it seem as if she were floating rather than walking. In her long red dress, her fiery tattoos were on display. It was hard to believe that she'd do something so rash. Years ago, when I was still mortal, she'd tried to kill me. But that was part of the initiation trials to enter the city, and since then, we'd been on good terms.

"Welcome back, Lydia," I said.

"I trust you enjoyed the eggs?"

"We're not here to talk about the eggs," said Orion evenly. "We're looking for our son. You were here this morning. Our oracle thought you might have an idea where he is."

"Me?" She put a finger to her lips. "Ah. My son used to go missing all the time. It was really very easy to find him."

I leaned forward over my belly. "How?"

She cupped her hands around her mouth and bellowed into the air, "Fig pudding!" Her voice echoed off the stones.

I stared at her, stunned. I'd never seen her do anything undignified before. But then, I supposed, I'd never seen her as a mom.

She turned to me, frowning. "That was a long time ago. Fig pudding was his favorite back then. What does your son like most in the world to eat?"

"Cotton candy," I said.

She cupped her hands to her mouth again. "The cotton candy will all be gone! Poor Nico won't have any left. Will everyone spread the word that the cotton candy is almost gone?"

He seemed to materialize from the shadows in the corners of the hall.

His face was tear-streaked, and his nose was runny. He'd obviously been crying. "I'm hungry, Daddy!"

Orion lifted Nico into the air and wrapped his arms around him. Nico was red-faced, already searching for the promised cotton candy. He was about to burst into hungry tears when he realized there was none here, but he was back with us all the same, and I couldn't be more relieved.

I actually hugged Lydia before she left, pressing her against my giant stomach.

And I turned to look at Nico, crying for the sugar he'd been expecting. Where the hells had he been?

THAT AFTERNOON, WE VISITED ISABEAU. IF ANYBODY could get to the bottom of what had happened to Nico, our mortal oracle friend was the one. We found her in her little cottage, her white hair threaded with flowers and seashells. She welcomed us all with tea.

For a few minutes, Isabeau sat with him and held his hands, letting her consciousness join with his to see the world through his eyes. At last, she nodded, leaning back a little in her chair. "Oh, yes, that's it," she exclaimed. "That's exactly it!" She released Nico's hands and beamed at him. "A very special young man."

I swallowed. "What, exactly, happened?"

"Let's show them," the old woman suggested, and she stood and offered a hand to our son. He took it, and they walked across her cluttered room together, a strange place full of animal skulls and dried flowers. When they reached the far wall, Nico turned and waved goodbye to us with a cheery smile—and the two of them proceeded to walk directly through the wall, out into the cobblestone street.

My stomach dropped, but in the next moment, they crossed back through the wall in the same way.

"How did you..." I began, but I was too astounded to finish. I crouched down over my stomach, pulling him close to me.

"I'm a ghost," he shouted with glee. "A big, big, *big*, huge ghost!" He stomped his feet for emphasis.

I looked up at Isabeau.

She shrugged. "I can't explain the magic behind it, exactly, but Nicodemus can walk through walls. Or, evidently, drop through floors. Into places like dungeons."

"Fuck," I muttered.

"Fuck," Nico repeated.

"Shh, no, baby." I placed a finger over his lips. "*Duck*. I said duck."

"He can *fall* through the floors?" asked Orion coolly.

"A strong emotion can trigger it," said Isabeau.

"A big duck ghost," a delighted Nico shouted to remind me.

I rose slowly. "So what do we do to keep him safe?"

Isabeau rubbed her hands together. "There are some great witches here at Belial to help him harness his gifts. But in the meantime..." She pulled out a tiny cloth bag tied to a piece of yarn. "Put this around his ankle. Yew leaves. They'll keep his magic subdued enough that it won't get out of control."

"Yes. Thank you," Orion agreed.

We left with a list of instructions from Isabeau and an entirely fresh set of worries to accompany those that concern every other set of new parents. How the fuck did you baby-proof a house for a child who could go through the walls?

❧

YEARS AGO, I WAS PLAGUED BY A TERRIBLE NIGHTMARE involving a little green-eyed, auburn-haired boy. About a horde of demons racing across the world, across *his* world, slaughtering everyone in sight. A demonic host led by my husband, Orion.

The dream was so vivid, it had struck fear into my heart.

Sometimes, the dream came back to me. But now, it was Kas unleashing horror on the mortal world. When the dreams were at their very worst, I'd picture that little boy as the sole survivor, see the terror in his eyes as everyone around him was killed and he had no one to turn to. I'd wake crying, reaching for Orion. I'd seek out Nico as he slept to make sure he was okay. Sometimes, I checked on him twice a night.

I'd love to say that as a parent, I lived in a world of bliss, where my anxiety went away and everything was contentment.

But I would never stop worrying about Nico, or the baby in my tummy who constantly had the hiccups.

There was no love without terror. The fear of loss.

But these three demons were my world, and I would gladly carry that fear to live in their warmth.

❦

THANK YOU FOR READING THE DEMON QUEEN TRIALS. If you want to stay updated to hear about any future spin off series, you can sign up to my newsletter.

Or, join the reader group to talk to other readers about Garden of Serpents and what to read next.

If you want a free standalone fantasy novel by C.N. Crawford and Katerina Martinez, you can download it here.

ALSO BY C.N. CRAWFORD

For a full list of our books, please check out our website, cncrawford.com.

Amazon and goodreads also have a full listing of our books. Reviews are appreciated!

Read on for a sample of a completed series—the Shadow Fae series—to see if that is what you want to read next!

ACKNOWLEDGMENTS

Thanks to Michael Omer and Nick for their feedback on the book, and helping me think about important plot points.

Lauren and Jean are my fabulous editors, who helped to make it shine.

Thanks to Linsey Hall, K.F. Breene, May Sage, and Laura Thalassa for moral support when writing.

Thanks to my advanced reader team for their help in making it truly shine, and to C.N. Crawford's Coven.

CPSIA information can be obtained
at www.ICGtesting.com
Printed in the USA
BVHW050945030722
641204BV00006B/310